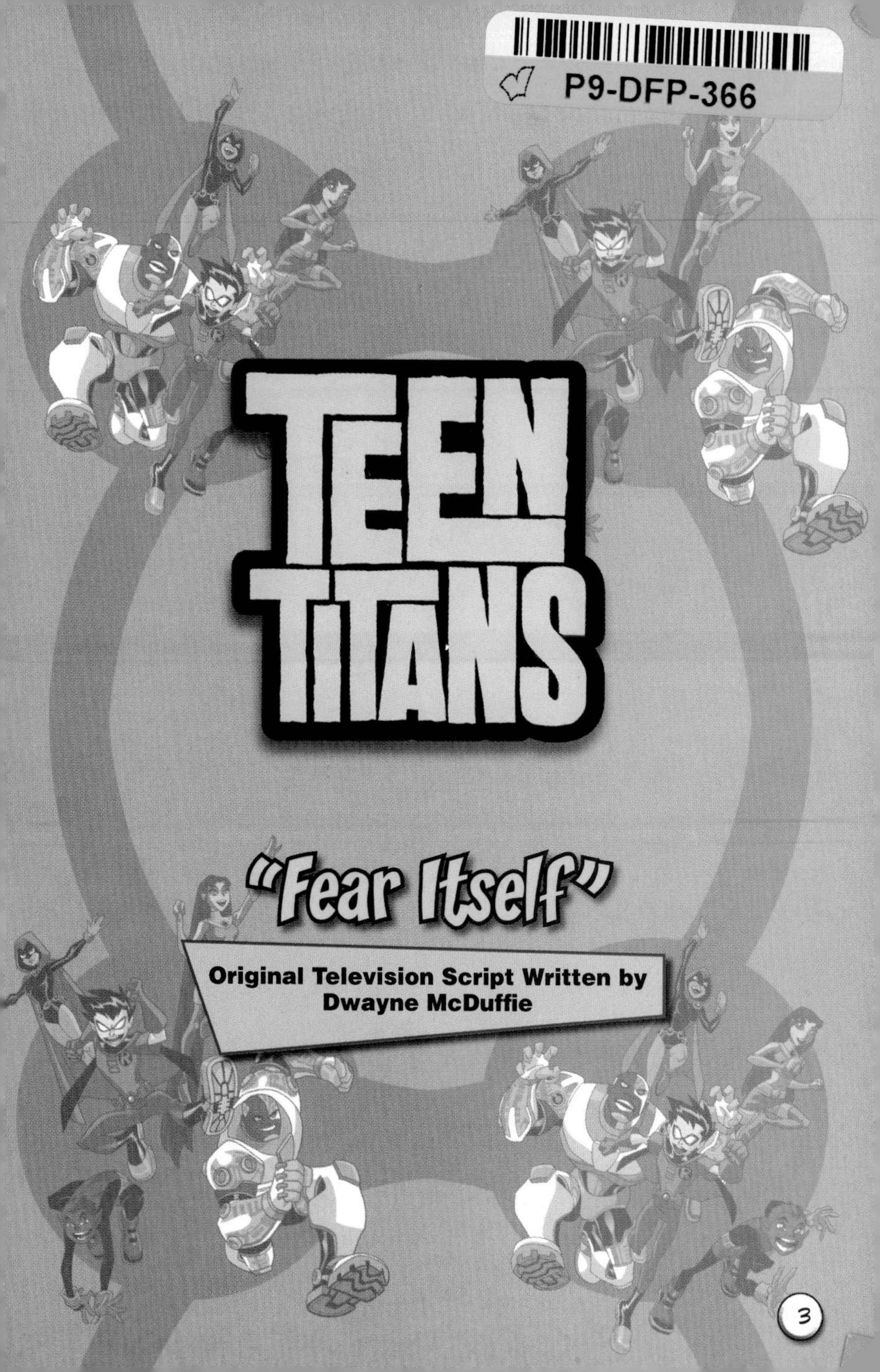

TEEN TITANS

"Fear Itself"

Original Television Script Written by
Dwayne McDuffie

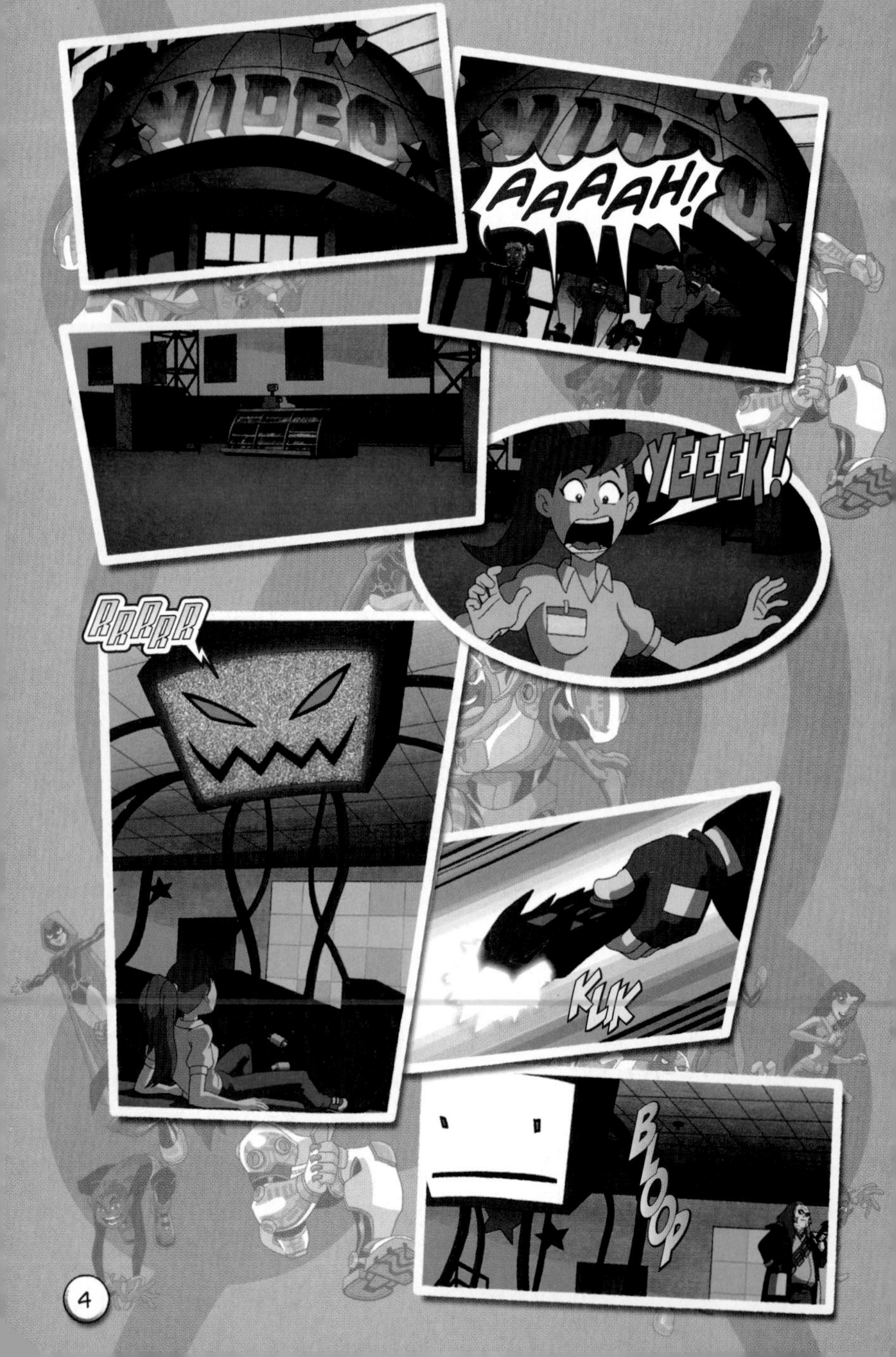
VIDEO
AAAAH!
YEEEK!
RRRRR
KLIK
BLOOP

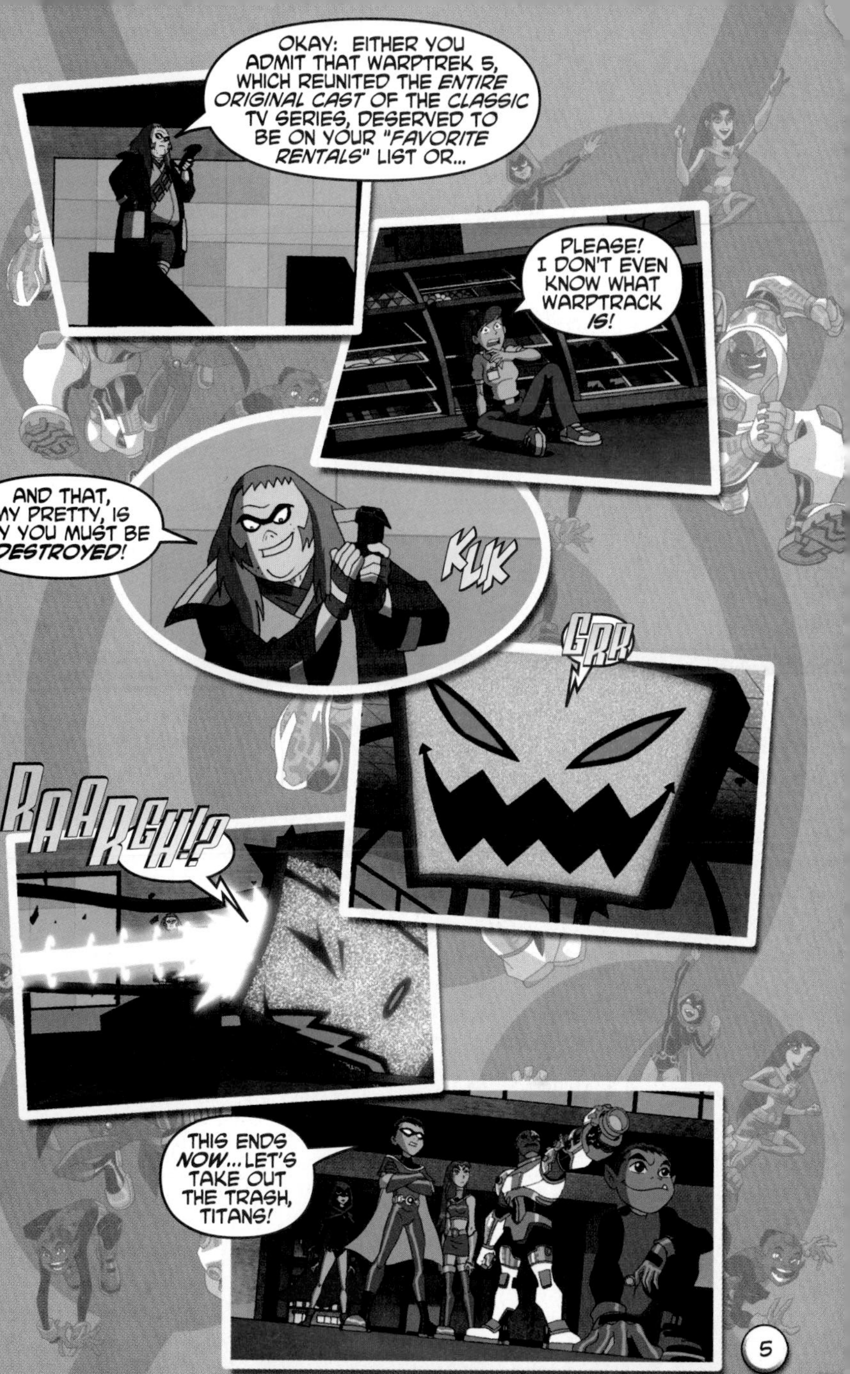
OKAY: EITHER YOU ADMIT THAT WARPTREK 5, WHICH REUNITED THE *ENTIRE ORIGINAL CAST* OF THE *CLASSIC* TV SERIES, DESERVED TO BE ON YOUR "*FAVORITE RENTALS*" LIST OR...
PLEASE! I DON'T EVEN KNOW WHAT WARPTRACK *IS*!
AND THAT, MY PRETTY, IS WHY YOU MUST BE *DESTROYED*!
KLIK
GRR
RAAARGH!?
THIS ENDS *NOW*... LET'S TAKE OUT THE TRASH, TITANS!

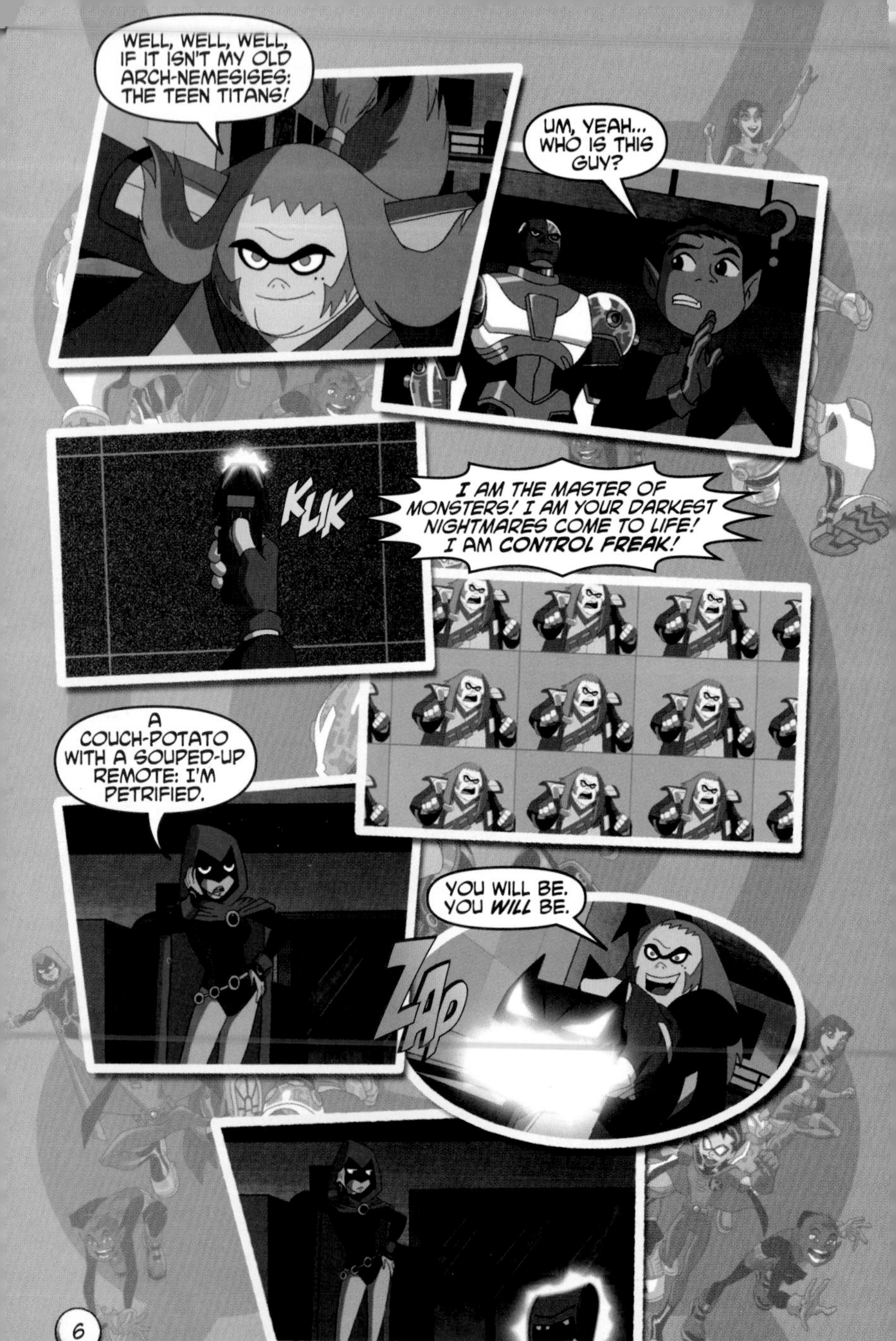
WELL, WELL, WELL, IF IT ISN'T MY OLD ARCH-NEMESISES: THE TEEN TITANS!
UM, YEAH... WHO IS THIS GUY?
KLIK
I AM THE MASTER OF MONSTERS! I AM YOUR DARKEST NIGHTMARES COME TO LIFE! I AM CONTROL FREAK!
A COUCH-POTATO WITH A SOUPED-UP REMOTE: I'M PETRIFIED.
YOU WILL BE. YOU WILL BE.
ZAP

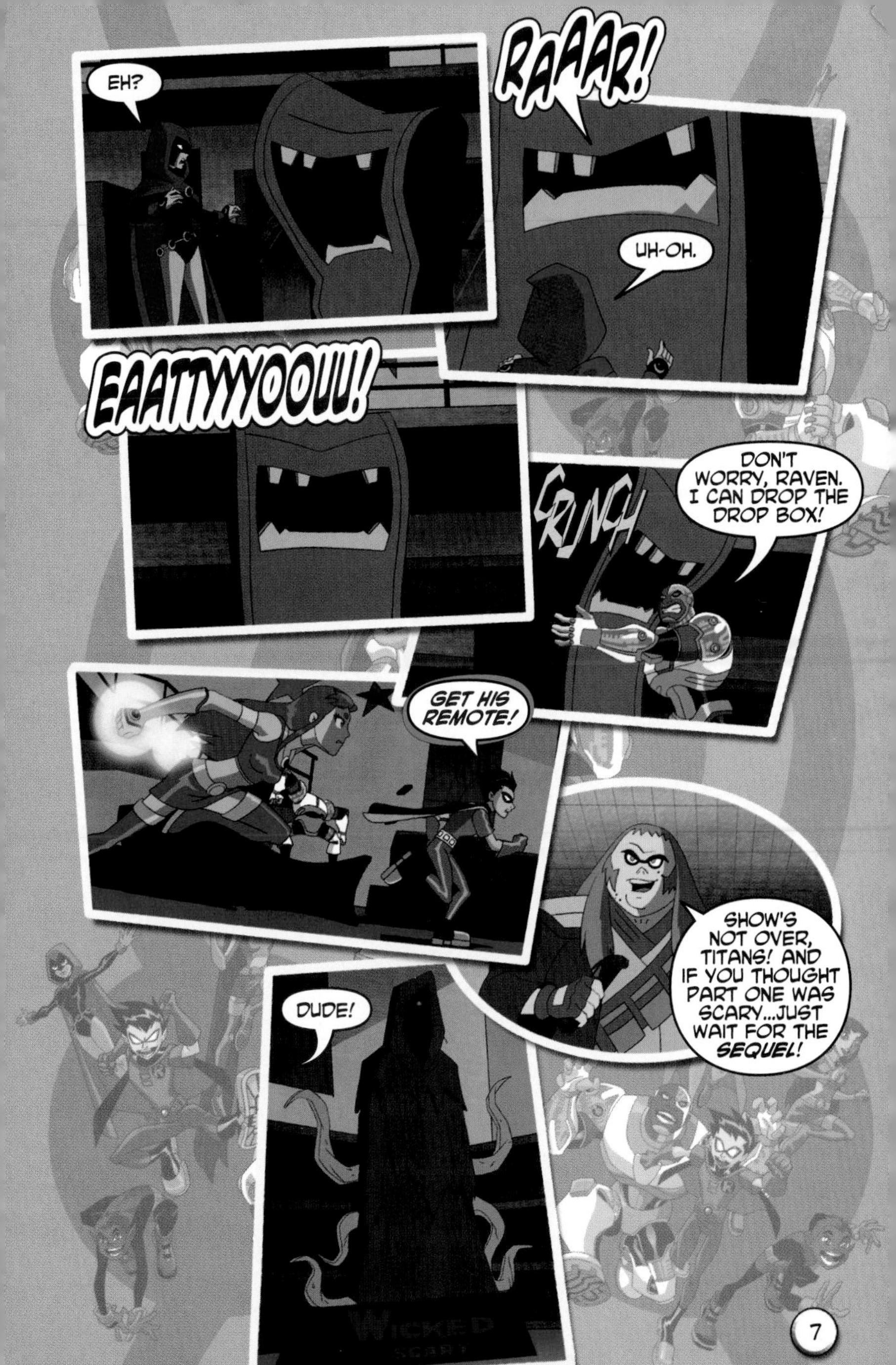
EH?
RAAAR!
UH-OH.
EAATTYYYOOUU!
CRUNCH
DON'T WORRY, RAVEN. I CAN DROP THE DROP BOX!
GET HIS REMOTE!
SHOW'S NOT OVER, TITANS! AND IF YOU THOUGHT PART ONE WAS SCARY...JUST WAIT FOR THE SEQUEL!
DUDE!

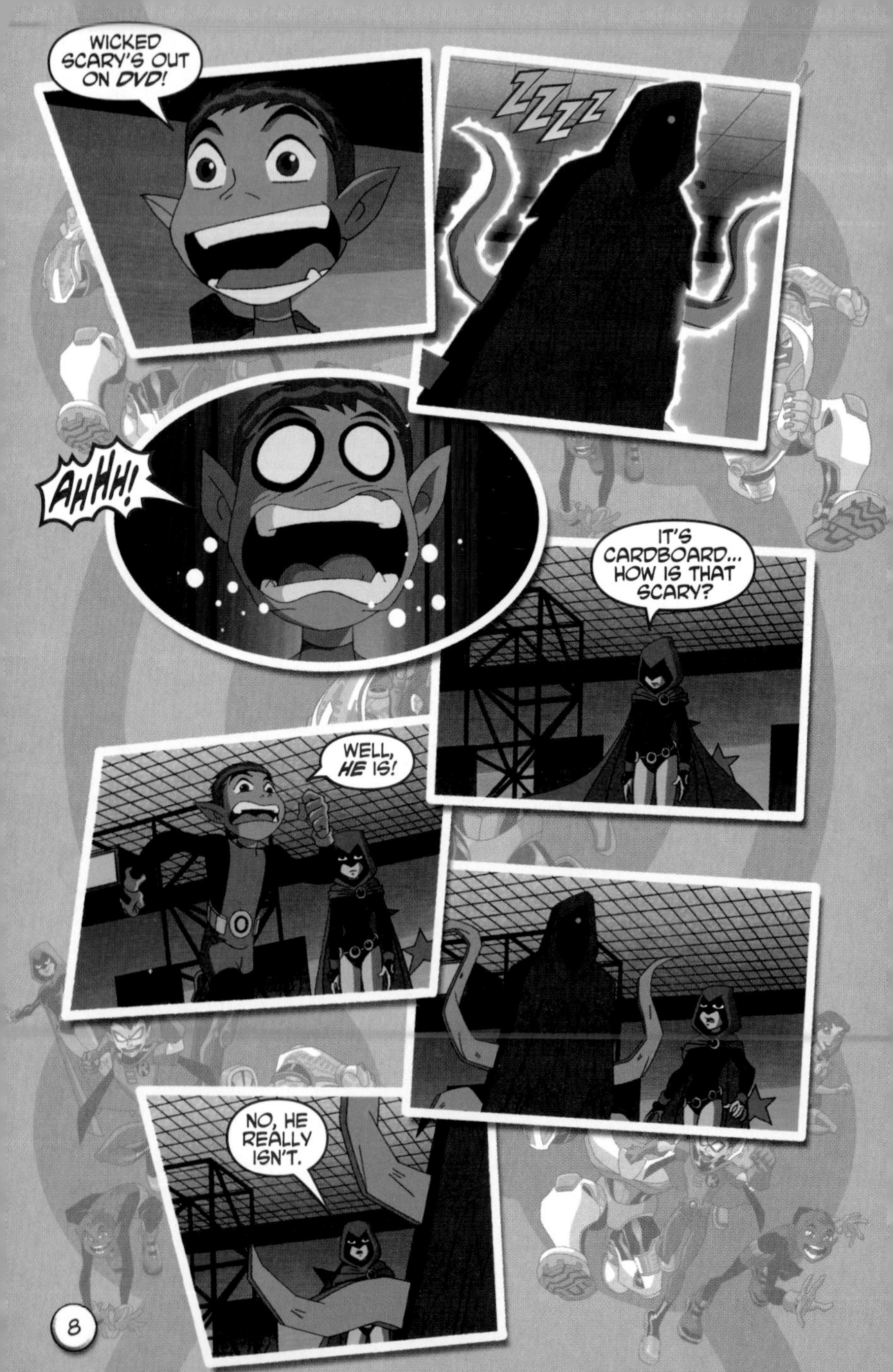

WICKED SCARY'S OUT ON *DVD*!
ZZZZ
AHHH!
IT'S CARDBOARD... HOW IS THAT SCARY?
WELL, *HE* IS!
NO, HE REALLY ISN'T.

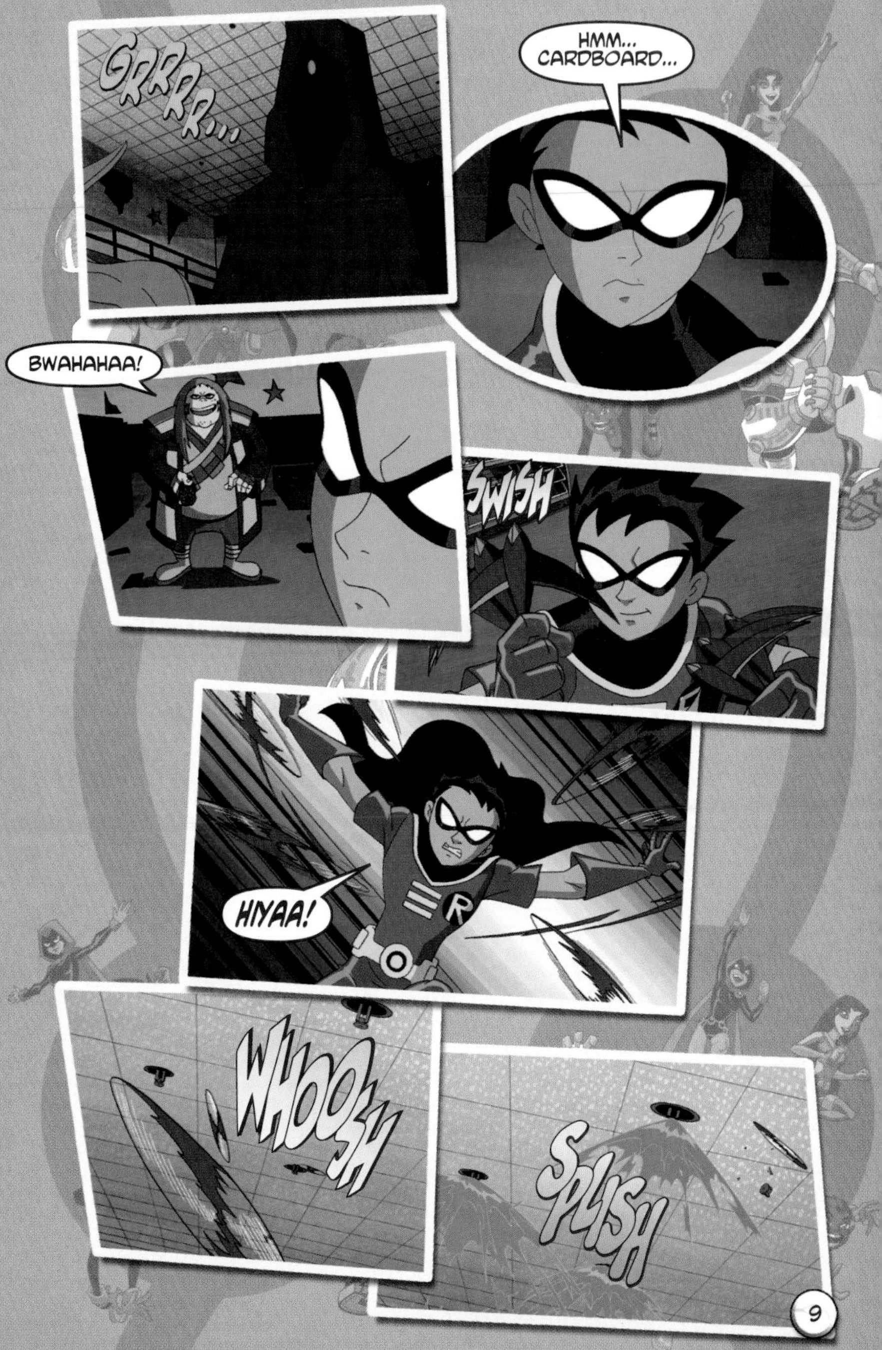
GRRRR...
HMM... CARDBOARD...
BWAHAHAA!
SWISH
HIYAA!
WHOOSH
SPLISH

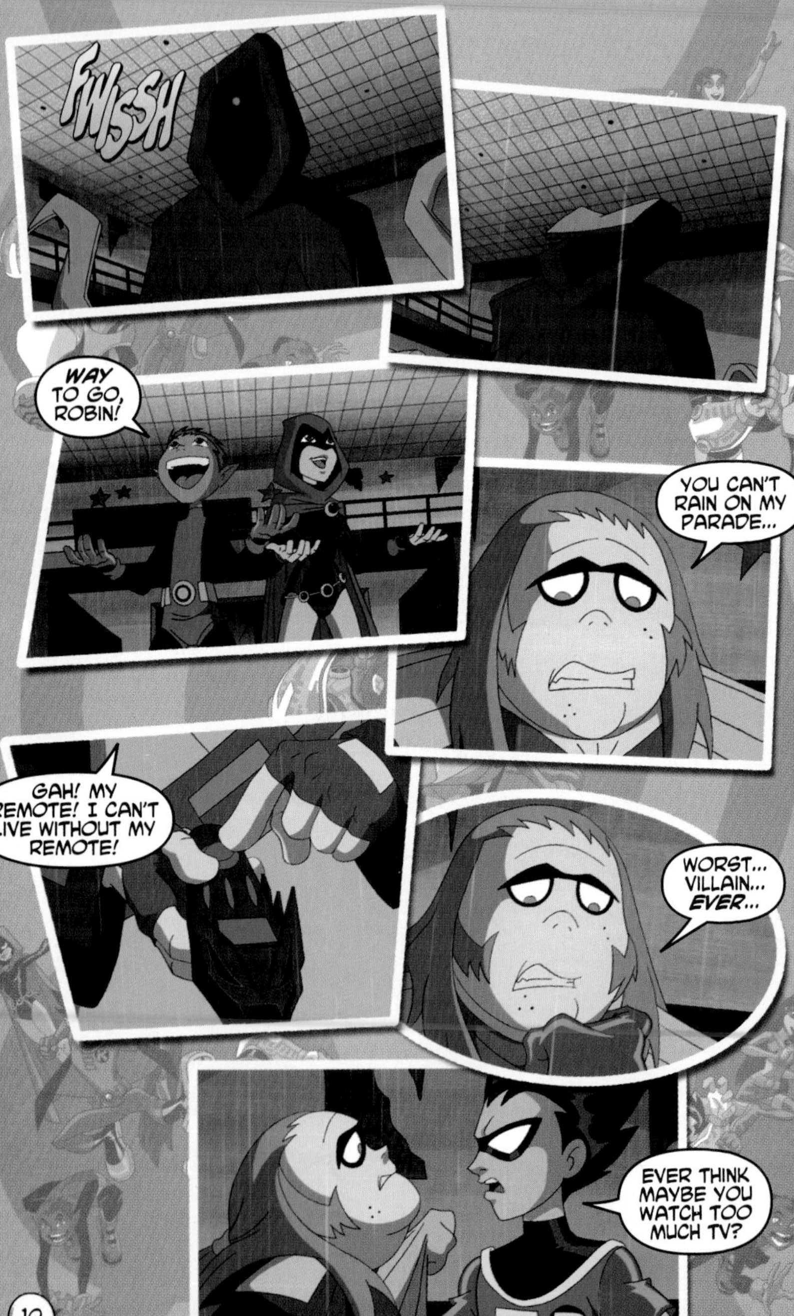
FWISSH
WAY TO GO, ROBIN!
YOU CAN'T RAIN ON MY PARADE...
GAH! MY REMOTE! I CAN'T LIVE WITHOUT MY REMOTE!
WORST... VILLAIN... EVER...
EVER THINK MAYBE YOU WATCH TOO MUCH TV?

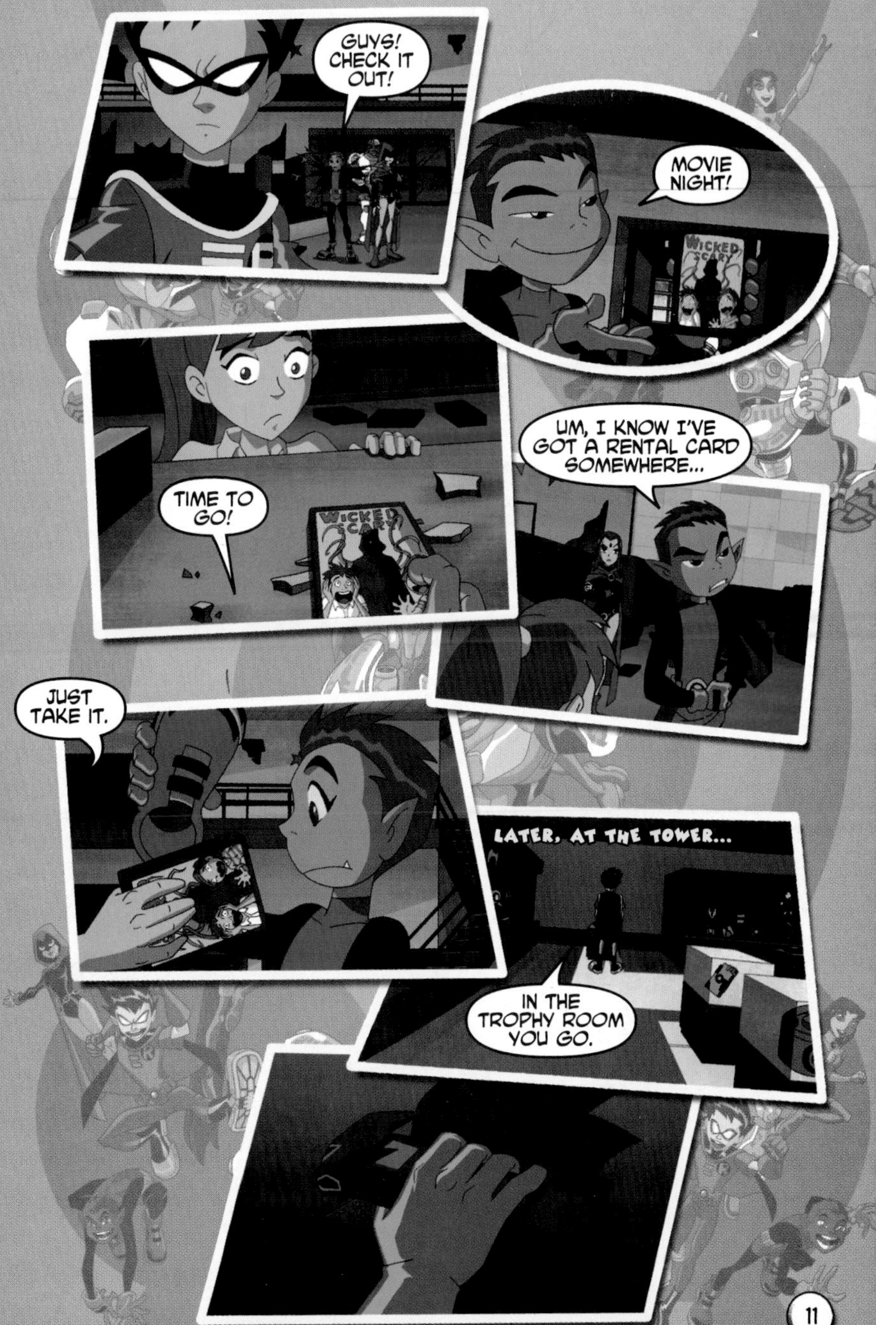
GUYS! CHECK IT OUT!
MOVIE NIGHT!
WICKED SCARY
TIME TO GO!
UM, I KNOW I'VE GOT A RENTAL CARD SOMEWHERE...
JUST TAKE IT.
LATER, AT THE TOWER...
IN THE TROPHY ROOM YOU GO.

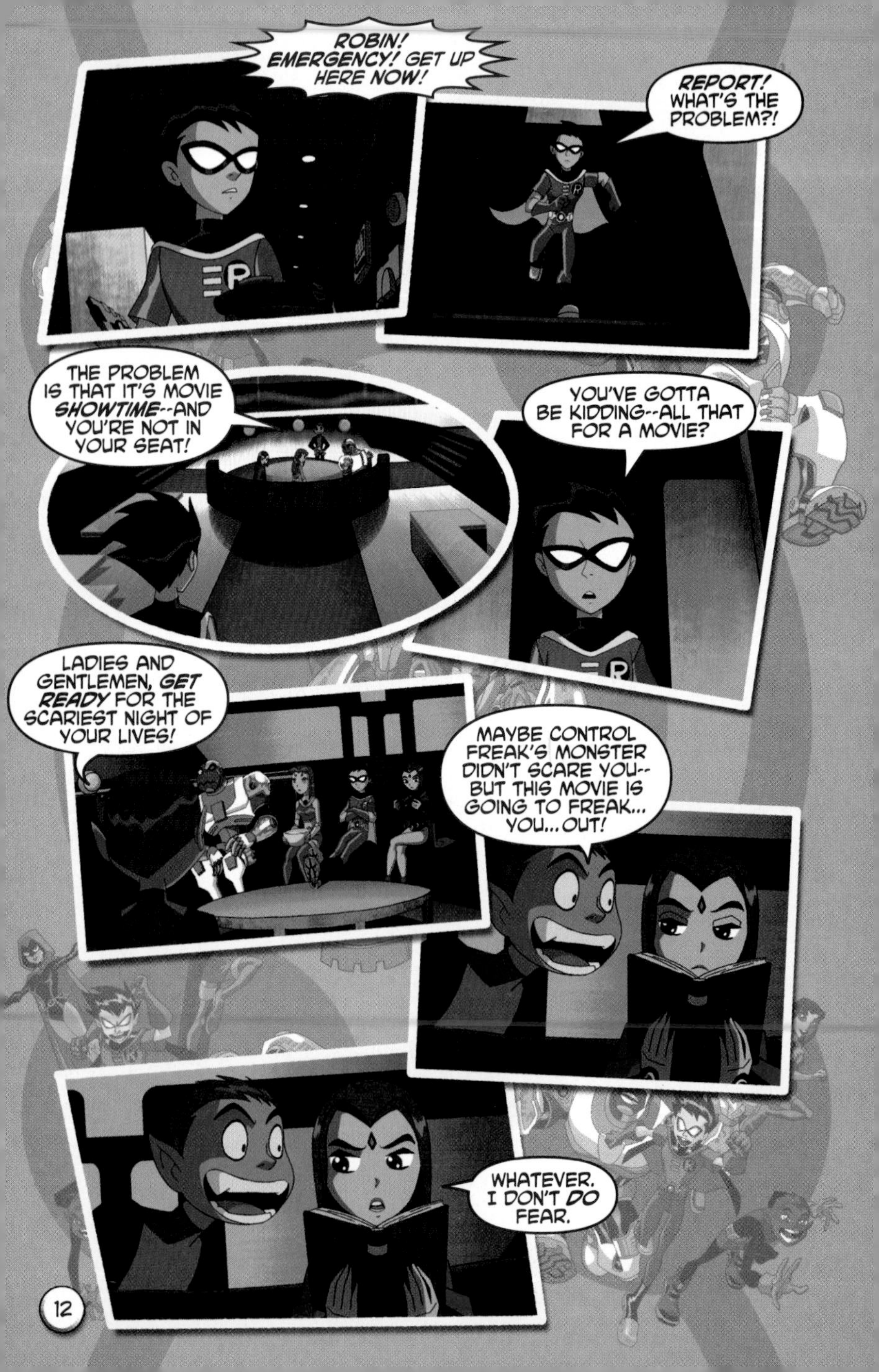
ROBIN! EMERGENCY! GET UP HERE NOW!
REPORT! WHAT'S THE PROBLEM?!
THE PROBLEM IS THAT IT'S MOVIE SHOWTIME--AND YOU'RE NOT IN YOUR SEAT!
YOU'VE GOTTA BE KIDDING--ALL THAT FOR A MOVIE?
LADIES AND GENTLEMEN, GET READY FOR THE SCARIEST NIGHT OF YOUR LIVES!
MAYBE CONTROL FREAK'S MONSTER DIDN'T SCARE YOU--BUT THIS MOVIE IS GOING TO FREAK... YOU...OUT!
WHATEVER. I DON'T DO FEAR.

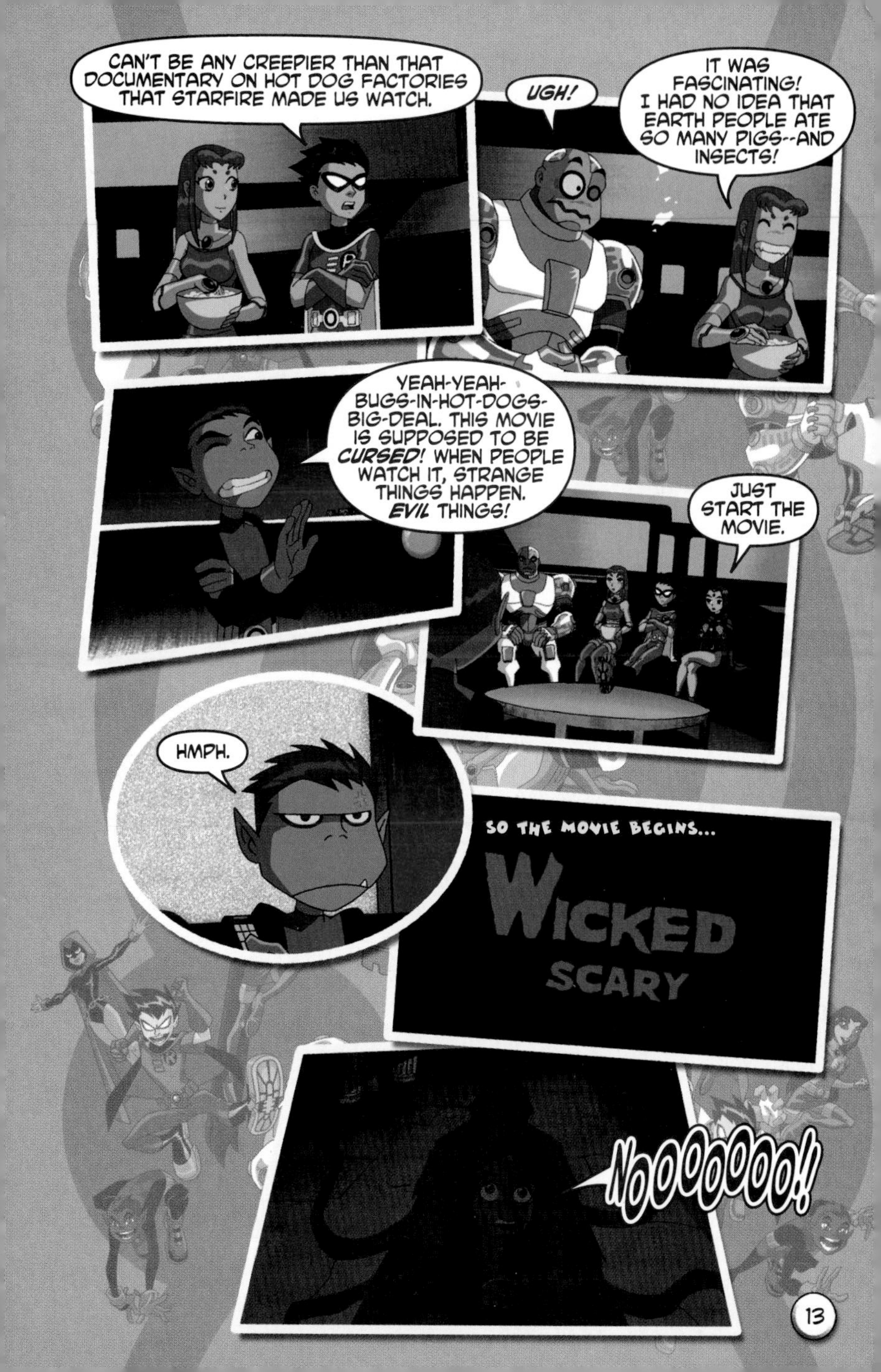

CAN'T BE ANY CREEPIER THAN THAT DOCUMENTARY ON HOT DOG FACTORIES THAT STARFIRE MADE US WATCH.
UGH!
IT WAS FASCINATING! I HAD NO IDEA THAT EARTH PEOPLE ATE SO MANY PIGS--AND INSECTS!
YEAH-YEAH-BUGS-IN-HOT-DOGS-BIG-DEAL. THIS MOVIE IS SUPPOSED TO BE CURSED! WHEN PEOPLE WATCH IT, STRANGE THINGS HAPPEN. EVIL THINGS!
JUST START THE MOVIE.
HMPH.
SO THE MOVIE BEGINS...
WICKED SCARY
NOOOOOOO!!

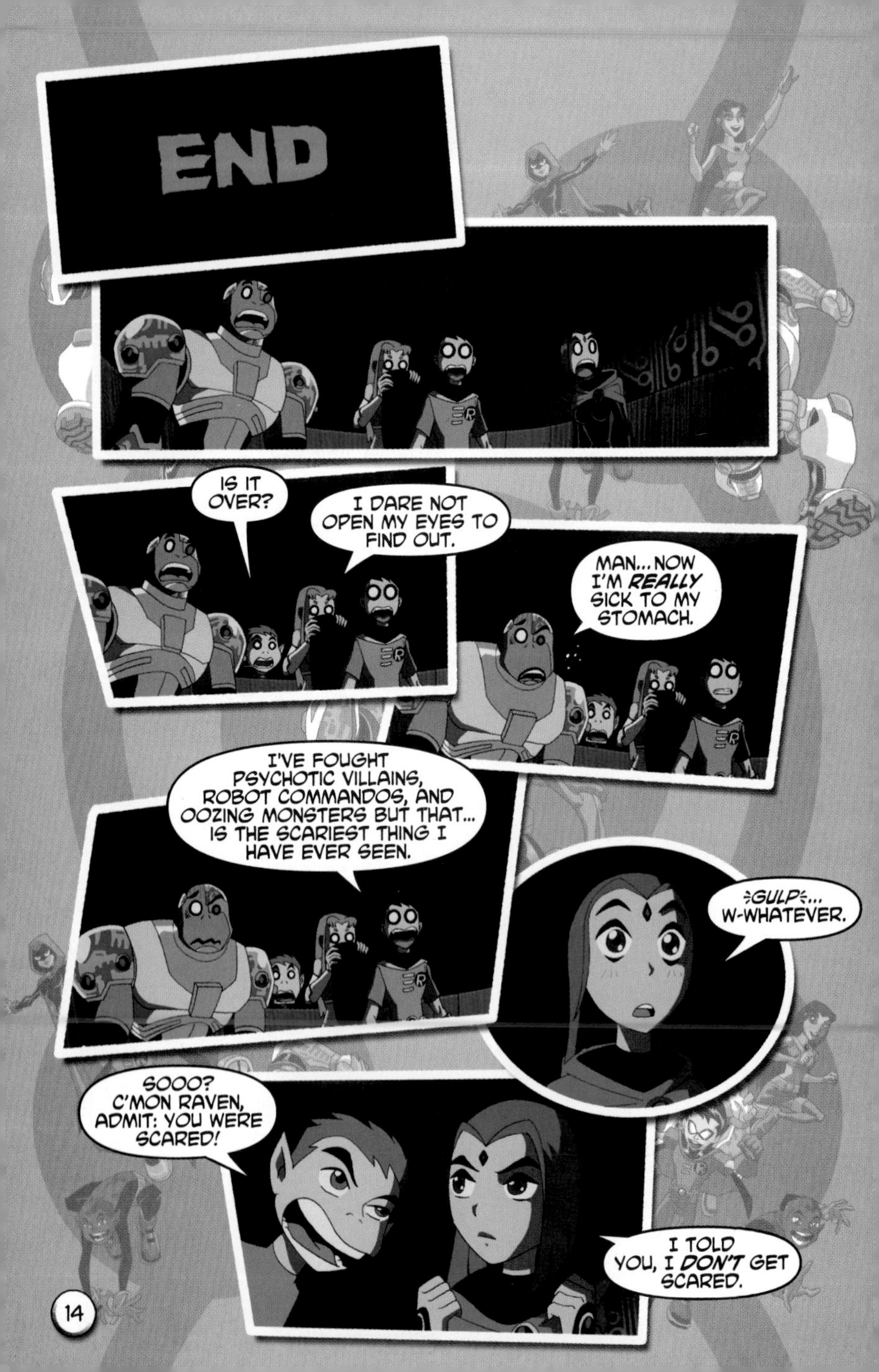

END
IS IT OVER?
I DARE NOT OPEN MY EYES TO FIND OUT.
MAN... NOW I'M *REALLY* SICK TO MY STOMACH.
I'VE FOUGHT PSYCHOTIC VILLAINS, ROBOT COMMANDOS, AND OOZING MONSTERS BUT THAT... IS THE SCARIEST THING I HAVE EVER SEEN.
GULP... W-WHATEVER.
SOOO? C'MON RAVEN, ADMIT: YOU WERE SCARED!
I TOLD YOU, I *DON'T* GET SCARED.

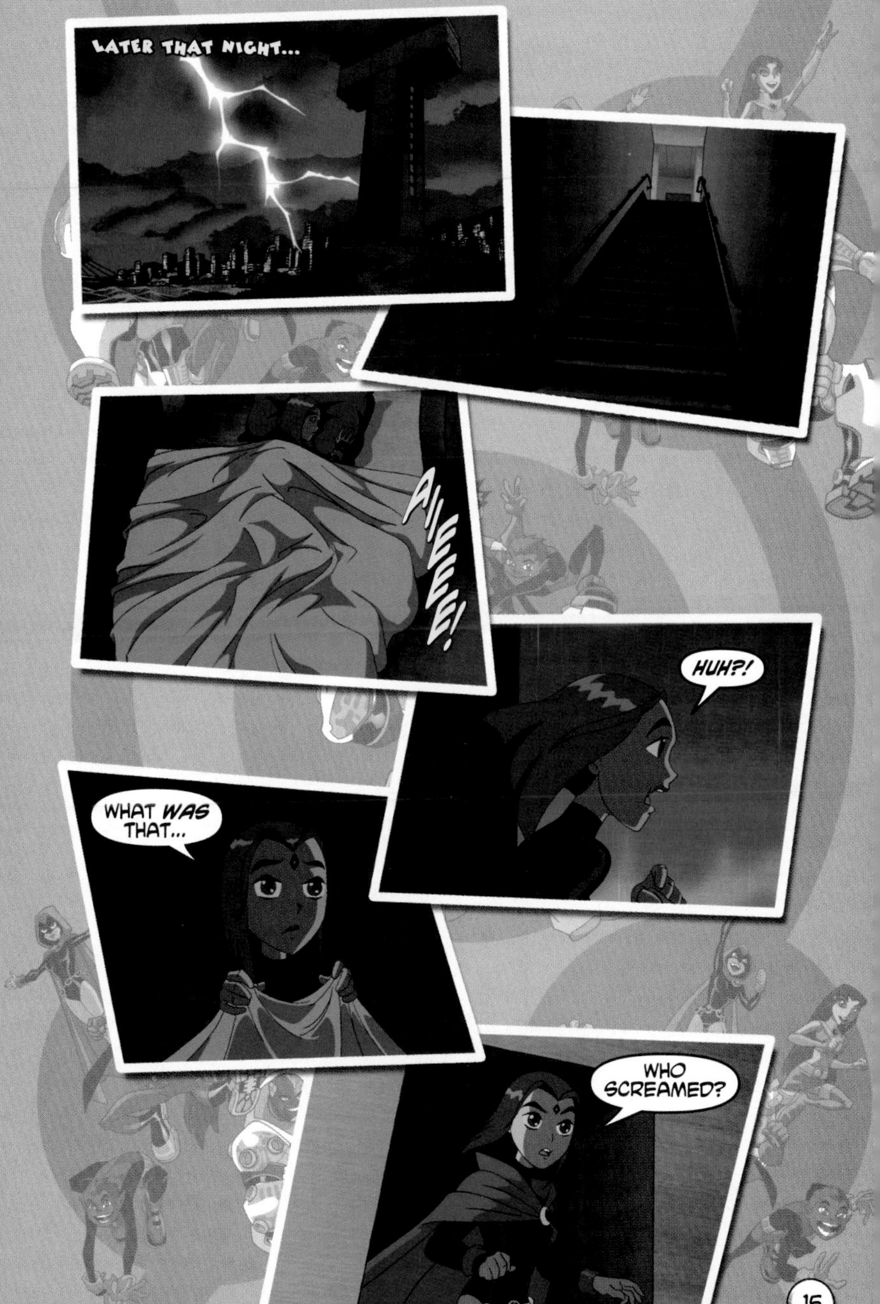
LATER THAT NIGHT...
AIIEEEE!
HUH?!
WHAT WAS THAT...
WHO SCREAMED?

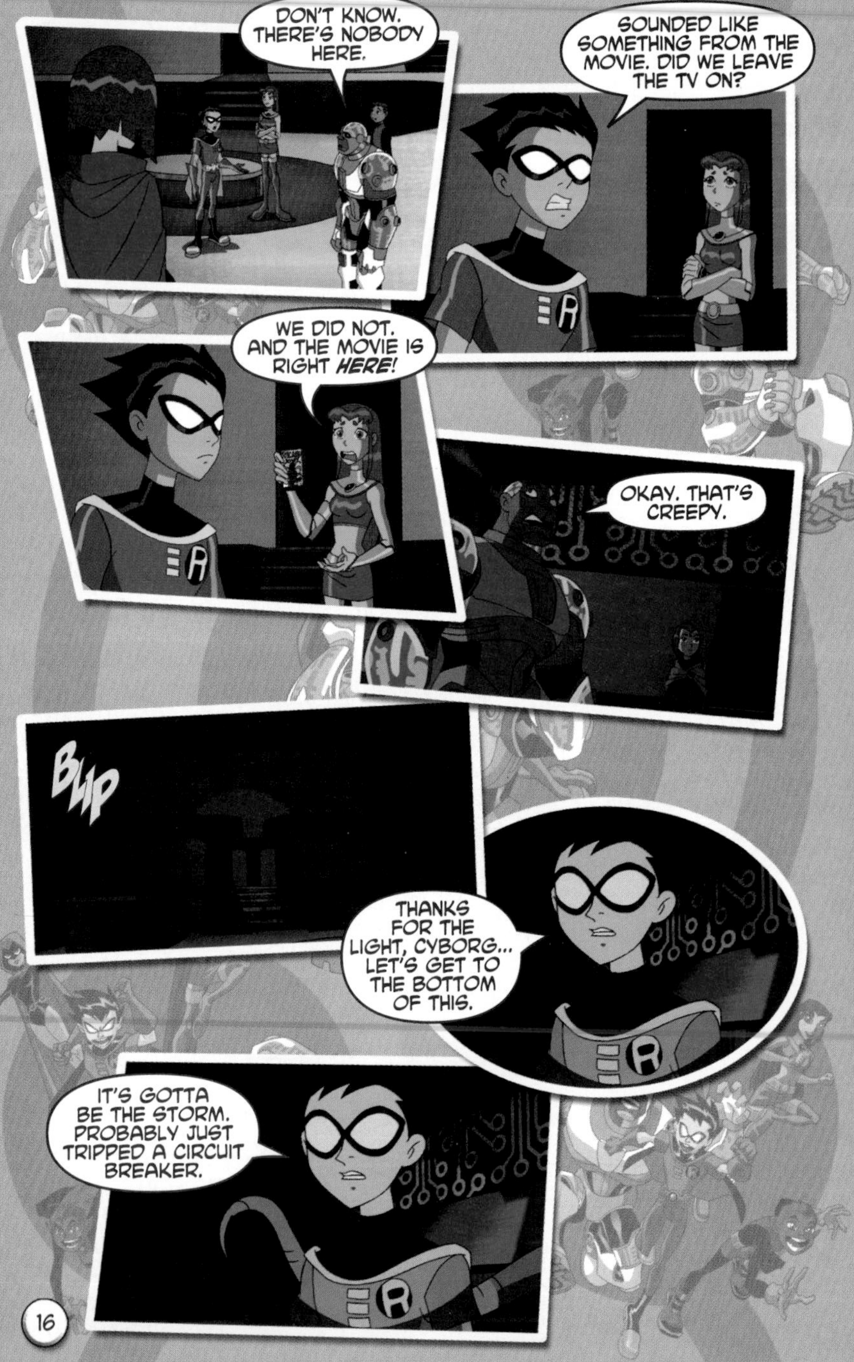
DON'T KNOW. THERE'S NOBODY HERE.
SOUNDED LIKE SOMETHING FROM THE MOVIE. DID WE LEAVE THE TV ON?
WE DID NOT. AND THE MOVIE IS RIGHT *HERE*!
OKAY. THAT'S CREEPY.
BLIP
THANKS FOR THE LIGHT, CYBORG... LET'S GET TO THE BOTTOM OF THIS.
IT'S GOTTA BE THE STORM. PROBABLY JUST TRIPPED A CIRCUIT BREAKER.

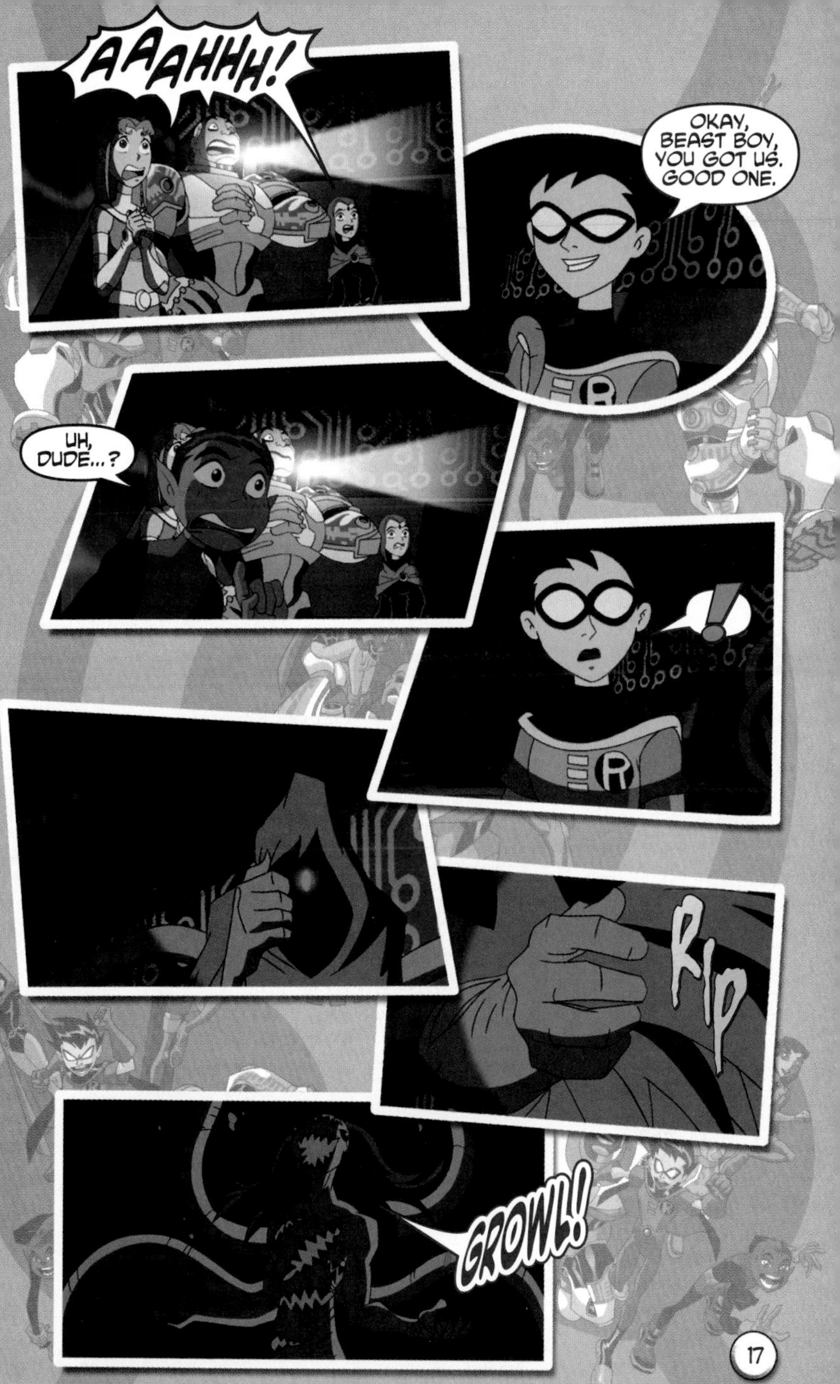
AAAHHH!
OKAY, BEAST BOY, YOU GOT US. GOOD ONE.
UH, DUDE...?
!
RIP
GROWL!

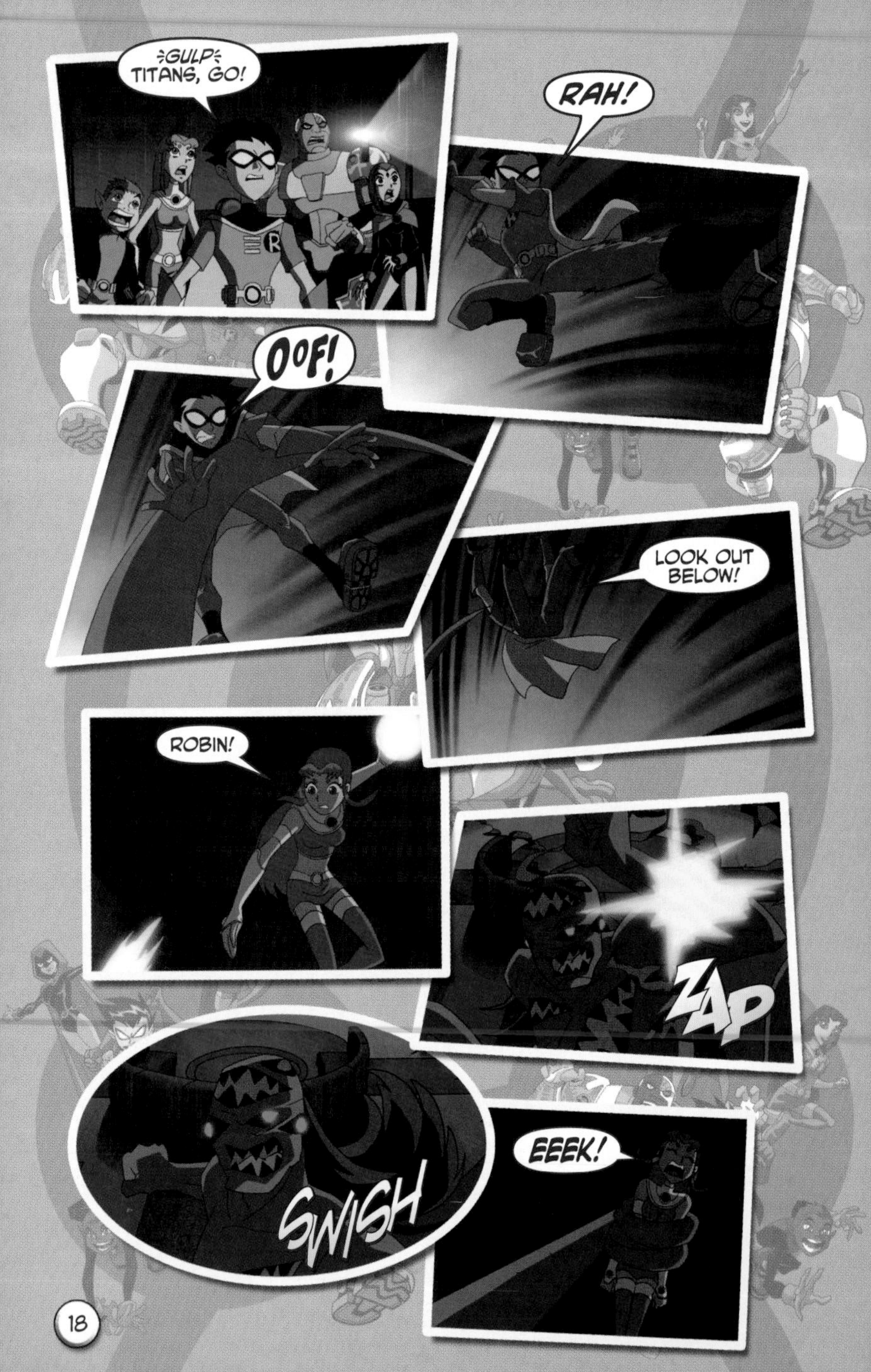
GULP
TITANS, GO!
RAH!
OOF!
LOOK OUT BELOW!
ROBIN!
ZAP
SWISH
EEEK!

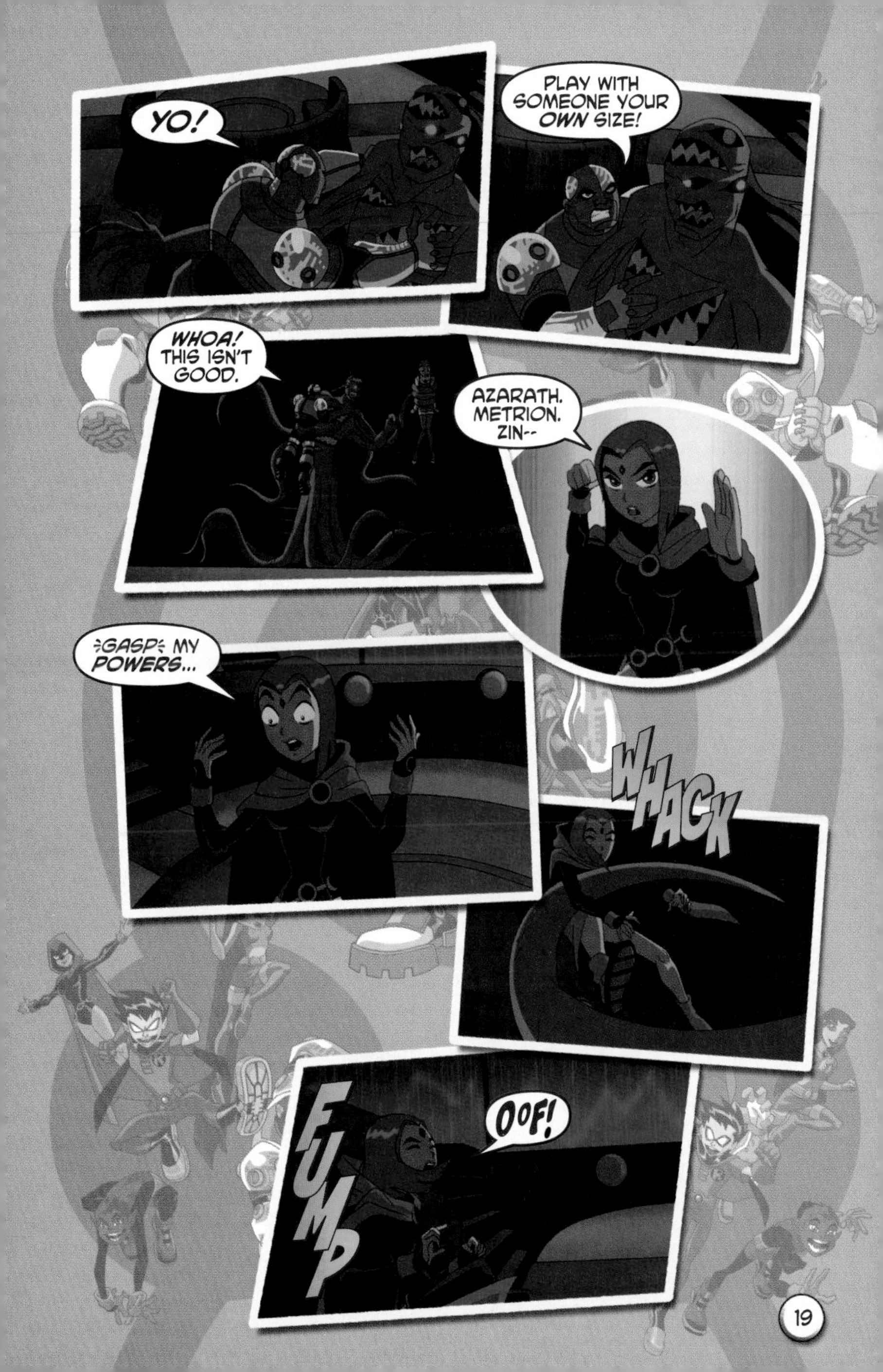
YO!
PLAY WITH SOMEONE YOUR OWN SIZE!
WHOA! THIS ISN'T GOOD.
AZARATH. METRION. ZIN--
GASP MY POWERS...
WHACK
FUMP
OOF!

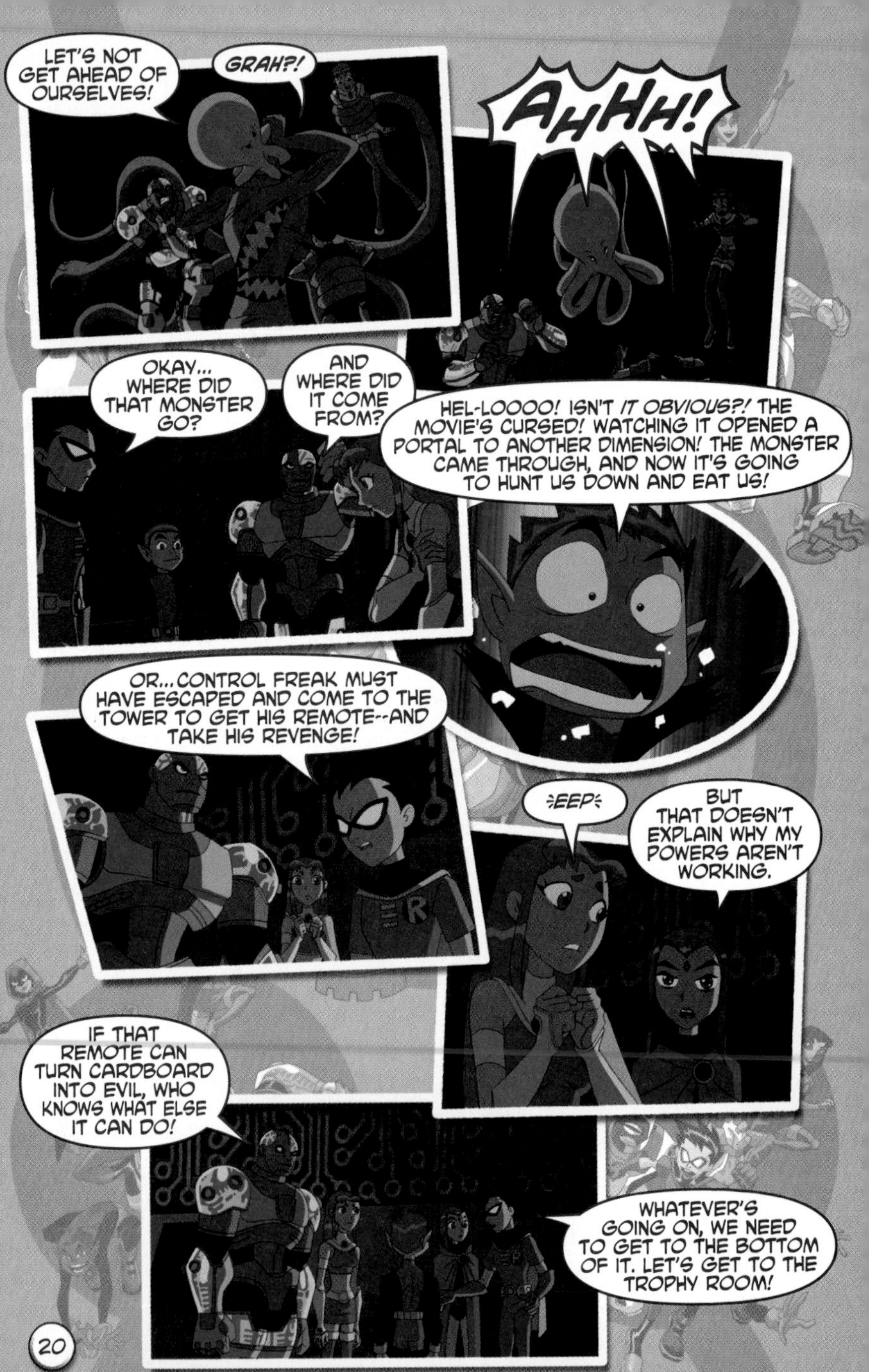
LET'S NOT GET AHEAD OF OURSELVES!
GRAH?!
AHHH!
OKAY... WHERE DID THAT MONSTER GO?
AND WHERE DID IT COME FROM?
HEL-LOOOO! ISN'T IT OBVIOUS?! THE MOVIE'S CURSED! WATCHING IT OPENED A PORTAL TO ANOTHER DIMENSION! THE MONSTER CAME THROUGH, AND NOW IT'S GOING TO HUNT US DOWN AND EAT US!
OR...CONTROL FREAK MUST HAVE ESCAPED AND COME TO THE TOWER TO GET HIS REMOTE--AND TAKE HIS REVENGE!
EEP
BUT THAT DOESN'T EXPLAIN WHY MY POWERS AREN'T WORKING.
IF THAT REMOTE CAN TURN CARDBOARD INTO EVIL, WHO KNOWS WHAT ELSE IT CAN DO!
WHATEVER'S GOING ON, WE NEED TO GET TO THE BOTTOM OF IT. LET'S GET TO THE TROPHY ROOM!

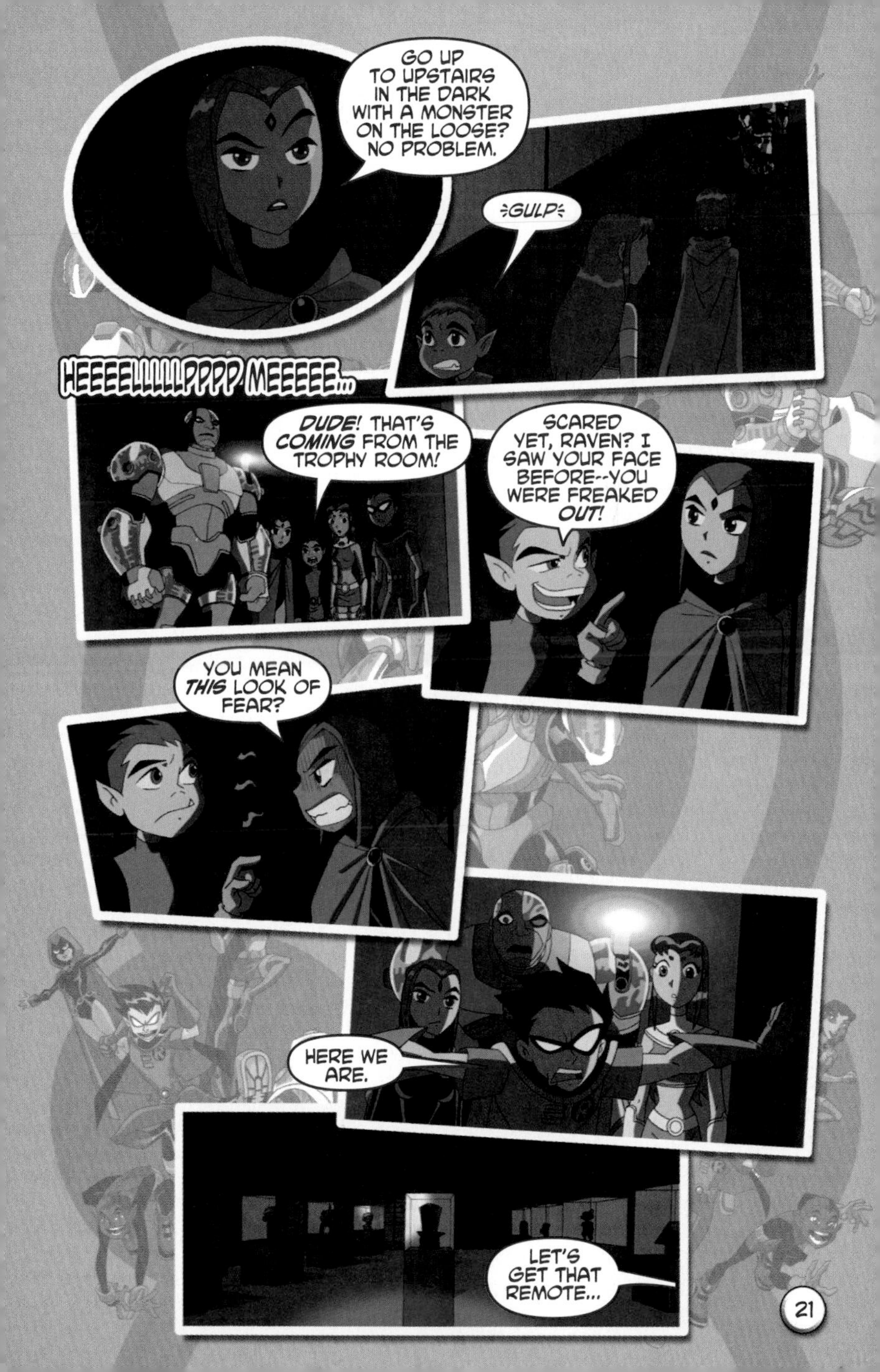
GO UP TO UPSTAIRS IN THE DARK WITH A MONSTER ON THE LOOSE? NO PROBLEM.
GULP
HEEEEELLLLLLPPPP MEEEEE...
DUDE! THAT'S COMING FROM THE TROPHY ROOM!
SCARED YET, RAVEN? I SAW YOUR FACE BEFORE--YOU WERE FREAKED OUT!
YOU MEAN THIS LOOK OF FEAR?
HERE WE ARE.
LET'S GET THAT REMOTE...

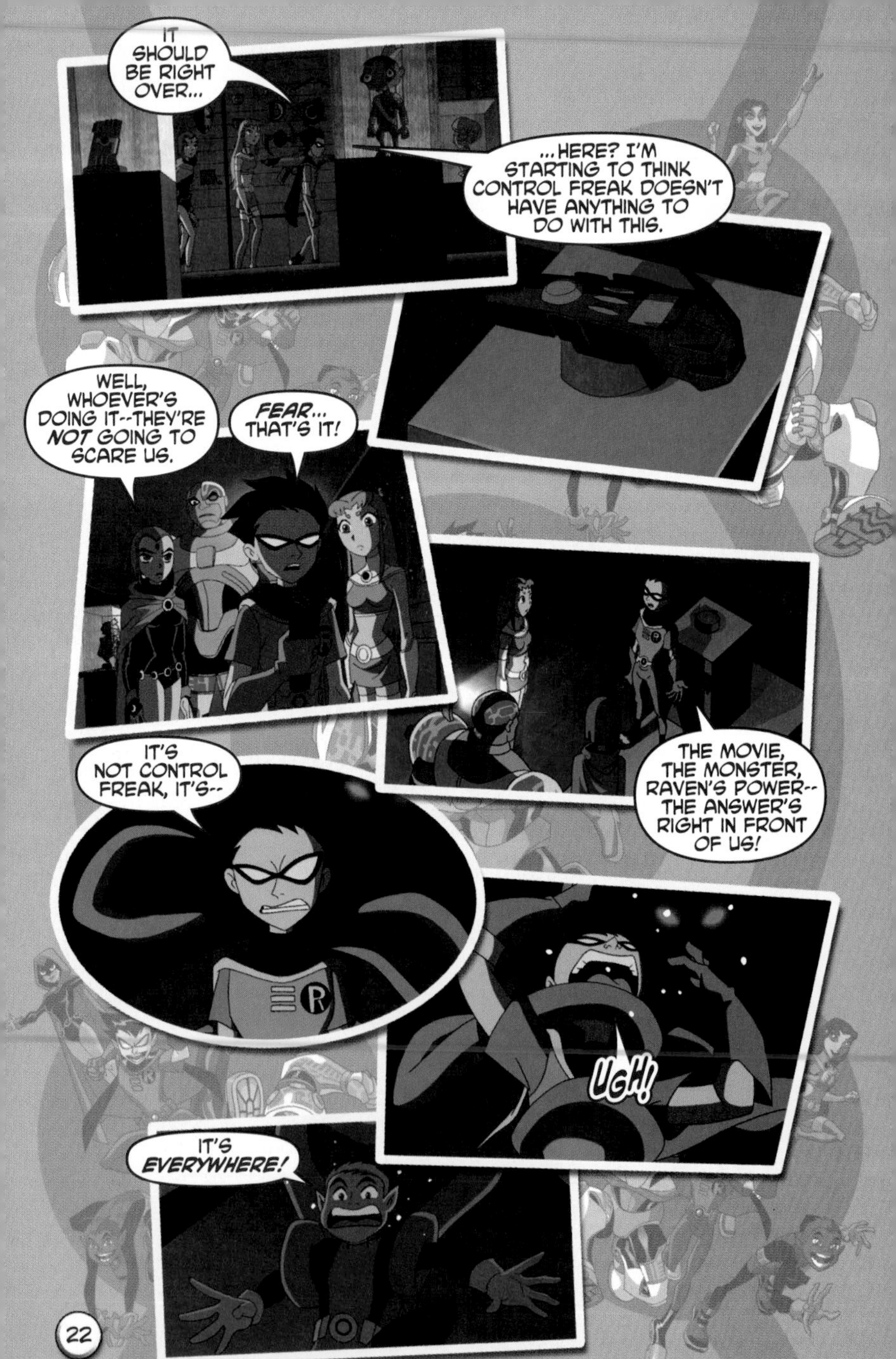
IT SHOULD BE RIGHT OVER...
...HERE? I'M STARTING TO THINK CONTROL FREAK DOESN'T HAVE ANYTHING TO DO WITH THIS.
WELL, WHOEVER'S DOING IT--THEY'RE *NOT* GOING TO SCARE US.
FEAR... THAT'S IT!
THE MOVIE, THE MONSTER, RAVEN'S POWER-- THE ANSWER'S RIGHT IN FRONT OF US!
IT'S NOT CONTROL FREAK, IT'S--
UGH!
IT'S *EVERYWHERE!*

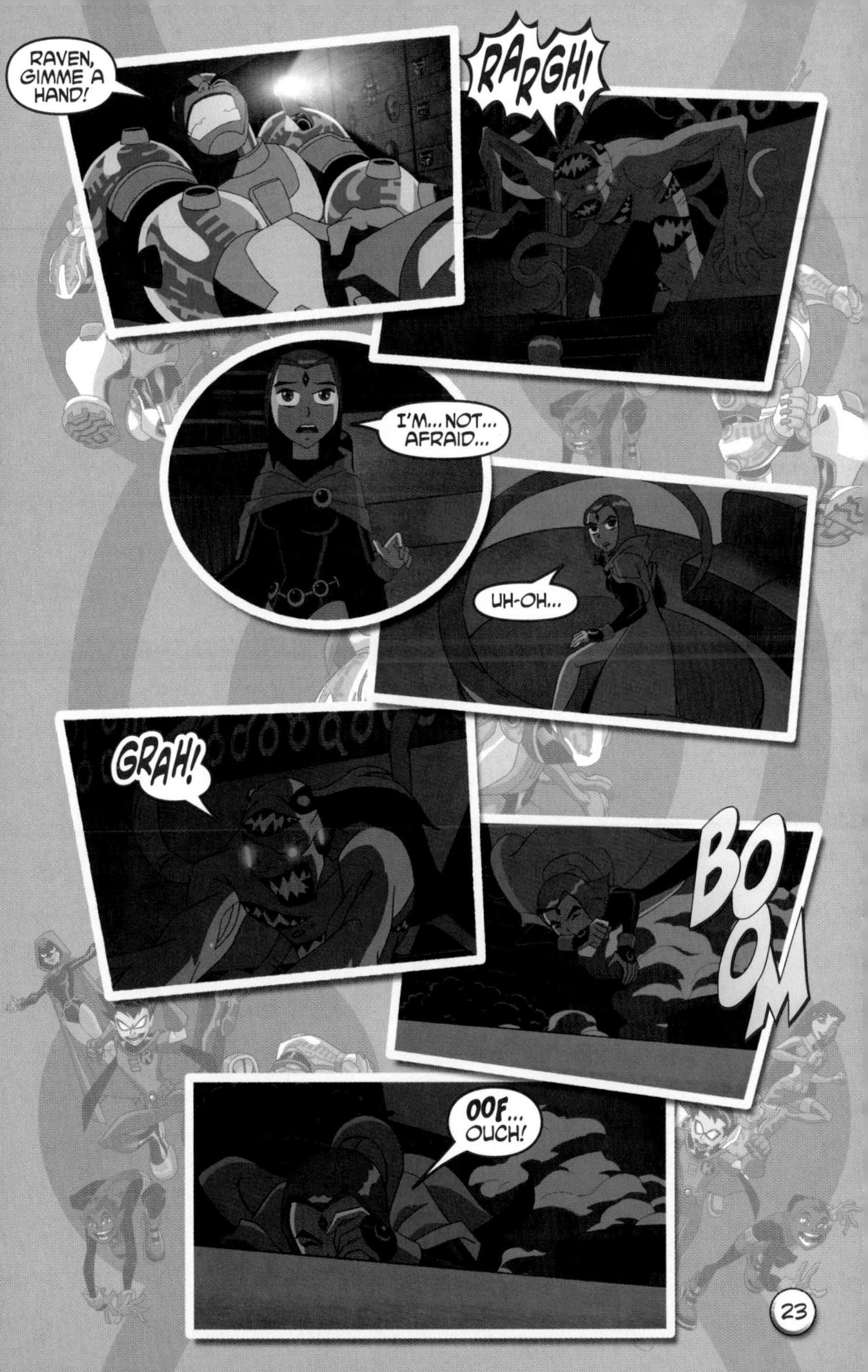
RAVEN, GIMME A HAND!
RARGH!
I'M... NOT... AFRAID...
UH-OH...
GRAH!
BOOM
OOF... OUCH!

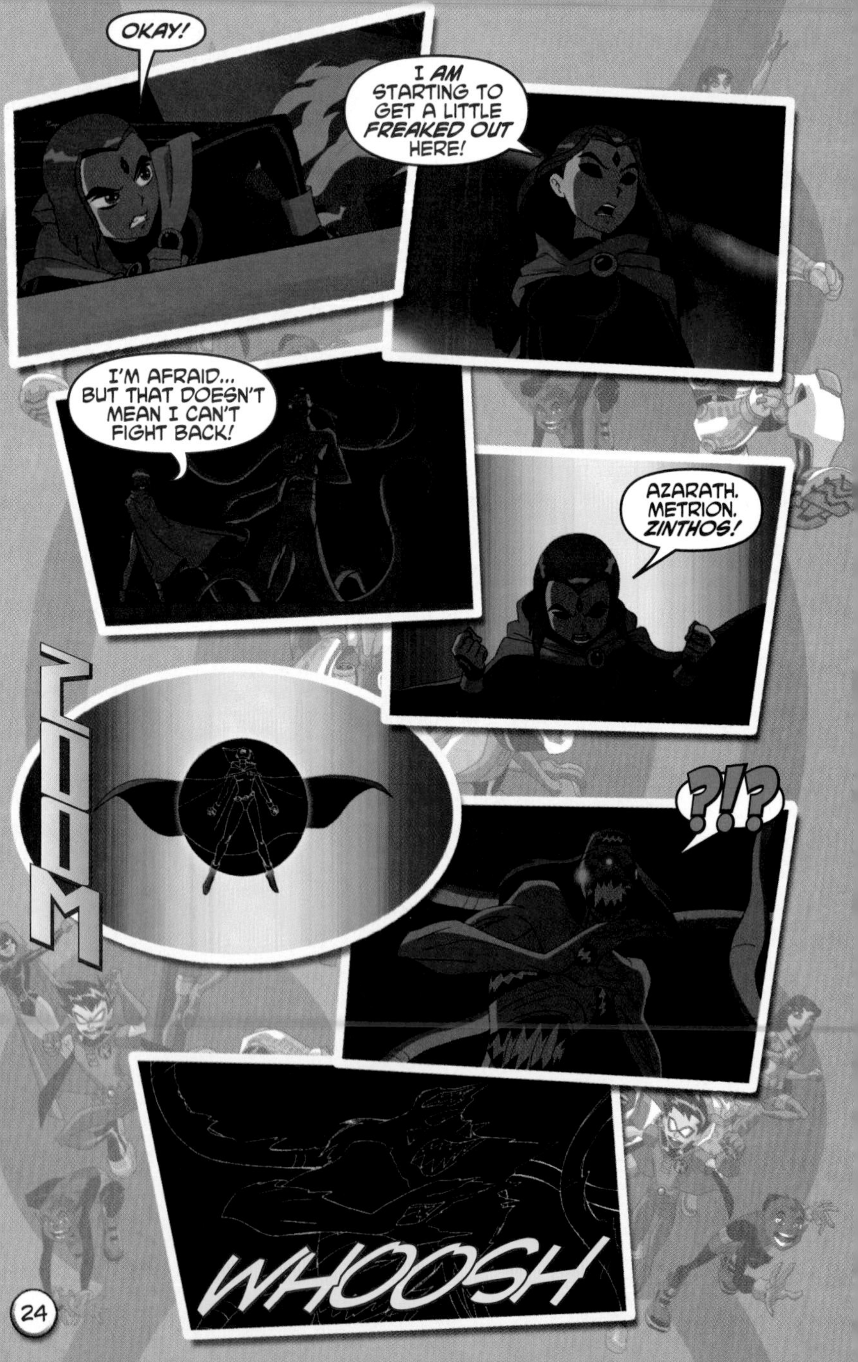
OKAY!
I AM STARTING TO GET A LITTLE FREAKED OUT HERE!
I'M AFRAID... BUT THAT DOESN'T MEAN I CAN'T FIGHT BACK!
AZARATH. METRION. ZINTHOS!
ZOOM
?!?
WHOOSH

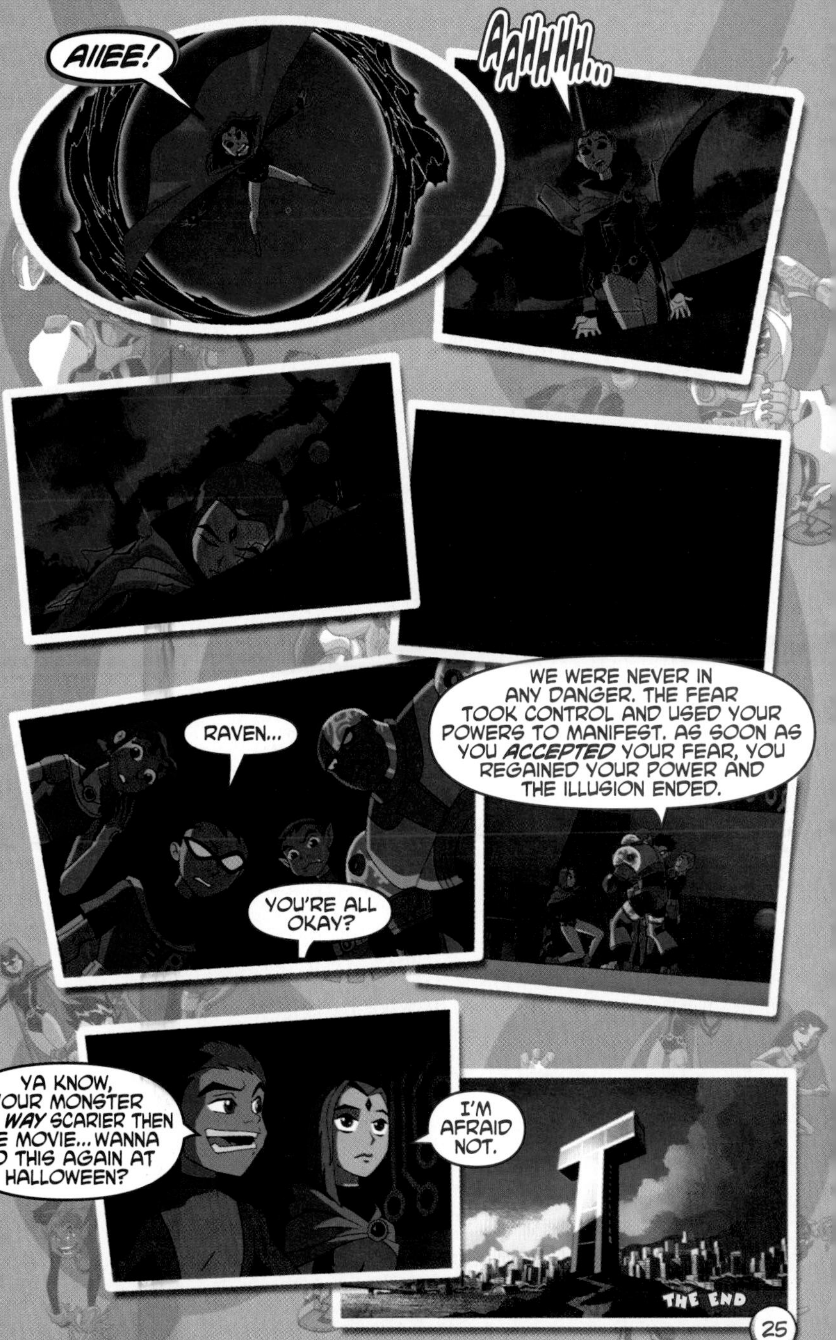
AIIEE!
AAHHHHH...
RAVEN...
YOU'RE ALL OKAY?
WE WERE NEVER IN ANY DANGER. THE FEAR TOOK CONTROL AND USED YOUR POWERS TO MANIFEST. AS SOON AS YOU *ACCEPTED* YOUR FEAR, YOU REGAINED YOUR POWER AND THE ILLUSION ENDED.
YA KNOW, YOUR MONSTER WAS *WAY* SCARIER THEN THE MOVIE...WANNA DO THIS AGAIN AT HALLOWEEN?
I'M AFRAID NOT.
THE END

¡MUCHA LUCHA!

"Getting Ahead"

Original Television Script Written by Peter Hastings

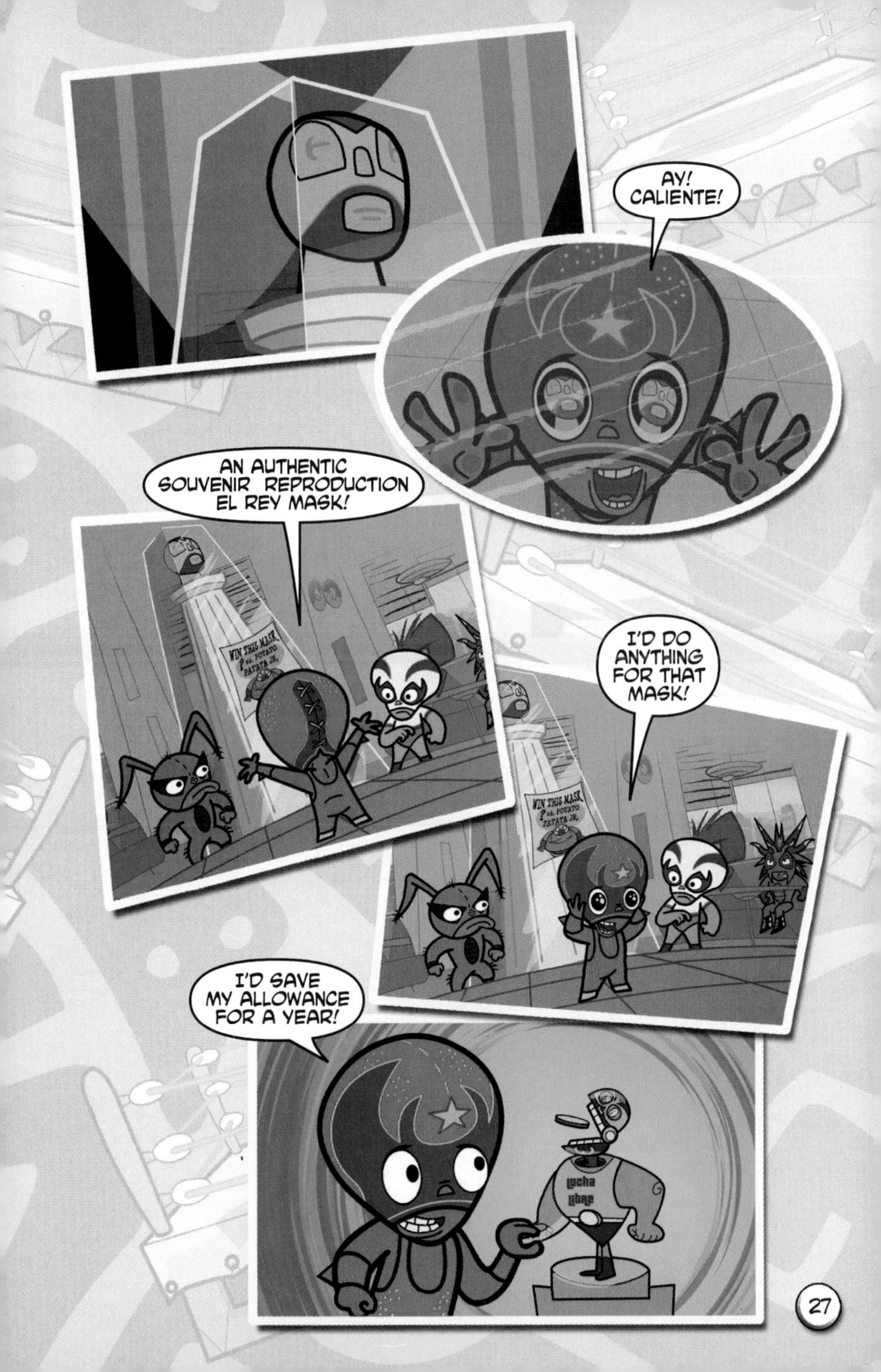
AY! CALIENTE!
AN AUTHENTIC SOUVENIR REPRODUCTION EL REY MASK!
WIN THIS MASK
I'D DO ANYTHING FOR THAT MASK!
I'D SAVE MY ALLOWANCE FOR A YEAR!
Lucha Libre

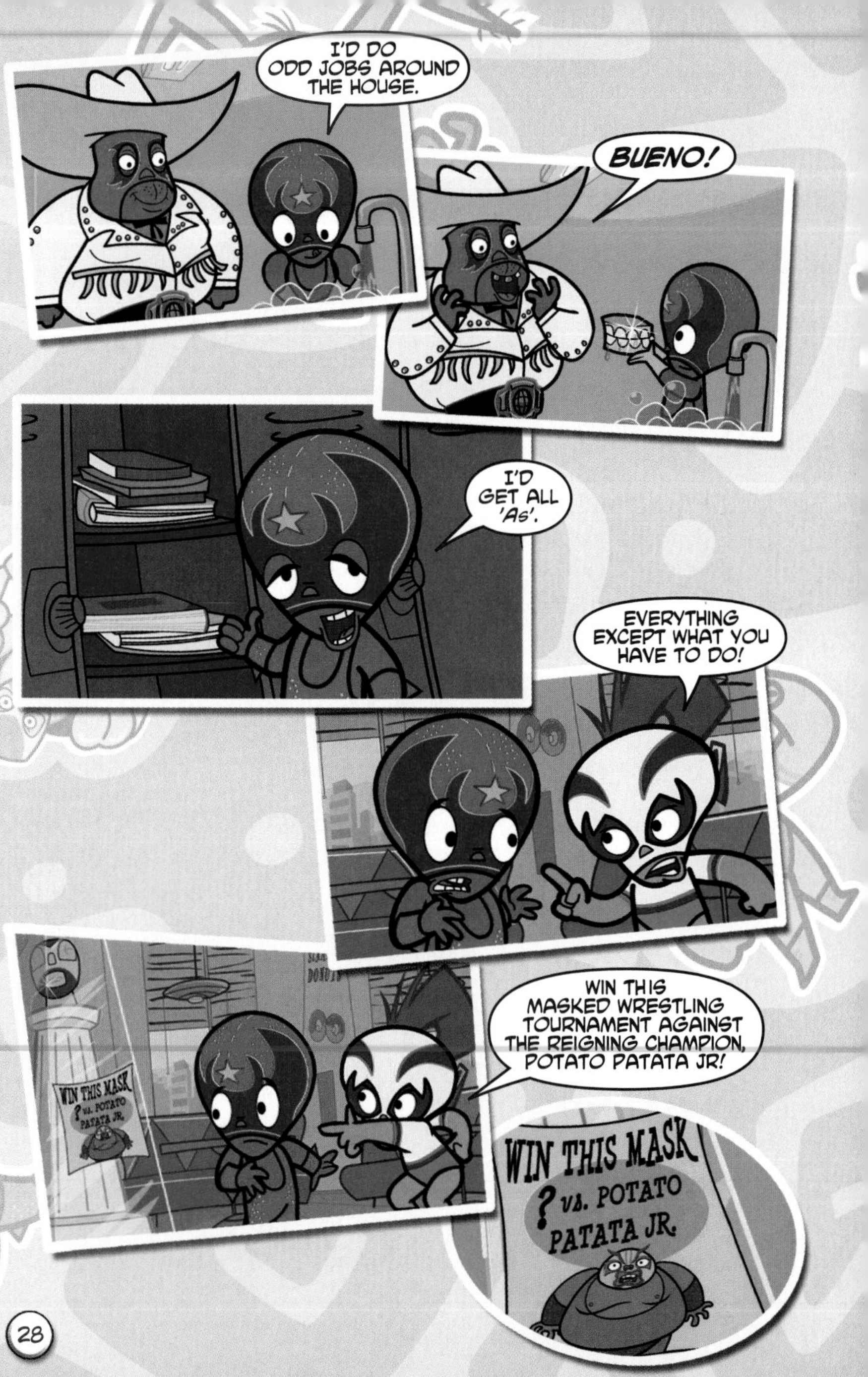
I'D DO ODD JOBS AROUND THE HOUSE.
BUENO!
I'D GET ALL 'As'.
EVERYTHING EXCEPT WHAT YOU HAVE TO DO!
WIN THIS MASKED WRESTLING TOURNAMENT AGAINST THE REIGNING CHAMPION, POTATO PATATA JR!
WIN THIS MASK ? vs. POTATO PATATA JR.

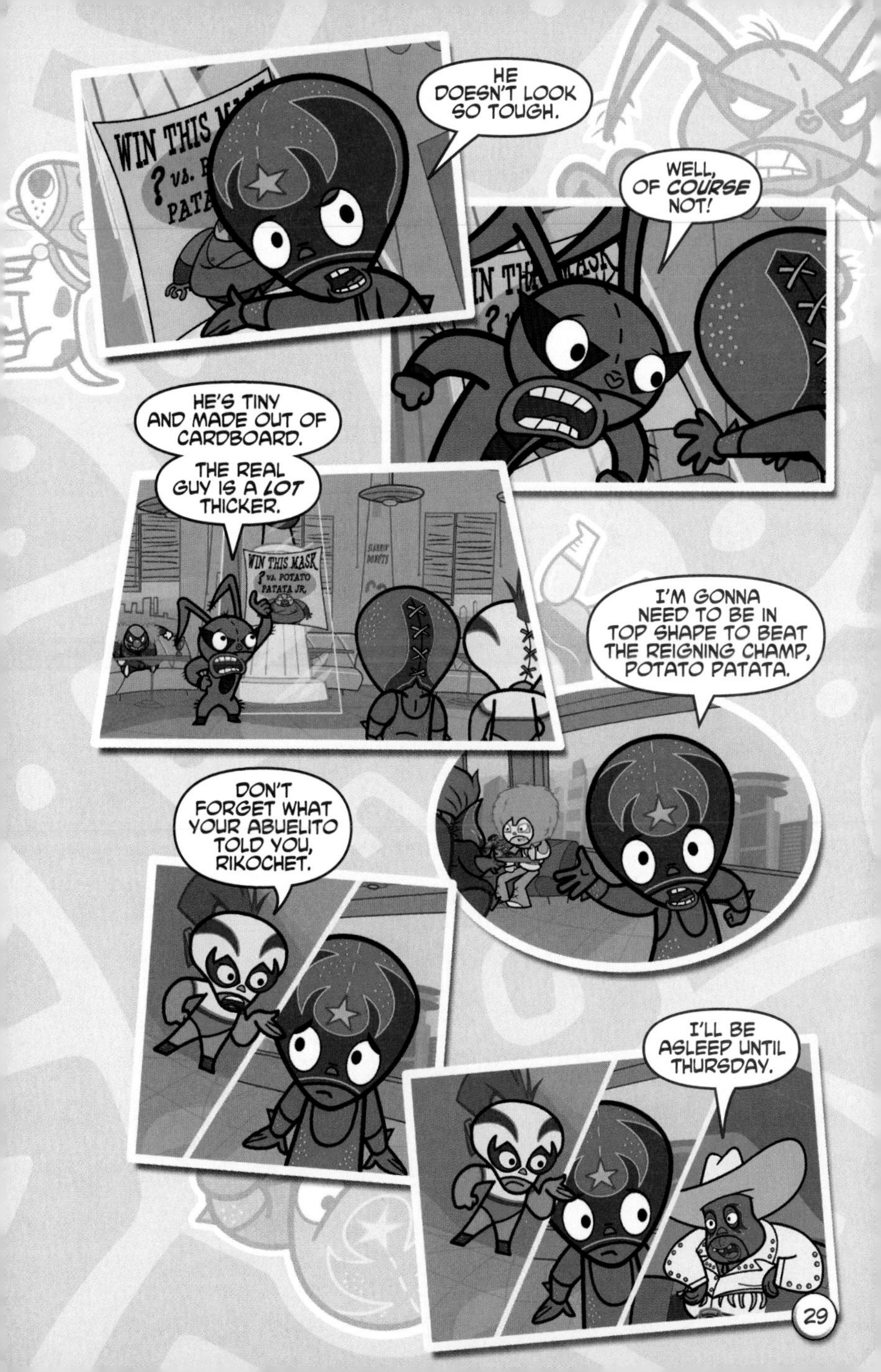

WIN THIS MASK
? vs. POTATO PATATA JR.
HE DOESN'T LOOK SO TOUGH.
WELL, OF *COURSE* NOT!
HE'S TINY AND MADE OUT OF CARDBOARD.
THE REAL GUY IS A *LOT* THICKER.
I'M GONNA NEED TO BE IN TOP SHAPE TO BEAT THE REIGNING CHAMP, POTATO PATATA.
DON'T FORGET WHAT YOUR ABUELITO TOLD YOU, RIKOCHET.
I'LL BE ASLEEP UNTIL THURSDAY.

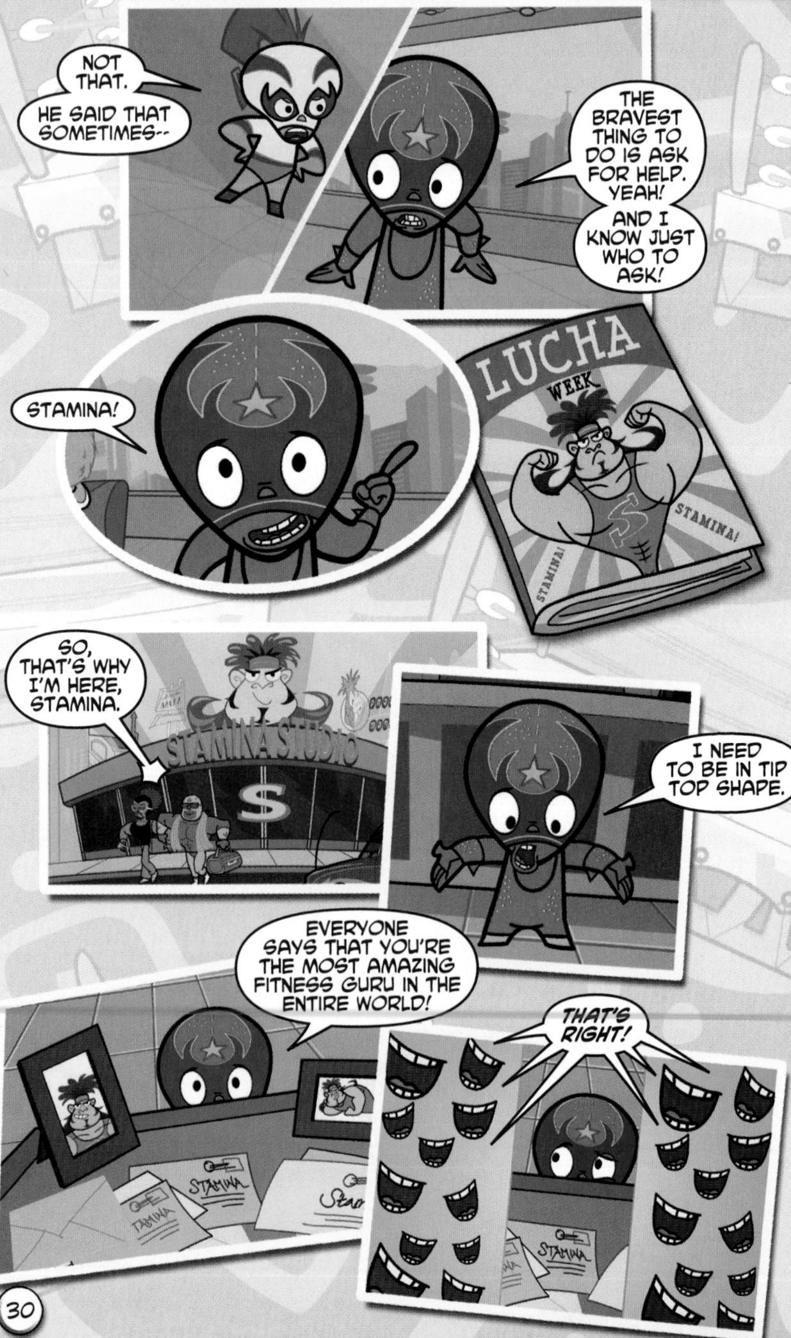
NOT THAT.
HE SAID THAT SOMETIMES--
THE BRAVEST THING TO DO IS ASK FOR HELP. YEAH!
AND I KNOW JUST WHO TO ASK!
STAMINA!
LUCHA WEEK
STAMINA!
STAMINA!
STAMINA!
SO, THAT'S WHY I'M HERE, STAMINA.
STAMINA STUDIO
I NEED TO BE IN TIP TOP SHAPE.
EVERYONE SAYS THAT YOU'RE THE MOST AMAZING FITNESS GURU IN THE ENTIRE WORLD!
THAT'S RIGHT!

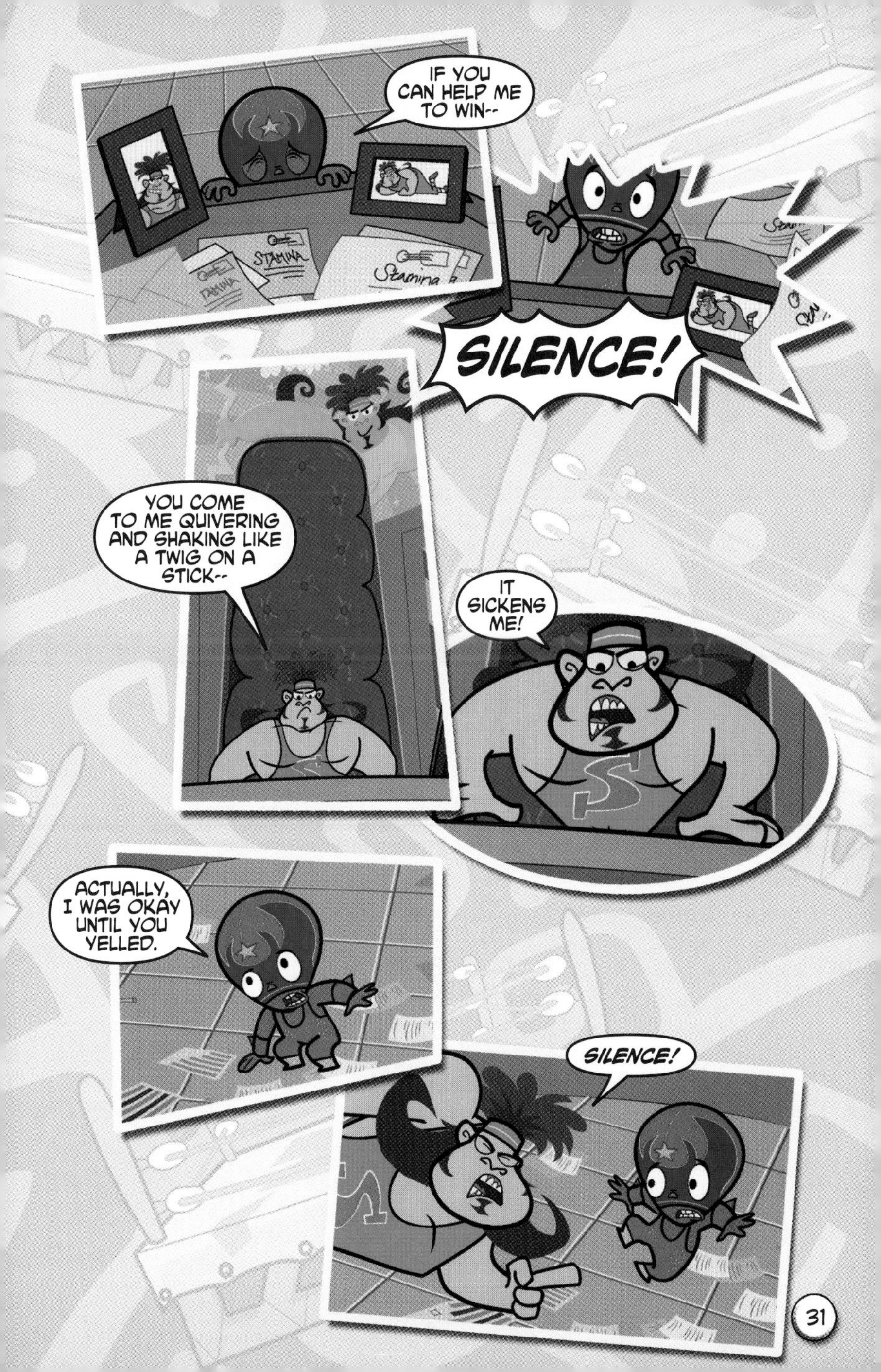
IF YOU CAN HELP ME TO WIN--
STAMINA
Stamina
SILENCE!
YOU COME TO ME QUIVERING AND SHAKING LIKE A TWIG ON A STICK--
IT SICKENS ME!
ACTUALLY, I WAS OKAY UNTIL YOU YELLED.
SILENCE!

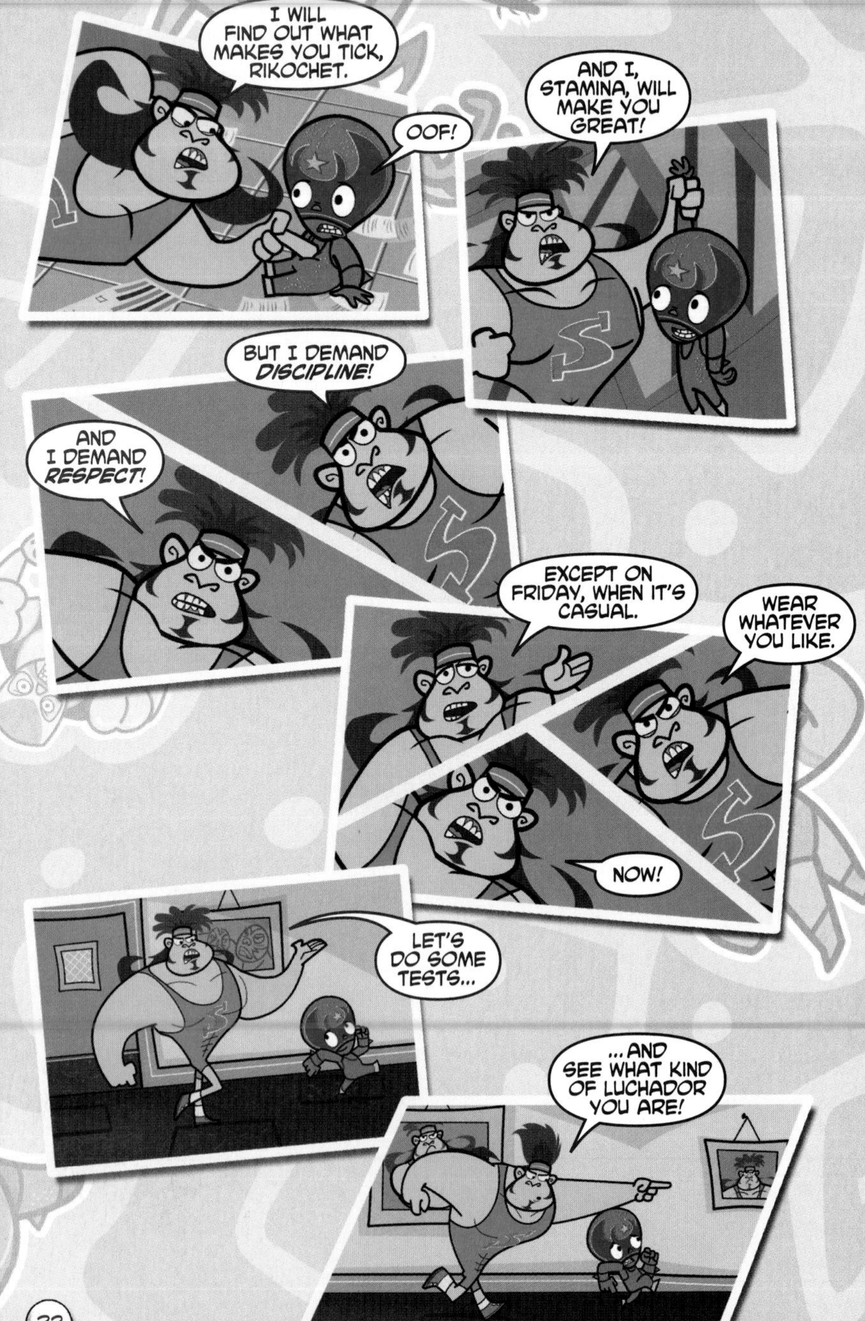
I WILL FIND OUT WHAT MAKES YOU TICK, RIKOCHET.
OOF!
AND I, STAMINA, WILL MAKE YOU GREAT!
BUT I DEMAND DISCIPLINE!
AND I DEMAND RESPECT!
EXCEPT ON FRIDAY, WHEN IT'S CASUAL.
WEAR WHATEVER YOU LIKE.
NOW!
LET'S DO SOME TESTS...
...AND SEE WHAT KIND OF LUCHADOR YOU ARE!

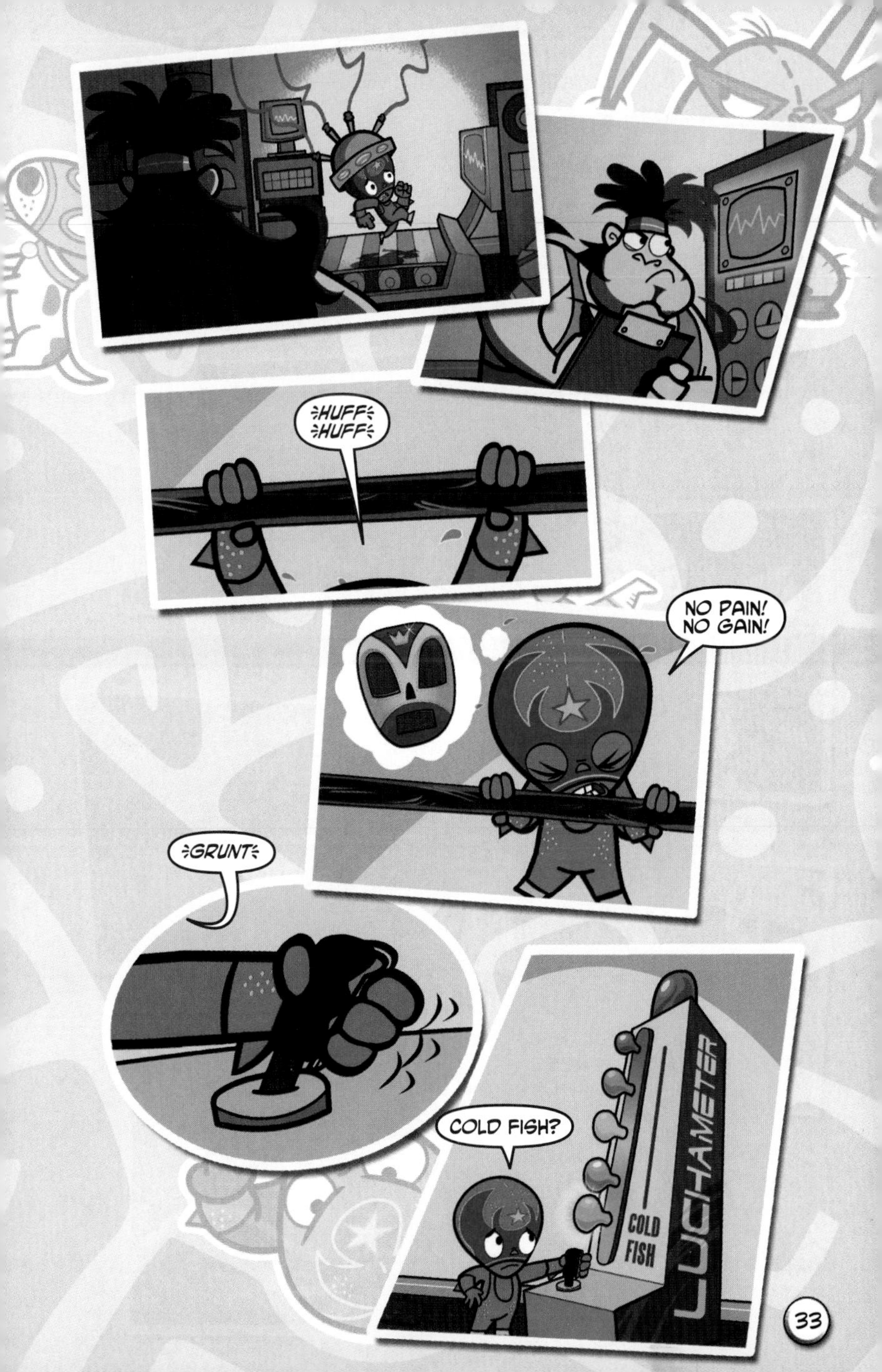

HUFF HUFF
NO PAIN! NO GAIN!
GRUNT
COLD FISH?
LUCHAMETER
COLD FISH

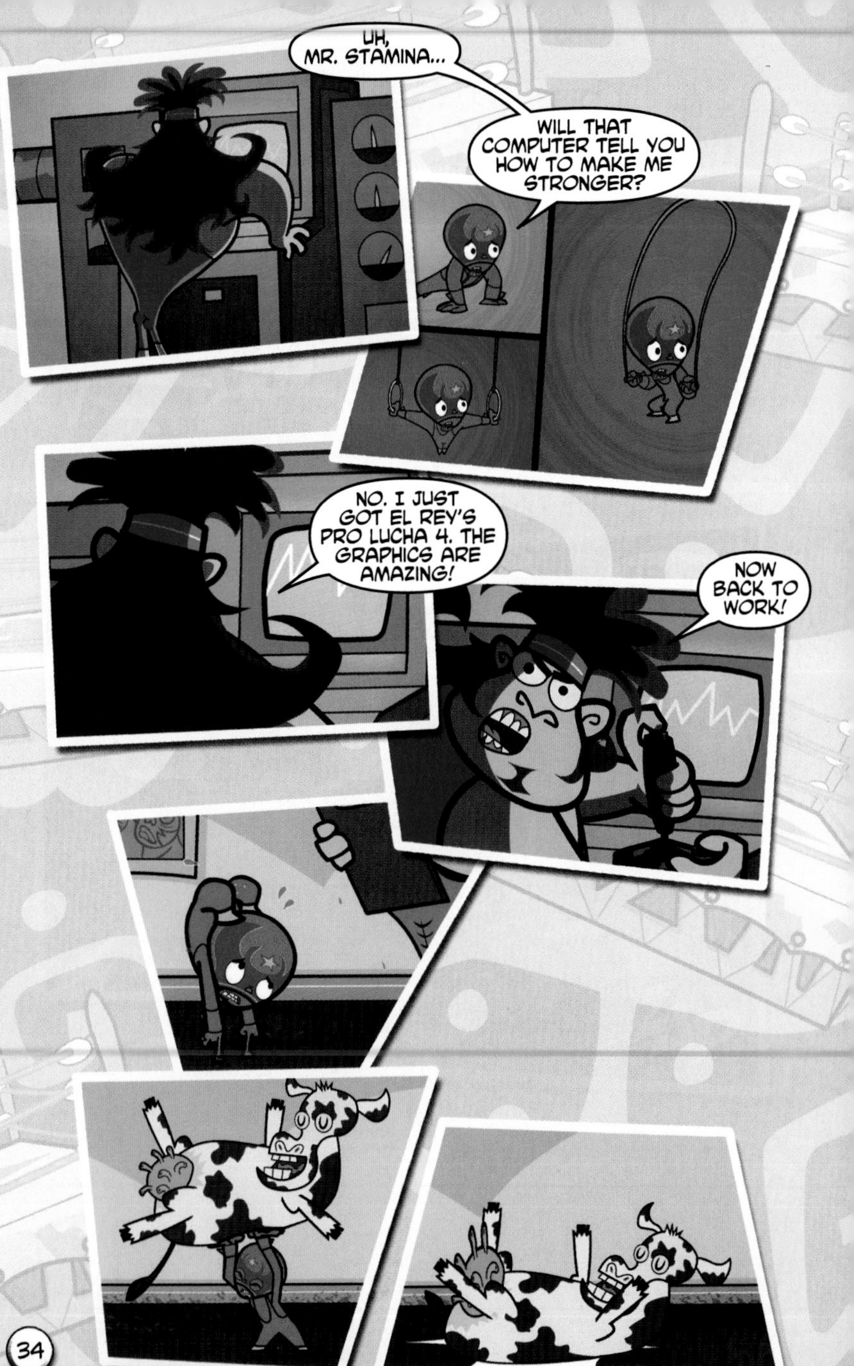
UH, MR. STAMINA...
WILL THAT COMPUTER TELL YOU HOW TO MAKE ME STRONGER?
NO. I JUST GOT EL REY'S PRO LUCHA 4. THE GRAPHICS ARE AMAZING!
NOW BACK TO WORK!

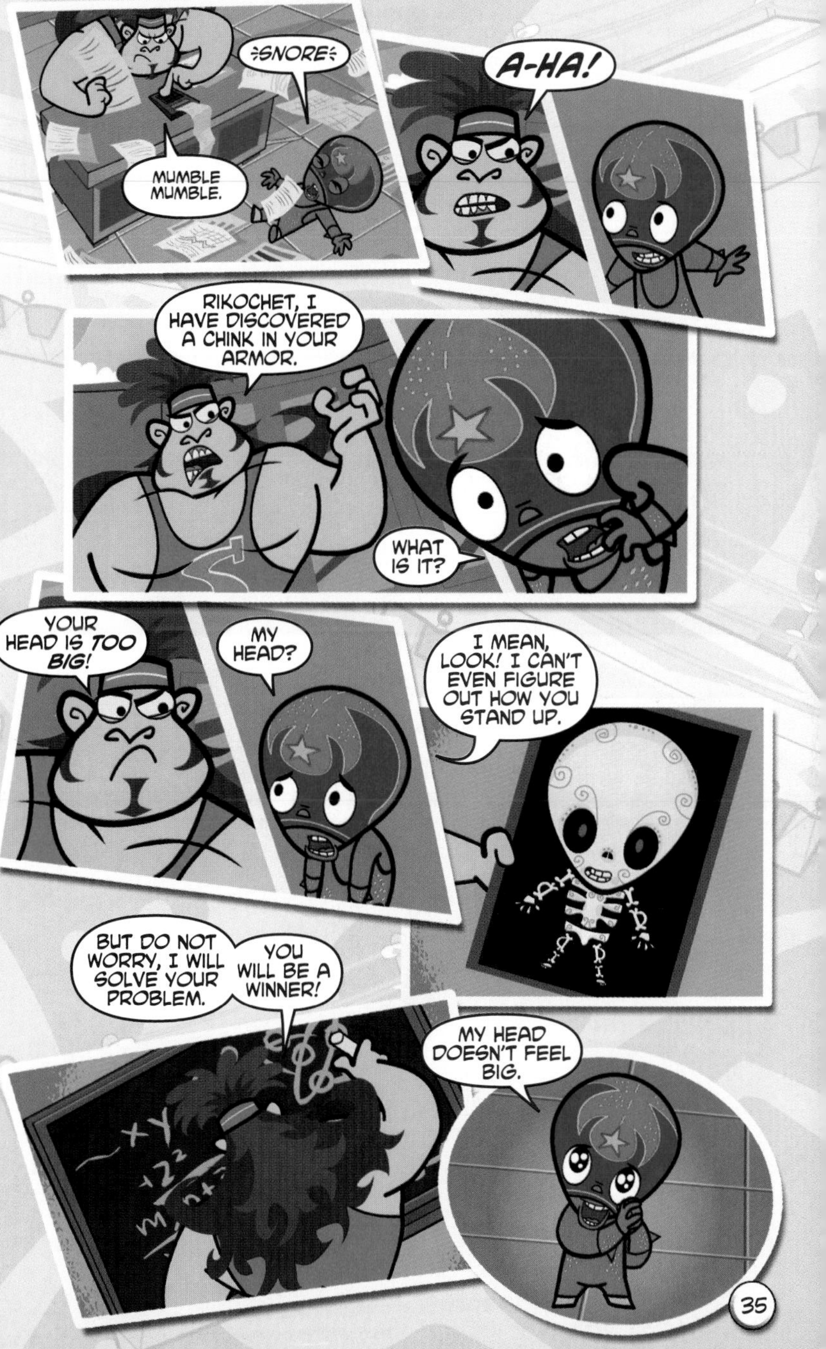
SNORE
MUMBLE MUMBLE.
A-HA!
RIKOCHET, I HAVE DISCOVERED A CHINK IN YOUR ARMOR.
WHAT IS IT?
YOUR HEAD IS *TOO BIG!*
MY HEAD?
I MEAN, LOOK! I CAN'T EVEN FIGURE OUT HOW YOU STAND UP.
BUT DO NOT WORRY, I WILL SOLVE YOUR PROBLEM.
YOU WILL BE A WINNER!
MY HEAD DOESN'T FEEL BIG.

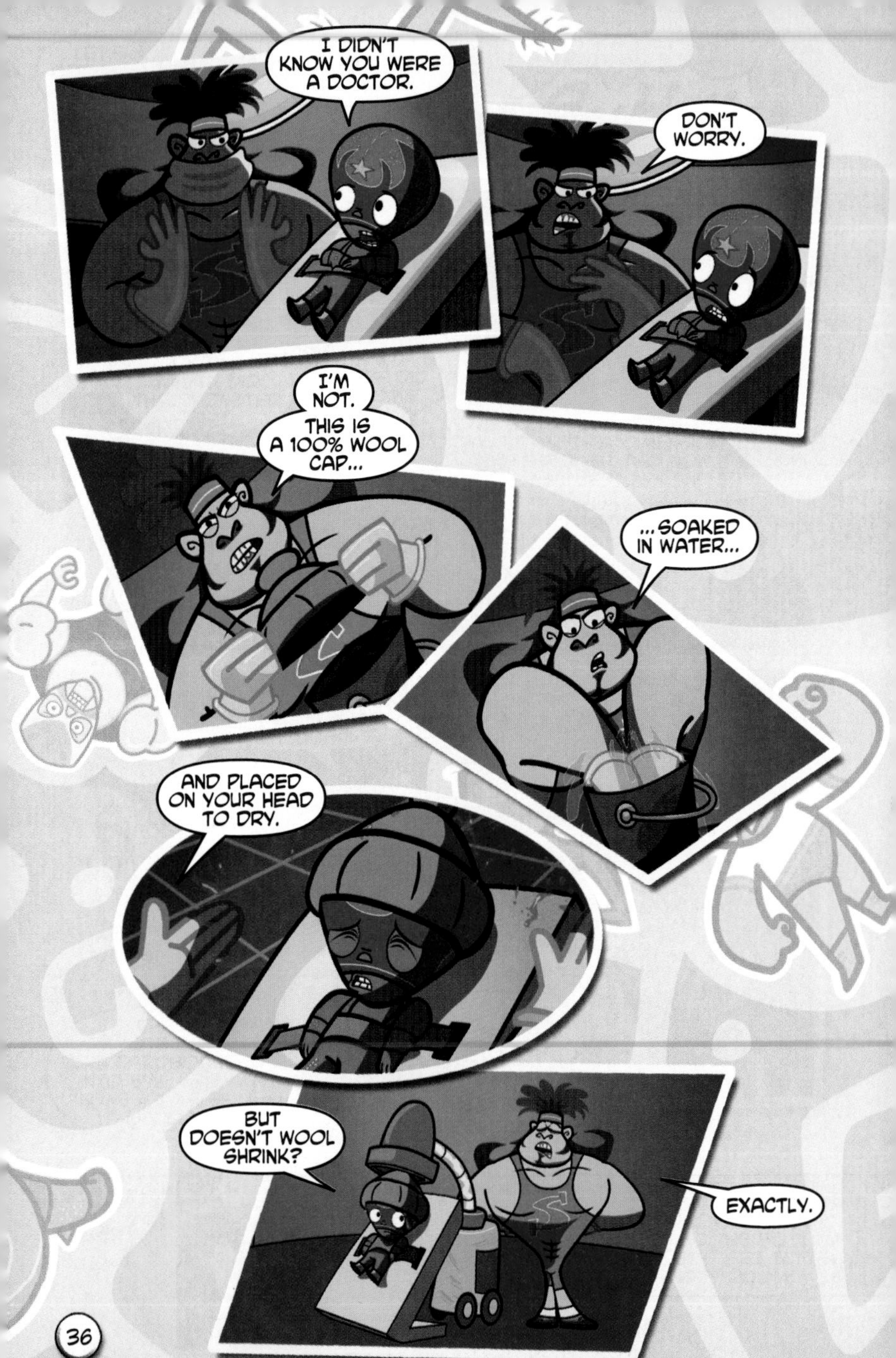
I DIDN'T KNOW YOU WERE A DOCTOR.
DON'T WORRY.
I'M NOT.
THIS IS A 100% WOOL CAP...
...SOAKED IN WATER...
AND PLACED ON YOUR HEAD TO DRY.
BUT DOESN'T WOOL SHRINK?
EXACTLY.

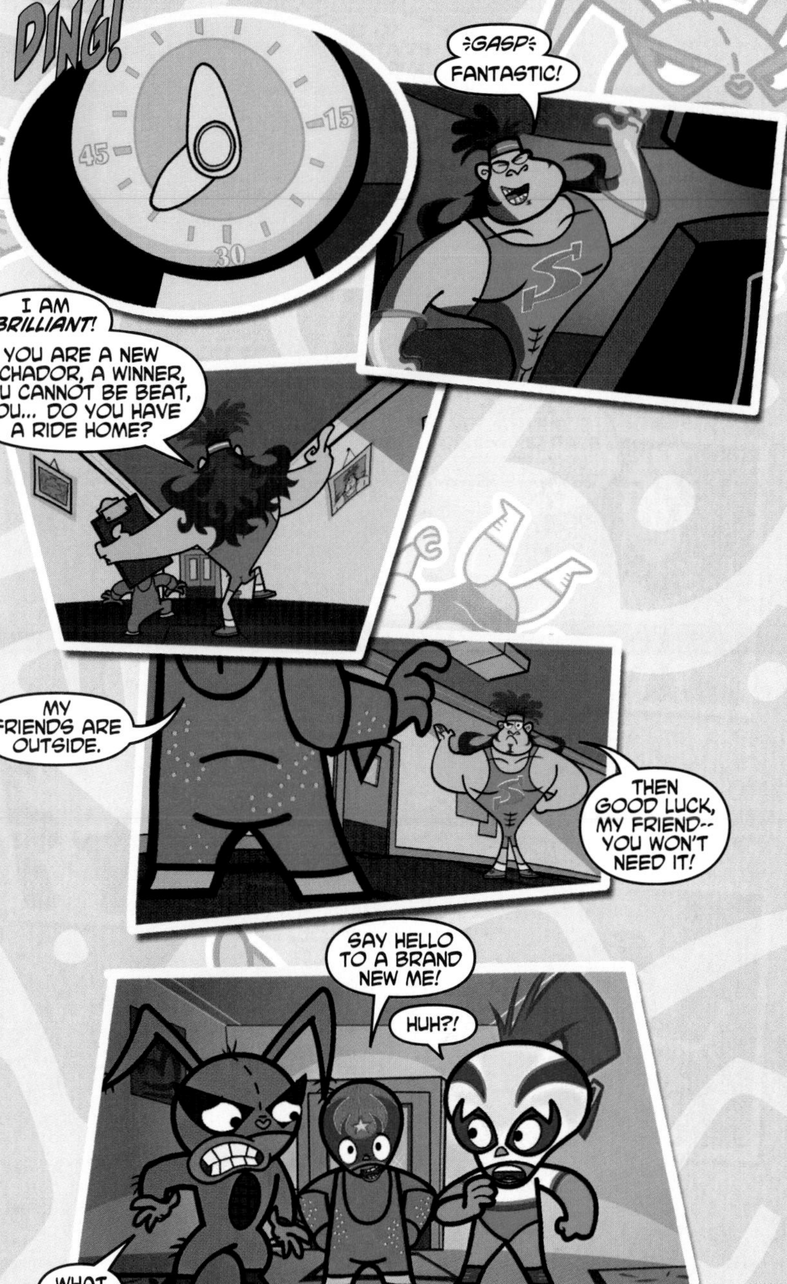
DING!
GASP
FANTASTIC!
I AM BRILLIANT!
YOU ARE A NEW LUCHADOR, A WINNER, YOU CANNOT BE BEAT, YOU... DO YOU HAVE A RIDE HOME?
MY FRIENDS ARE OUTSIDE.
THEN GOOD LUCK, MY FRIEND-- YOU WON'T NEED IT!
SAY HELLO TO A BRAND NEW ME!
HUH?!
WHAT TH--?!

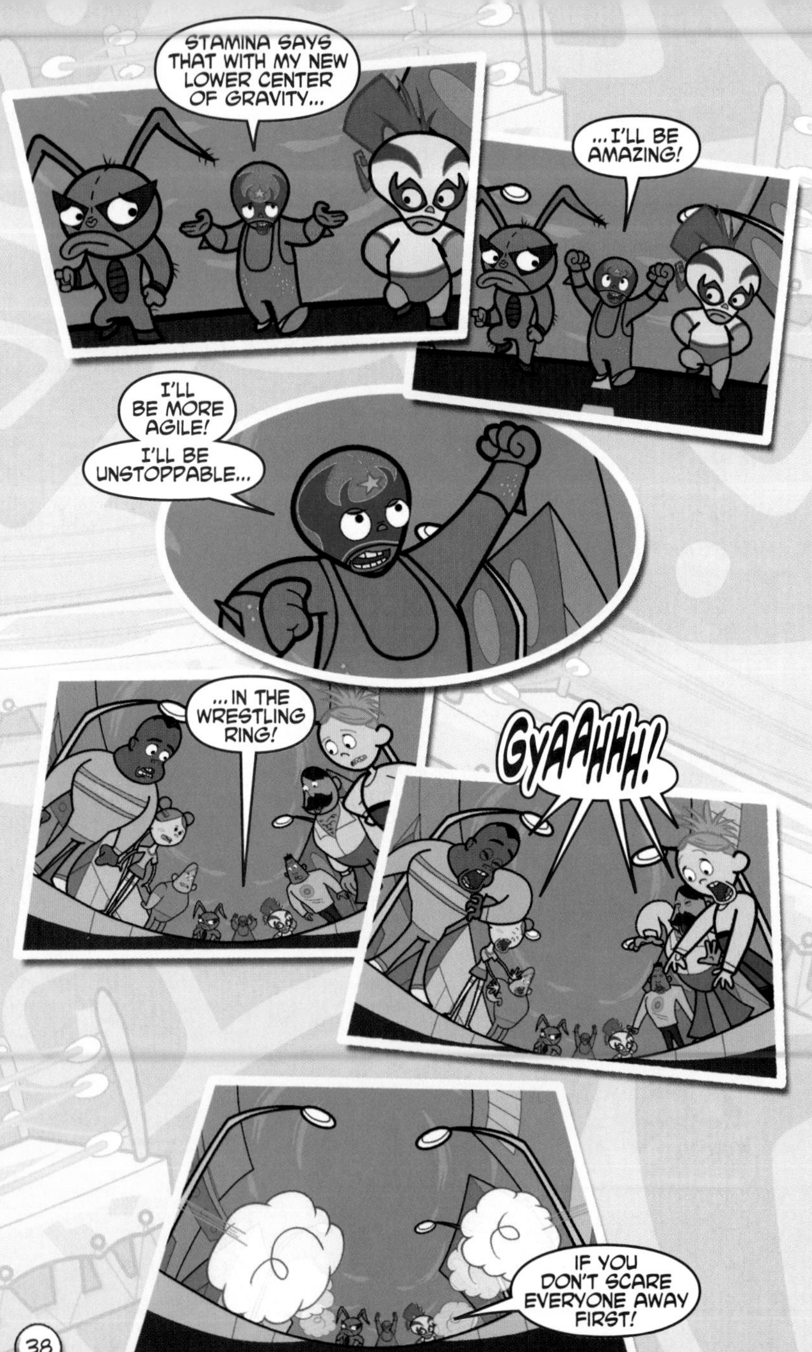
STAMINA SAYS THAT WITH MY NEW LOWER CENTER OF GRAVITY...
...I'LL BE AMAZING!
I'LL BE MORE AGILE!
I'LL BE UNSTOPPABLE...
...IN THE WRESTLING RING!
GYAAHHH!
IF YOU DON'T SCARE EVERYONE AWAY FIRST!

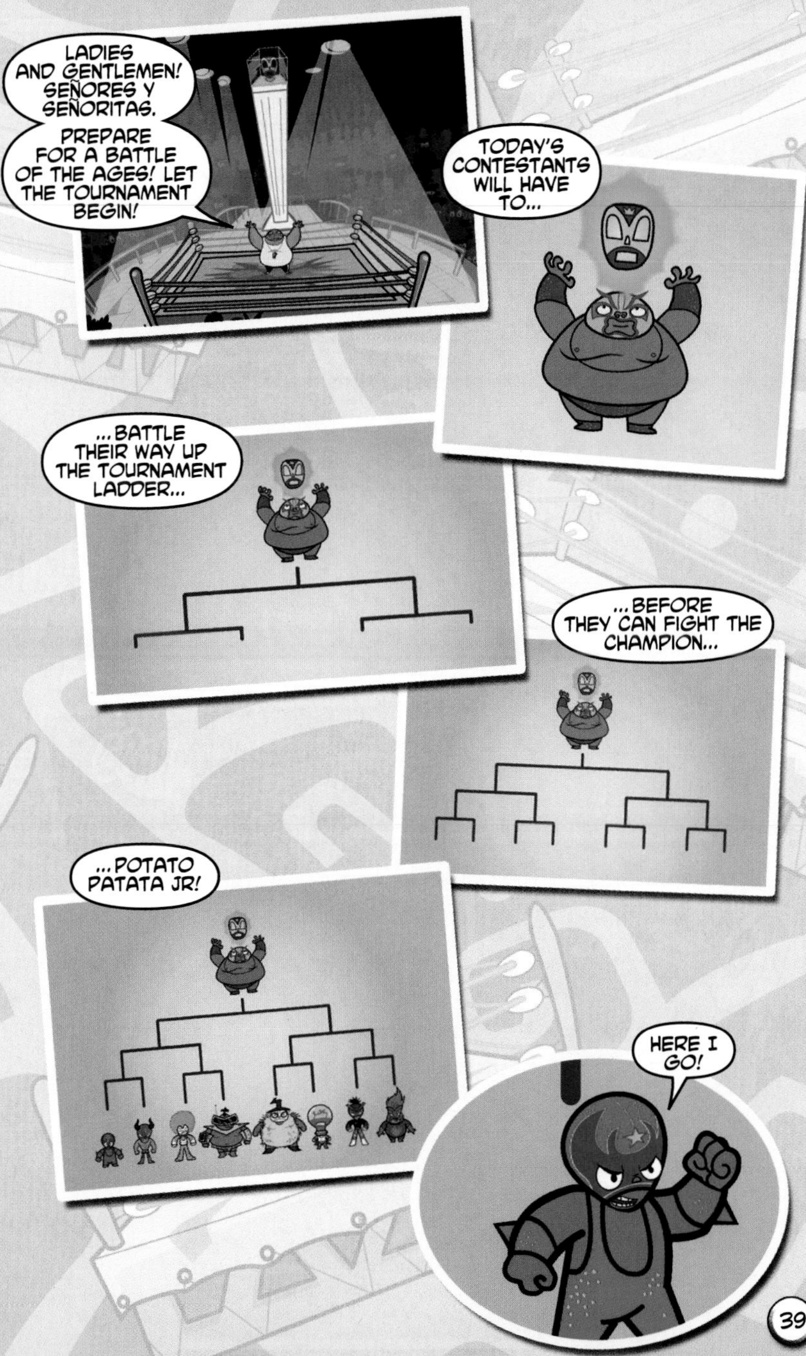
LADIES AND GENTLEMEN! SEÑORES Y SEÑORITAS.
PREPARE FOR A BATTLE OF THE AGES! LET THE TOURNAMENT BEGIN!
TODAY'S CONTESTANTS WILL HAVE TO...
...BATTLE THEIR WAY UP THE TOURNAMENT LADDER...
...BEFORE THEY CAN FIGHT THE CHAMPION...
...POTATO PATATA JR!
HERE I GO!

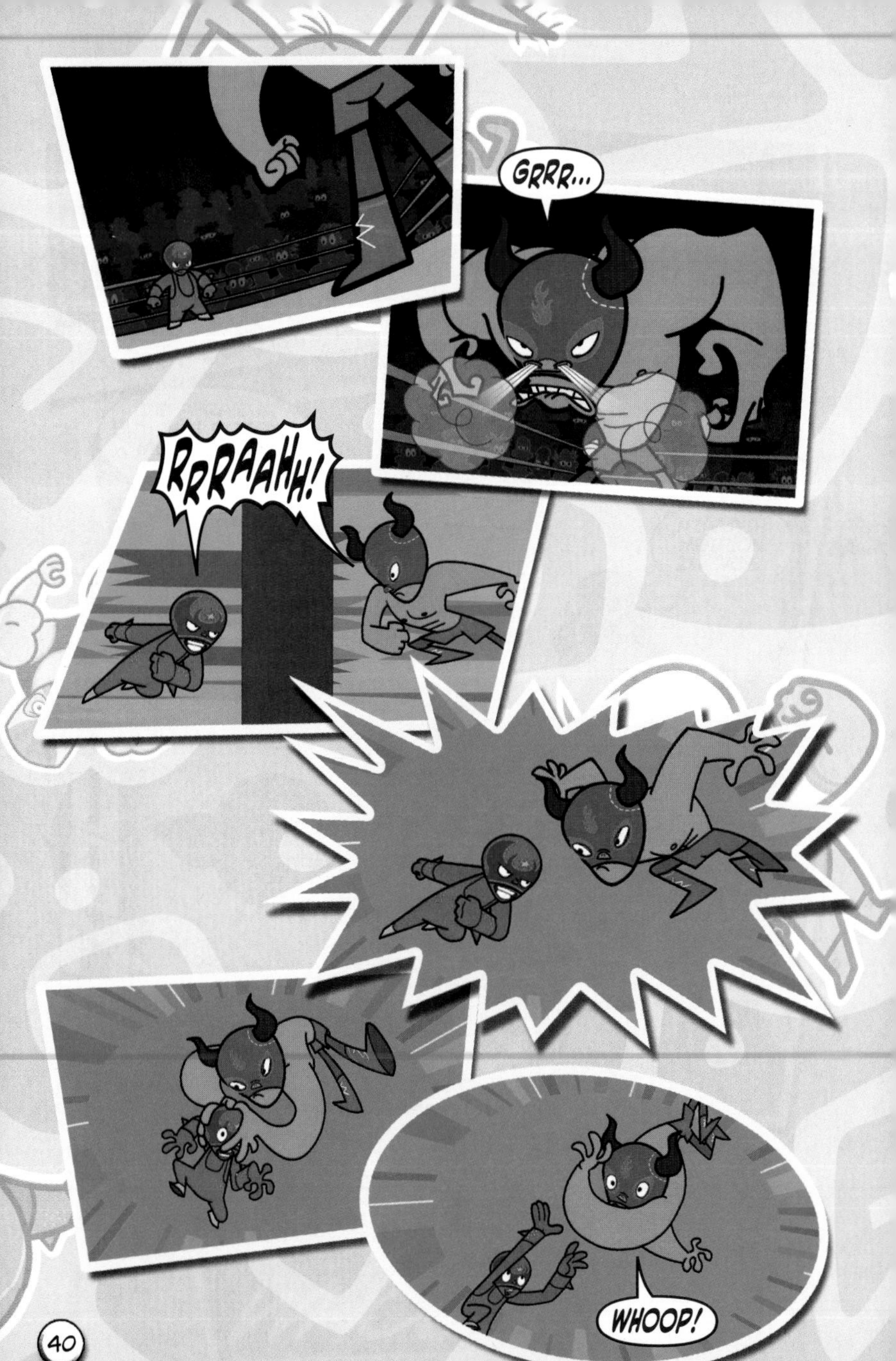
GRRR...
RRRAAHH!
WHOOP!

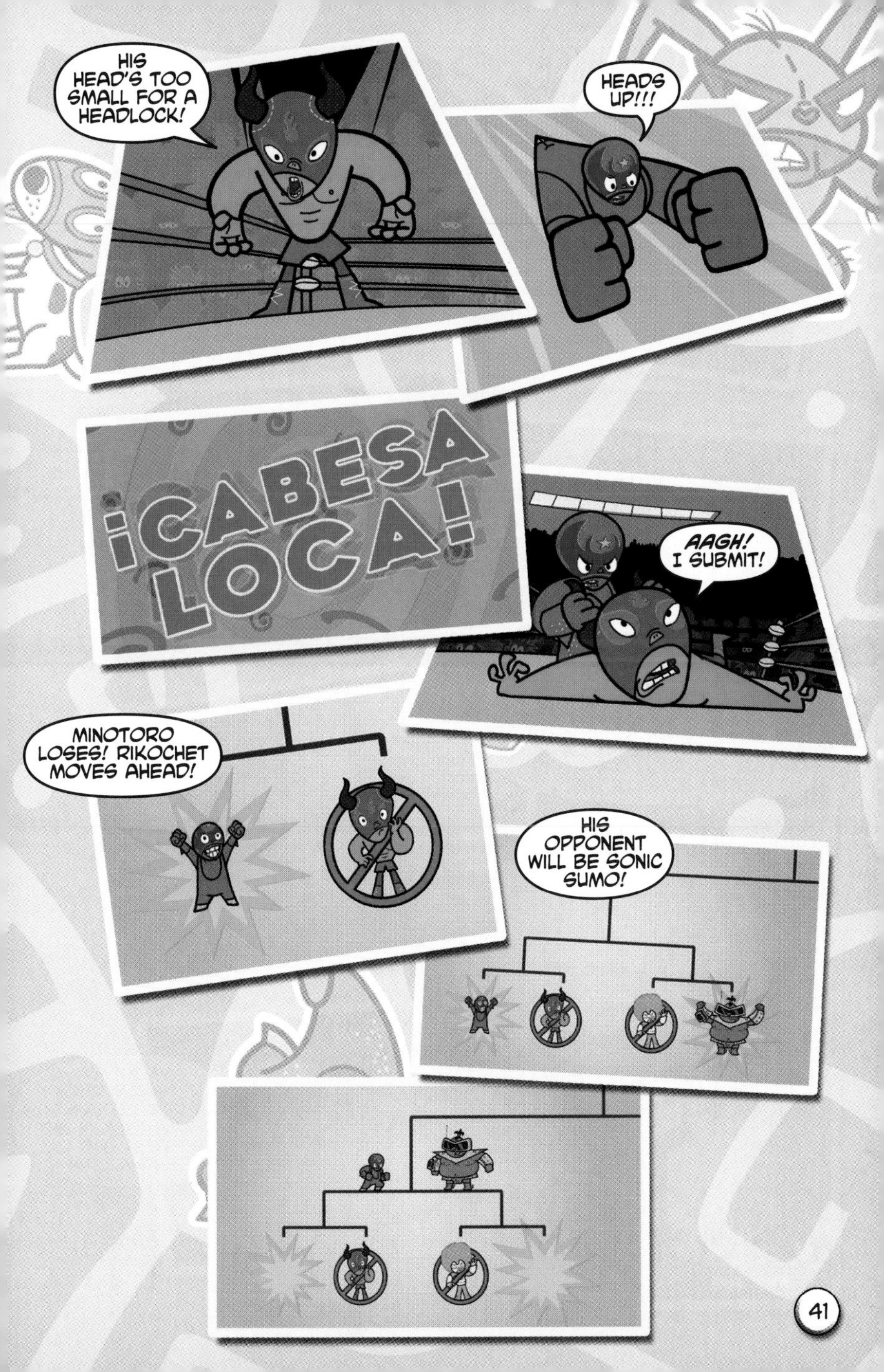
HIS HEAD'S TOO SMALL FOR A HEADLOCK!
HEADS UP!!!
¡CABESA LOCA!
AAGH! I SUBMIT!
MINOTORO LOSES! RIKOCHET MOVES AHEAD!
HIS OPPONENT WILL BE SONIC SUMO!

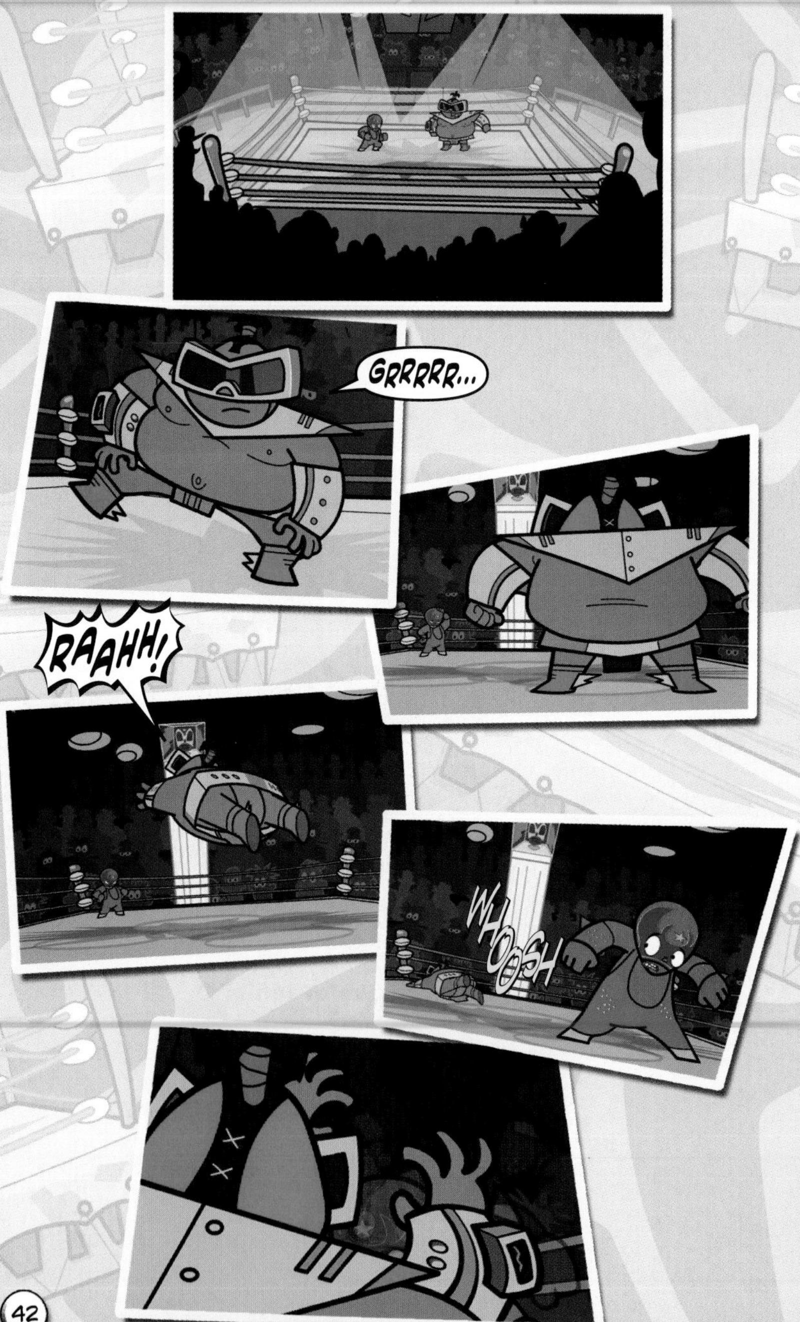
GRRRRR...
RAAHH!
WHOOSH

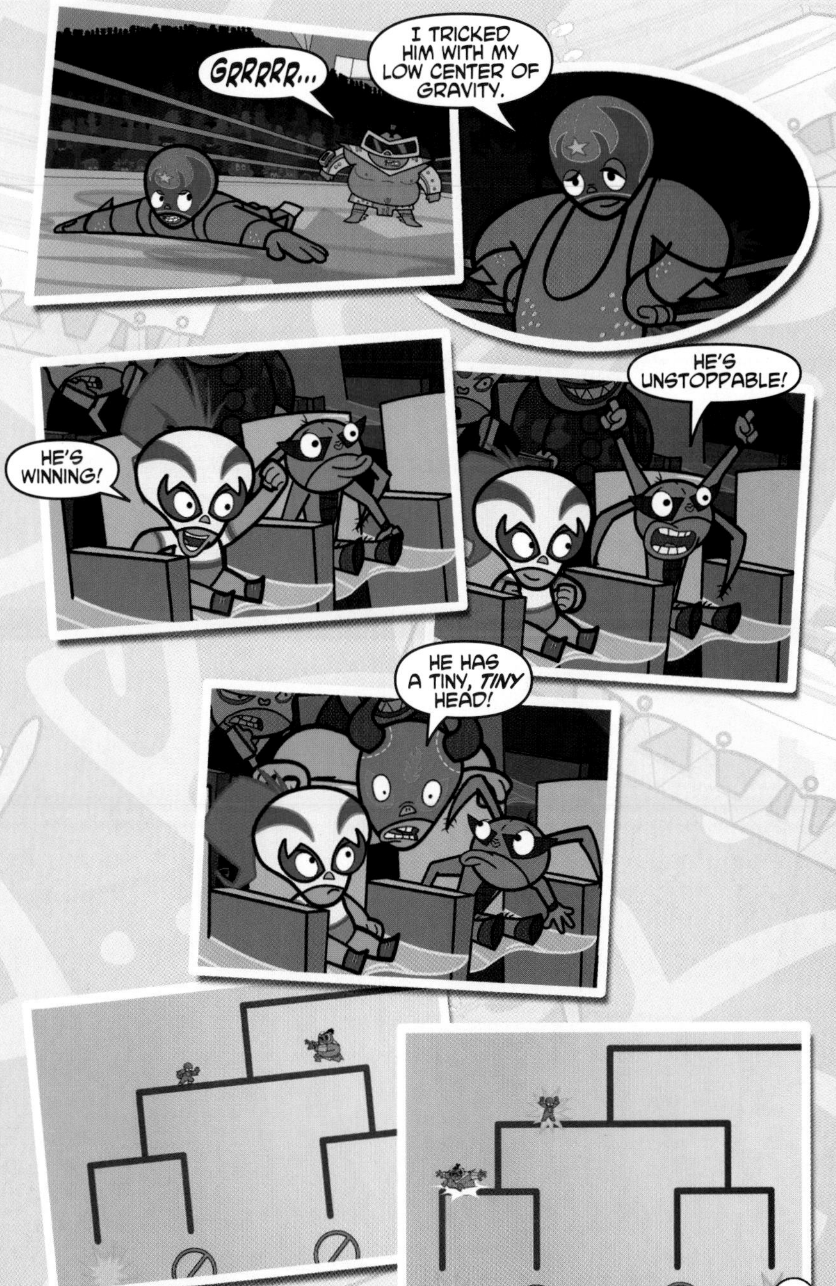
GRRRRR...
I TRICKED HIM WITH MY LOW CENTER OF GRAVITY.
HE'S WINNING!
HE'S UNSTOPPABLE!
HE HAS A TINY, *TINY* HEAD!

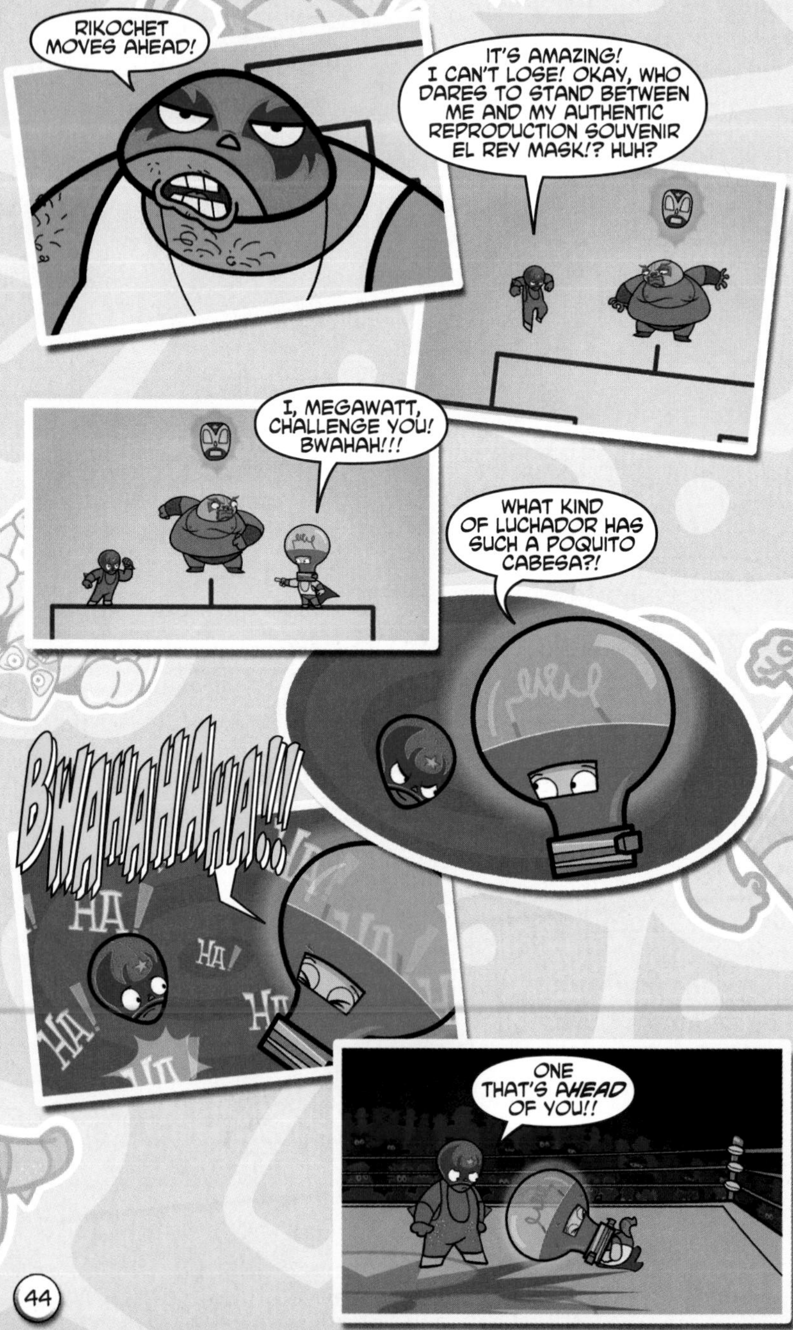
RIKOCHET MOVES AHEAD!
IT'S AMAZING! I CAN'T LOSE! OKAY, WHO DARES TO STAND BETWEEN ME AND MY AUTHENTIC REPRODUCTION SOUVENIR EL REY MASK!? HUH?
I, MEGAWATT, CHALLENGE YOU! BWAHAH!!!
WHAT KIND OF LUCHADOR HAS SUCH A POQUITO CABESA?!
BWAHAHAHAHA!!!..
HA!
HA!
HA!
ONE THAT'S AHEAD OF YOU!!

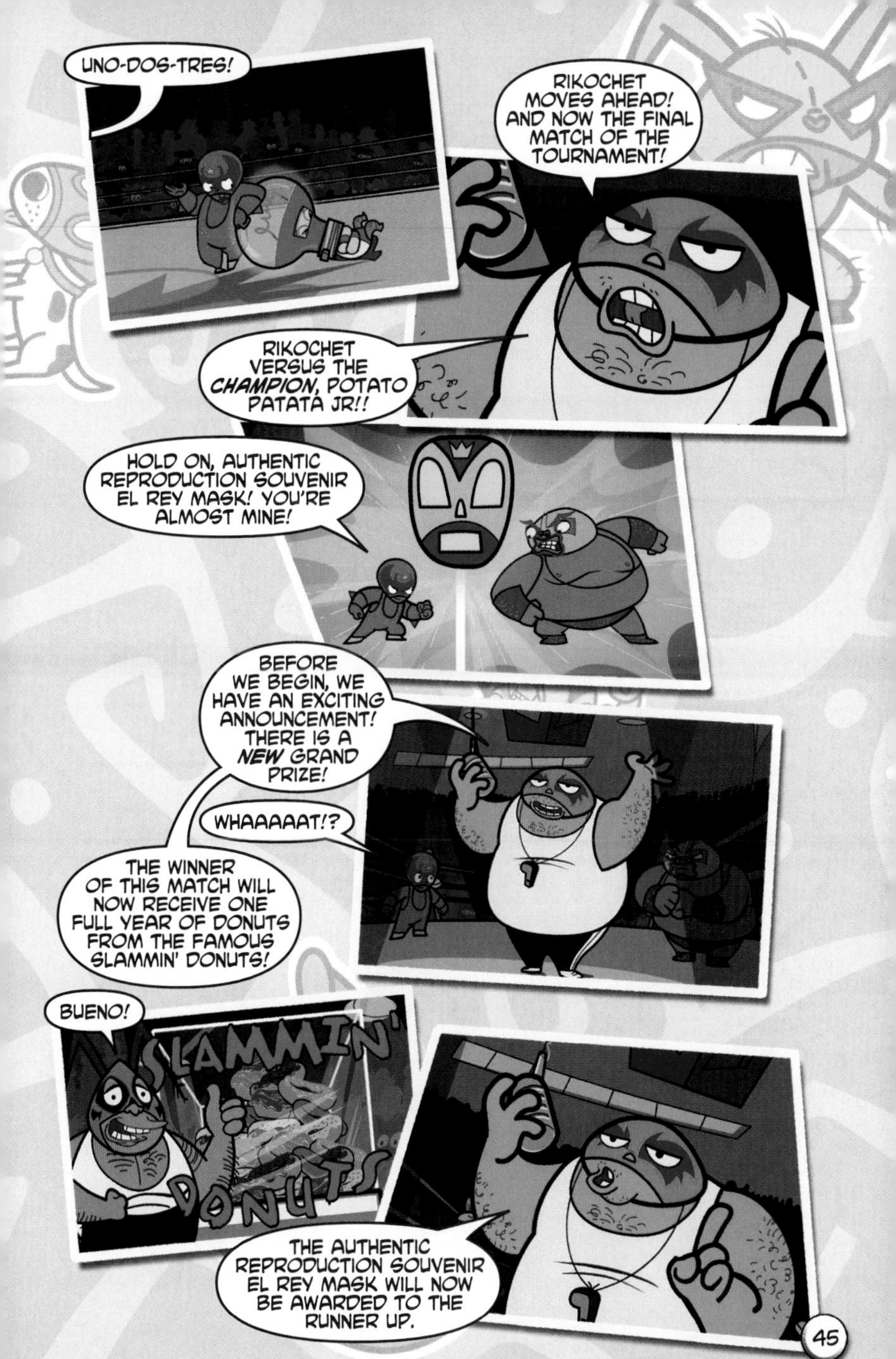
UNO-DOS-TRES!
RIKOCHET MOVES AHEAD! AND NOW THE FINAL MATCH OF THE TOURNAMENT!
RIKOCHET VERSUS THE *CHAMPION*, POTATO PATATA JR!!
HOLD ON, AUTHENTIC REPRODUCTION SOUVENIR EL REY MASK! YOU'RE ALMOST MINE!
BEFORE WE BEGIN, WE HAVE AN EXCITING ANNOUNCEMENT! THERE IS A *NEW* GRAND PRIZE!
WHAAAAAT!?
THE WINNER OF THIS MATCH WILL NOW RECEIVE ONE FULL YEAR OF DONUTS FROM THE FAMOUS SLAMMIN' DONUTS!
BUENO!
SLAMMIN'
DONUTS
THE AUTHENTIC REPRODUCTION SOUVENIR EL REY MASK WILL NOW BE AWARDED TO THE RUNNER UP.

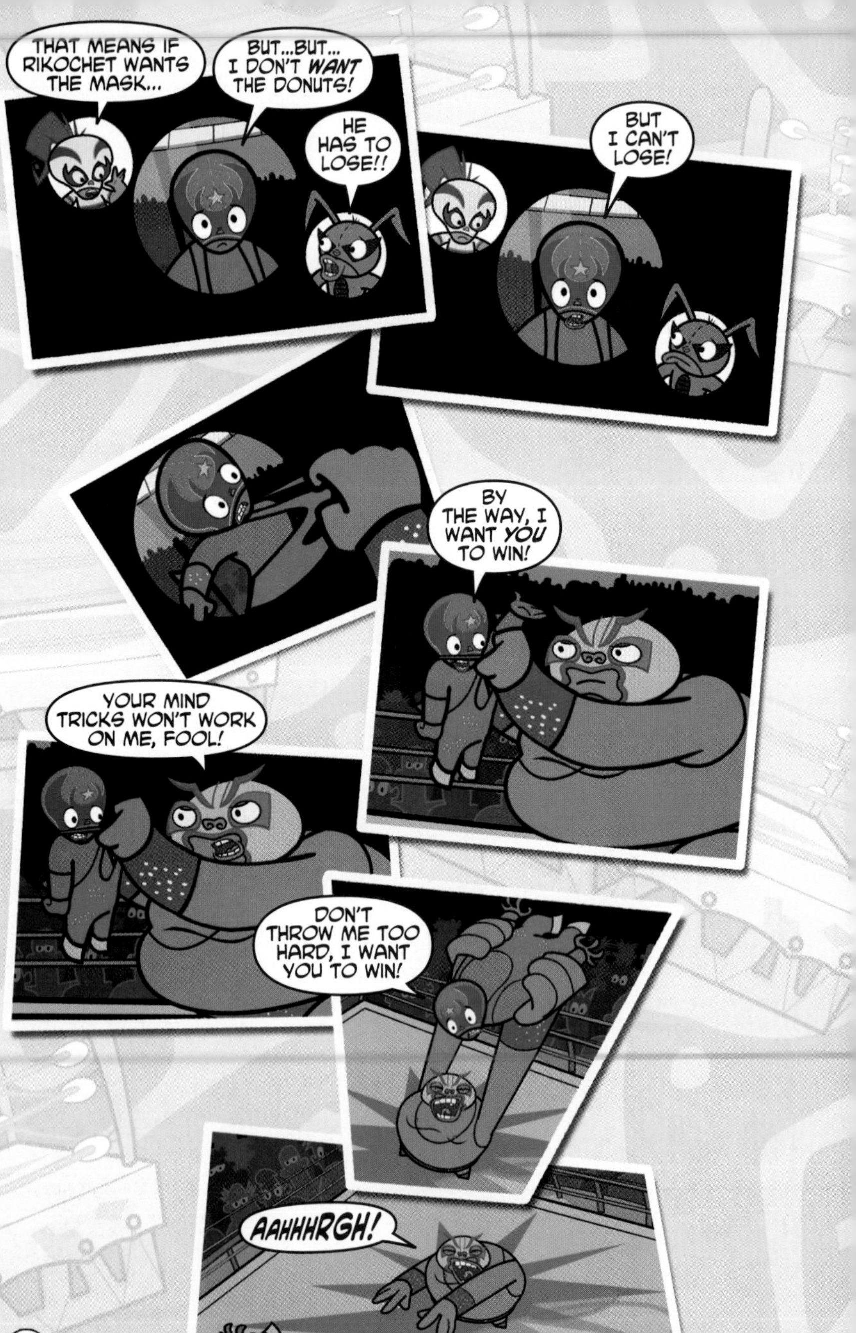

THAT MEANS IF RIKOCHET WANTS THE MASK...
BUT...BUT... I DON'T *WANT* THE DONUTS!
HE HAS TO LOSE!!
BUT I CAN'T LOSE!
BY THE WAY, I WANT *YOU* TO WIN!
YOUR MIND TRICKS WON'T WORK ON ME, FOOL!
DON'T THROW ME TOO HARD, I WANT YOU TO WIN!
AAHHHRGH!

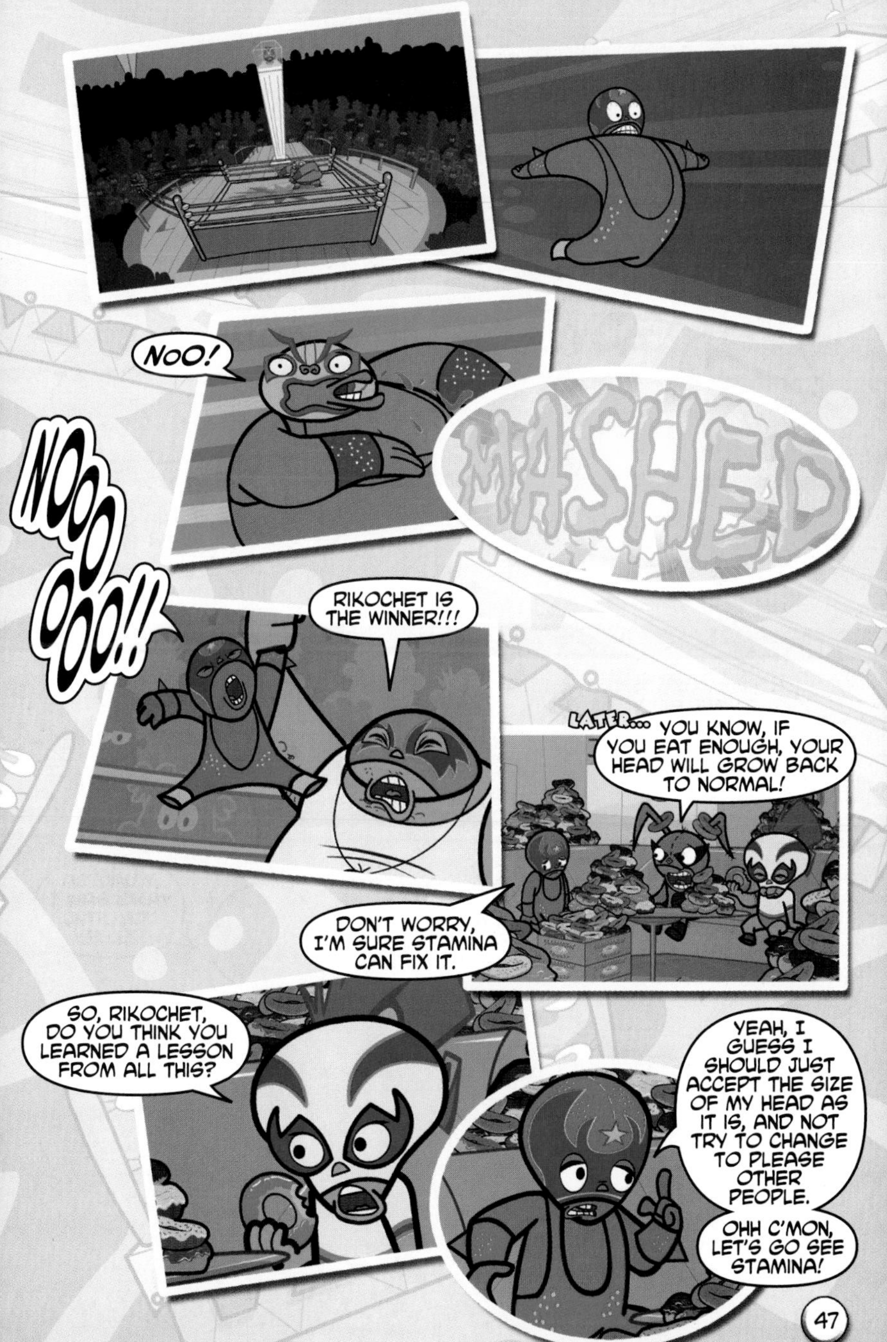

NoO!
MASHED
NOOOOOOO!!
RIKOCHET IS THE WINNER!!!
LATER...
YOU KNOW, IF YOU EAT ENOUGH, YOUR HEAD WILL GROW BACK TO NORMAL!
DON'T WORRY, I'M SURE STAMINA CAN FIX IT.
SO, RIKOCHET, DO YOU THINK YOU LEARNED A LESSON FROM ALL THIS?
YEAH, I GUESS I SHOULD JUST ACCEPT THE SIZE OF MY HEAD AS IT IS, AND NOT TRY TO CHANGE TO PLEASE OTHER PEOPLE.
OHH C'MON, LET'S GO SEE STAMINA!

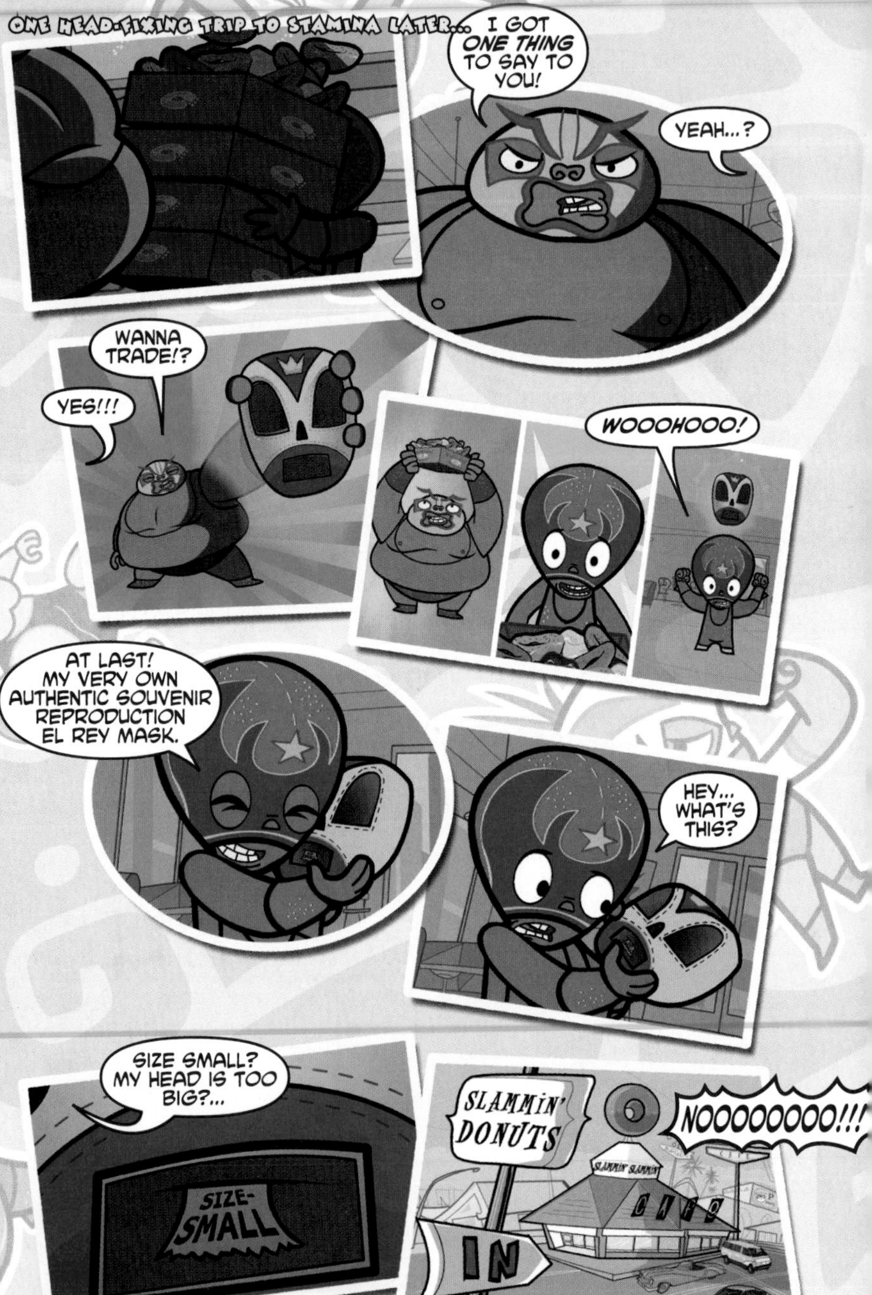
ONE HEAD-FIXING TRIP TO STAMINA LATER...
I GOT ONE THING TO SAY TO YOU!
YEAH...?
WANNA TRADE!?
YES!!!
WOOOHOOO!
AT LAST! MY VERY OWN AUTHENTIC SOUVENIR REPRODUCTION EL REY MASK.
HEY... WHAT'S THIS?
SIZE SMALL? MY HEAD IS TOO BIG?...
SIZE-SMALL
SLAMMIN' DONUTS
NOOOOOOOO!!!
IN
THE END

SCOOBY-DOO!

"Mummy Scares Best"

Original Television Script Written by
Ed Scharlach

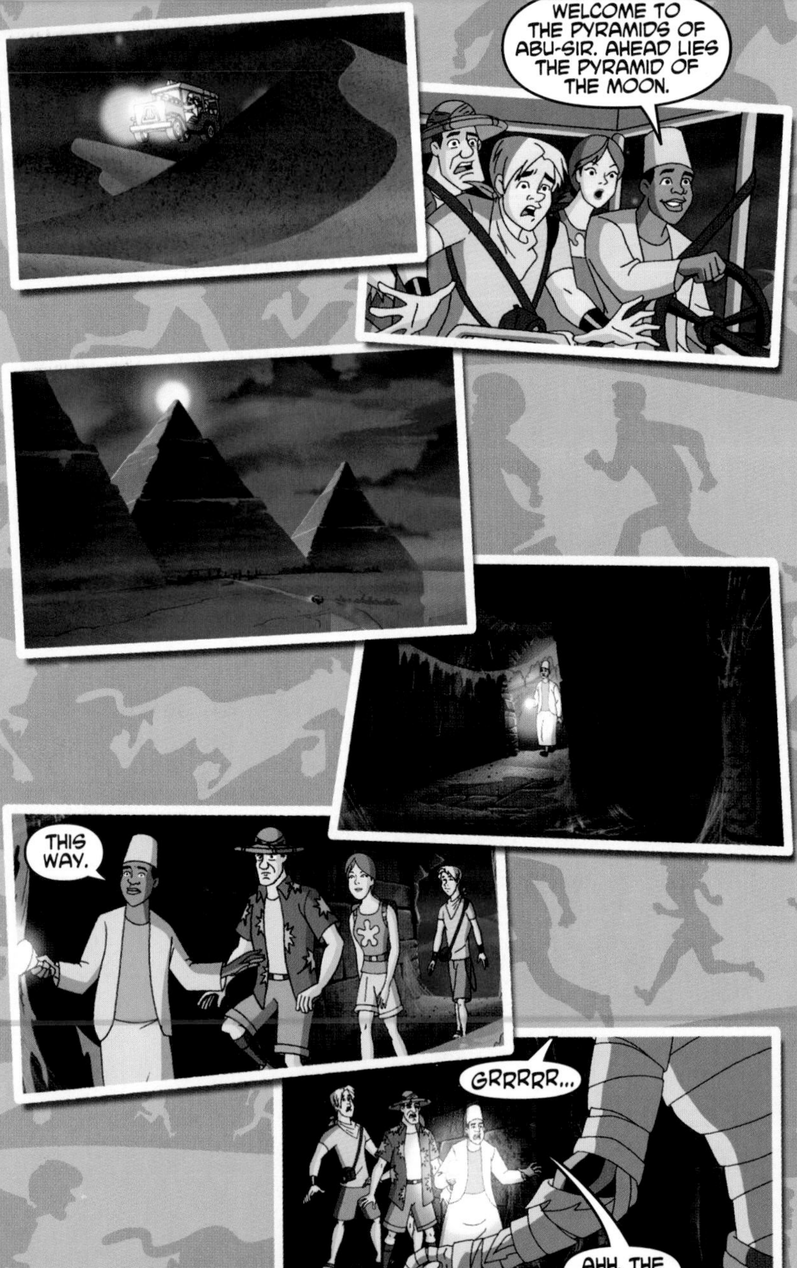
WELCOME TO THE PYRAMIDS OF ABU-SIR. AHEAD LIES THE PYRAMID OF THE MOON.
THIS WAY.
GRRRRR...
AHH, THE *MUMMY!*

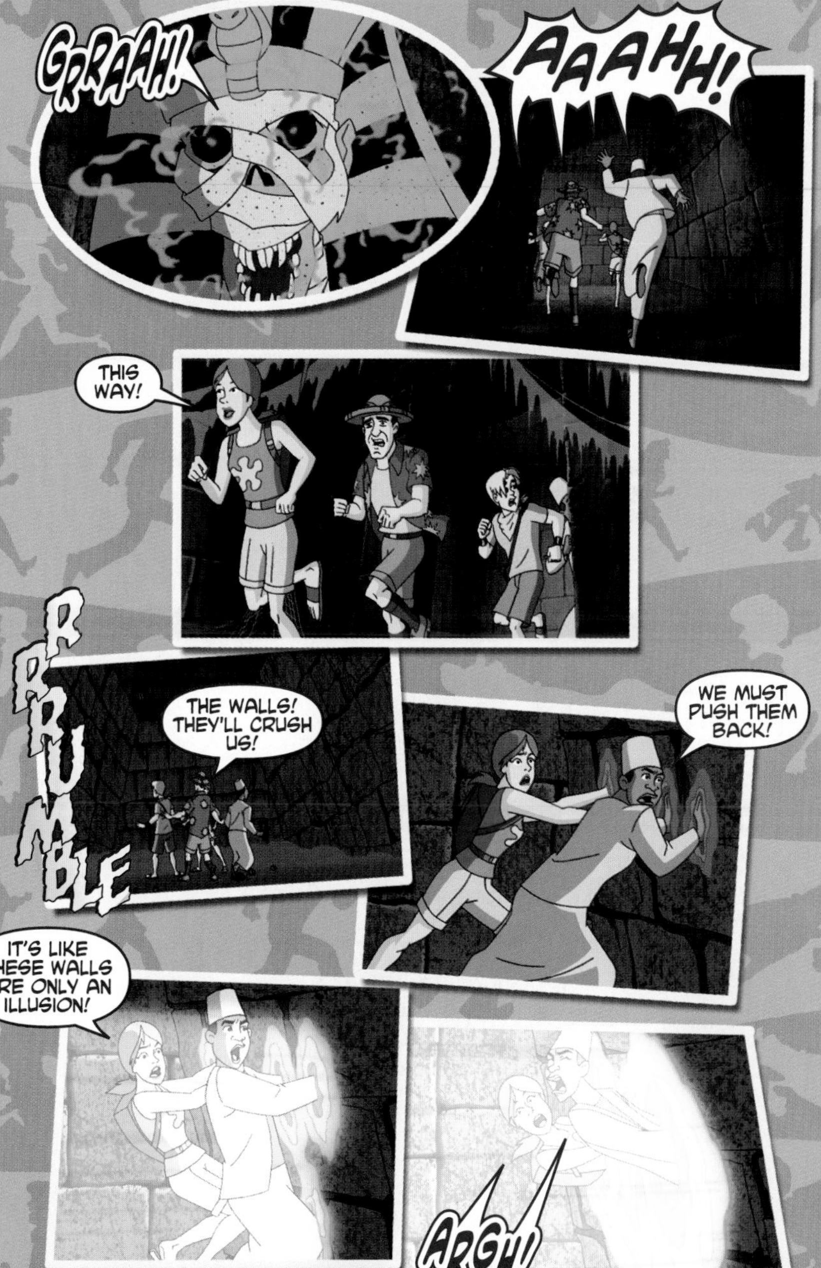
GRRAAAH!
AAAHH!
THIS WAY!
RRRUMBLE
THE WALLS! THEY'LL CRUSH US!
WE MUST PUSH THEM BACK!
IT'S LIKE THESE WALLS ARE ONLY AN ILLUSION!
ARGH!

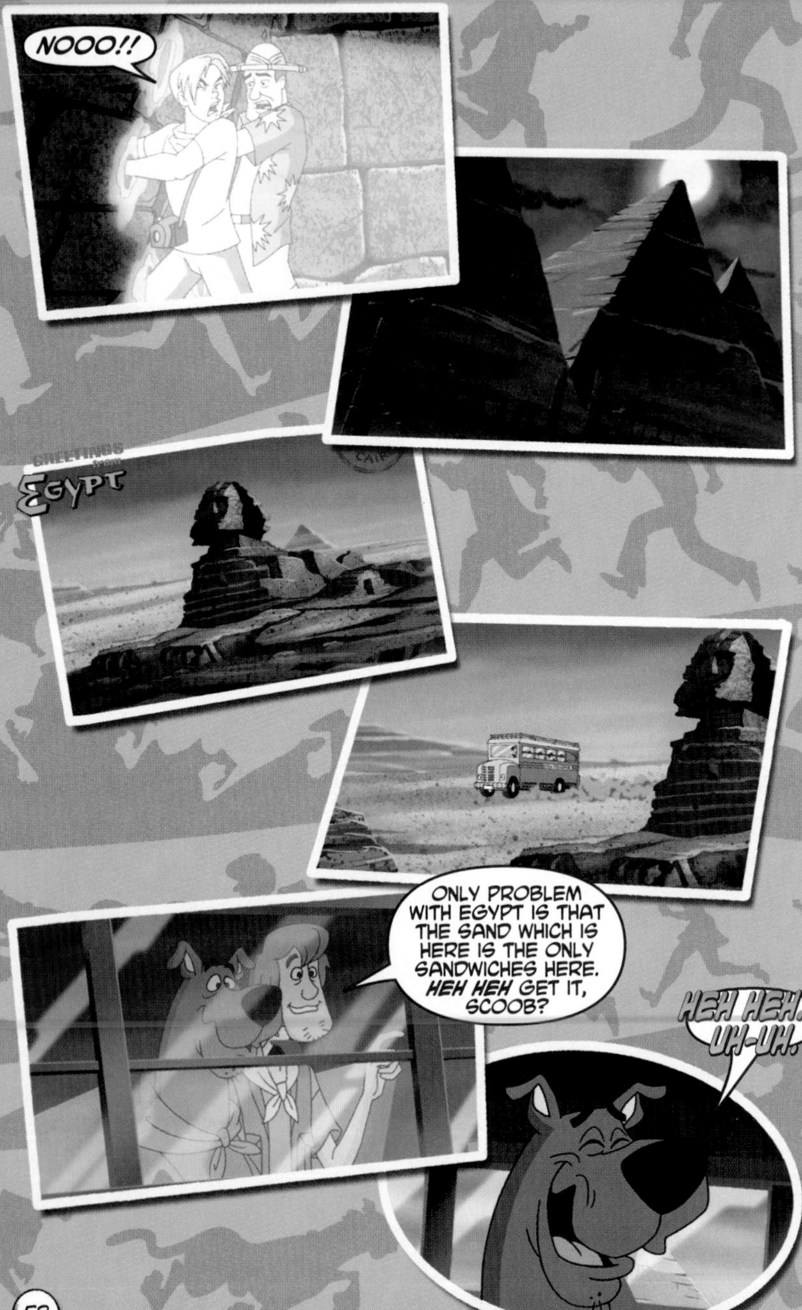
NOOO!!
GREETINGS from
EGYPT
ONLY PROBLEM WITH EGYPT IS THAT THE SAND WHICH IS HERE IS THE ONLY SANDWICHES HERE. ***HEH HEH*** GET IT, SCOOB?
HEH HEH... UH-UH.

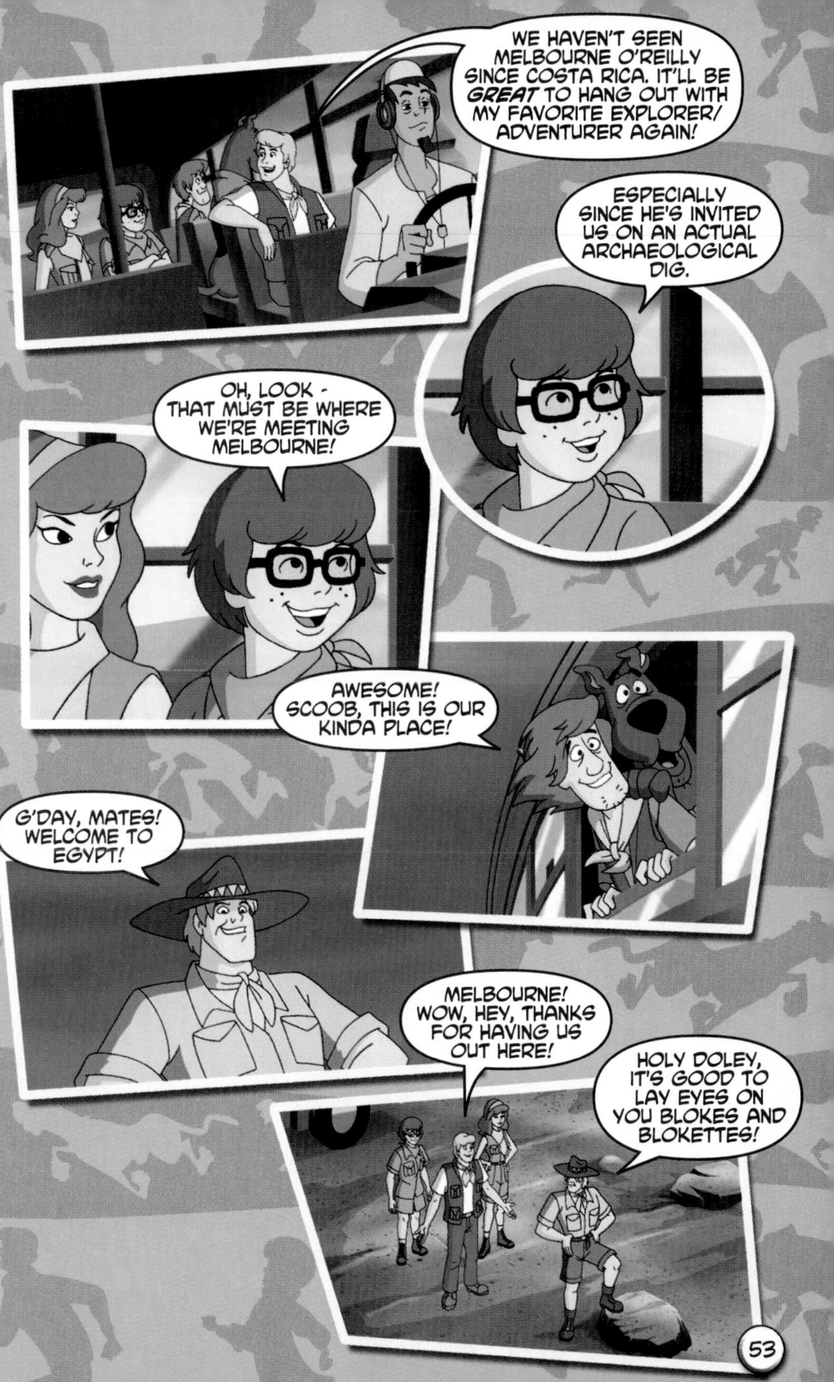
WE HAVEN'T SEEN MELBOURNE O'REILLY SINCE COSTA RICA. IT'LL BE *GREAT* TO HANG OUT WITH MY FAVORITE EXPLORER/ ADVENTURER AGAIN!
ESPECIALLY SINCE HE'S INVITED US ON AN ACTUAL ARCHAEOLOGICAL DIG.
OH, LOOK - THAT MUST BE WHERE WE'RE MEETING MELBOURNE!
AWESOME! SCOOB, THIS IS OUR KINDA PLACE!
G'DAY, MATES! WELCOME TO EGYPT!
MELBOURNE! WOW, HEY, THANKS FOR HAVING US OUT HERE!
HOLY DOLEY, IT'S GOOD TO LAY EYES ON YOU BLOKES AND BLOKETTES!

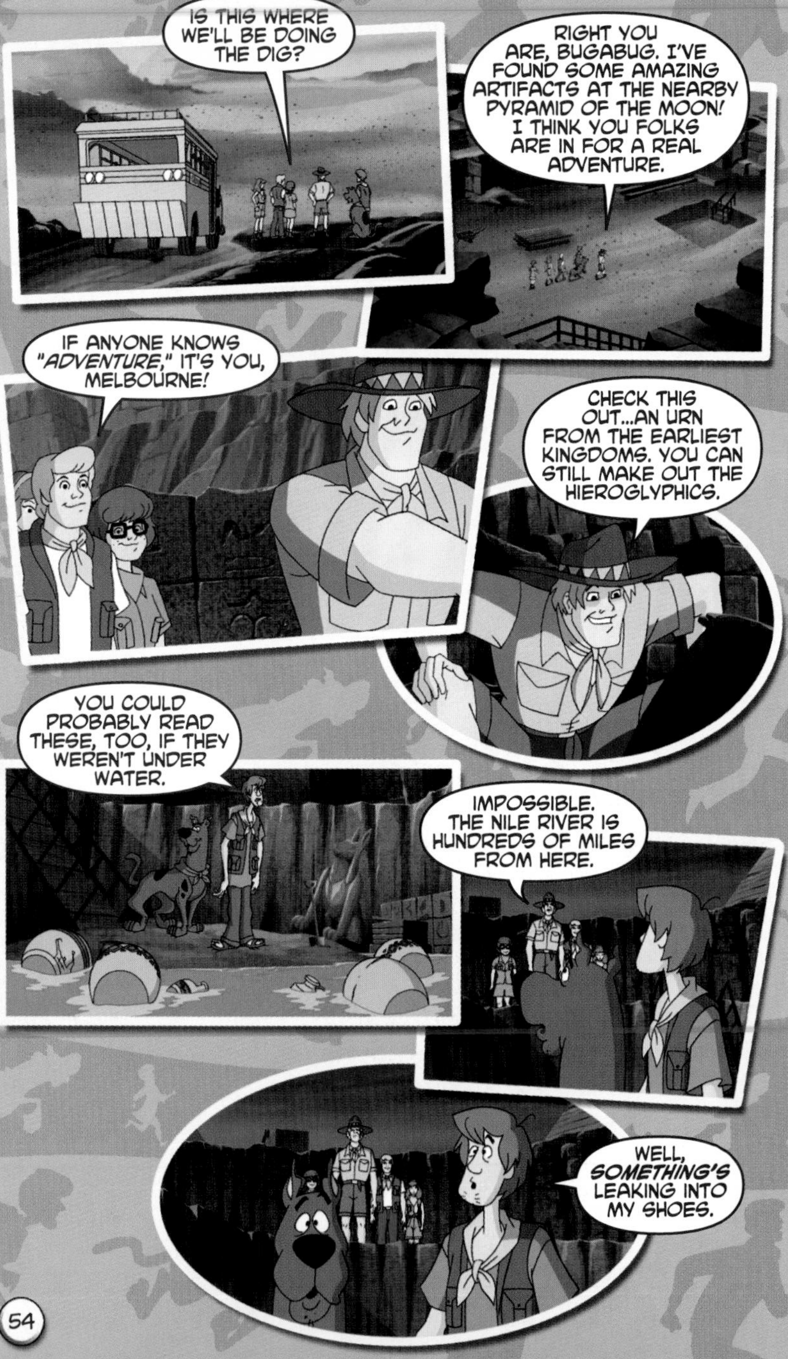
IS THIS WHERE WE'LL BE DOING THE DIG?
RIGHT YOU ARE, BUGABUG. I'VE FOUND SOME AMAZING ARTIFACTS AT THE NEARBY PYRAMID OF THE MOON! I THINK YOU FOLKS ARE IN FOR A REAL ADVENTURE.
IF ANYONE KNOWS "*ADVENTURE*," IT'S YOU, MELBOURNE!
CHECK THIS OUT...AN URN FROM THE EARLIEST KINGDOMS. YOU CAN STILL MAKE OUT THE HIEROGLYPHICS.
YOU COULD PROBABLY READ THESE, TOO, IF THEY WEREN'T UNDER WATER.
IMPOSSIBLE. THE NILE RIVER IS HUNDREDS OF MILES FROM HERE.
WELL, ***SOMETHING'S*** LEAKING INTO MY SHOES.

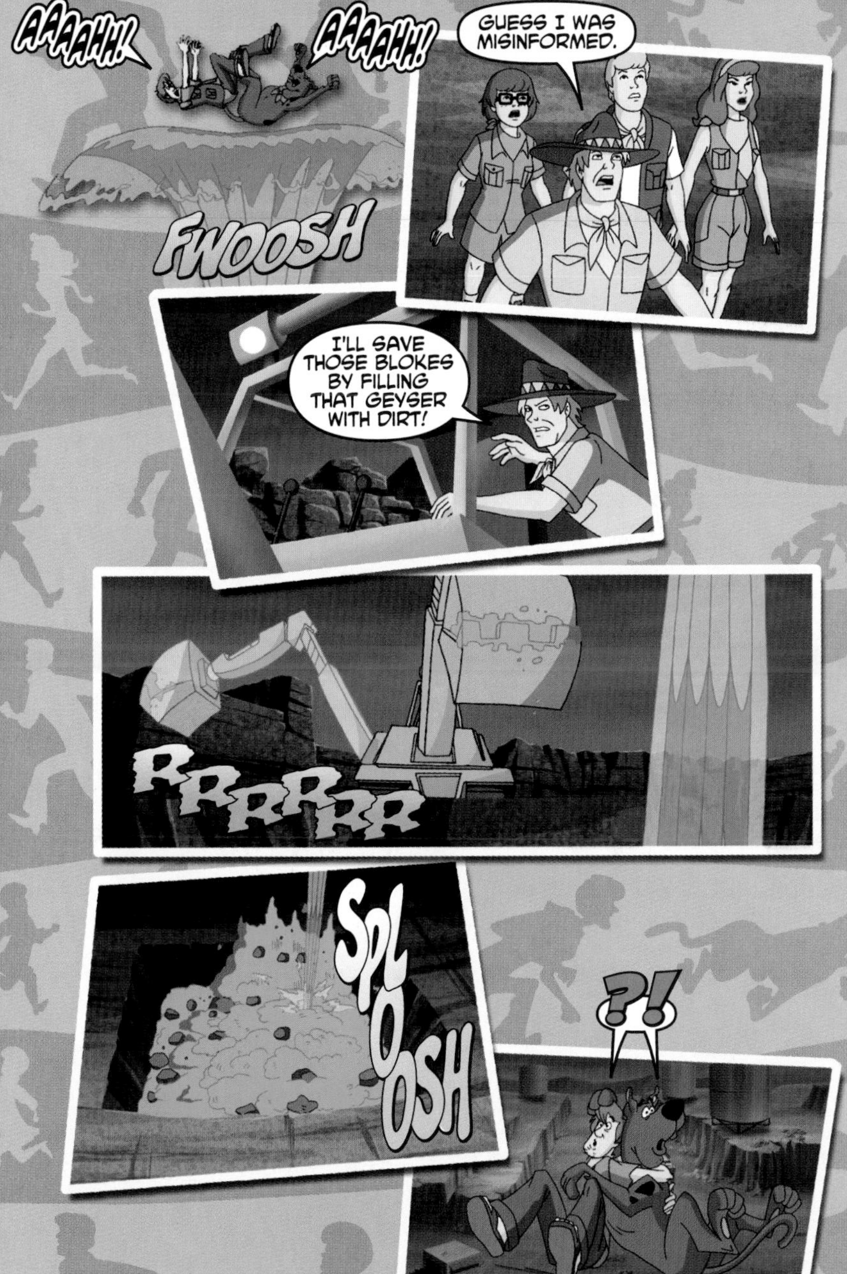
AAAAHH!
AAAAHH!
GUESS I WAS MISINFORMED.
FWOOSH
I'LL SAVE THOSE BLOKES BY FILLING THAT GEYSER WITH DIRT!
RRRRRR
SPLOOSH
?!

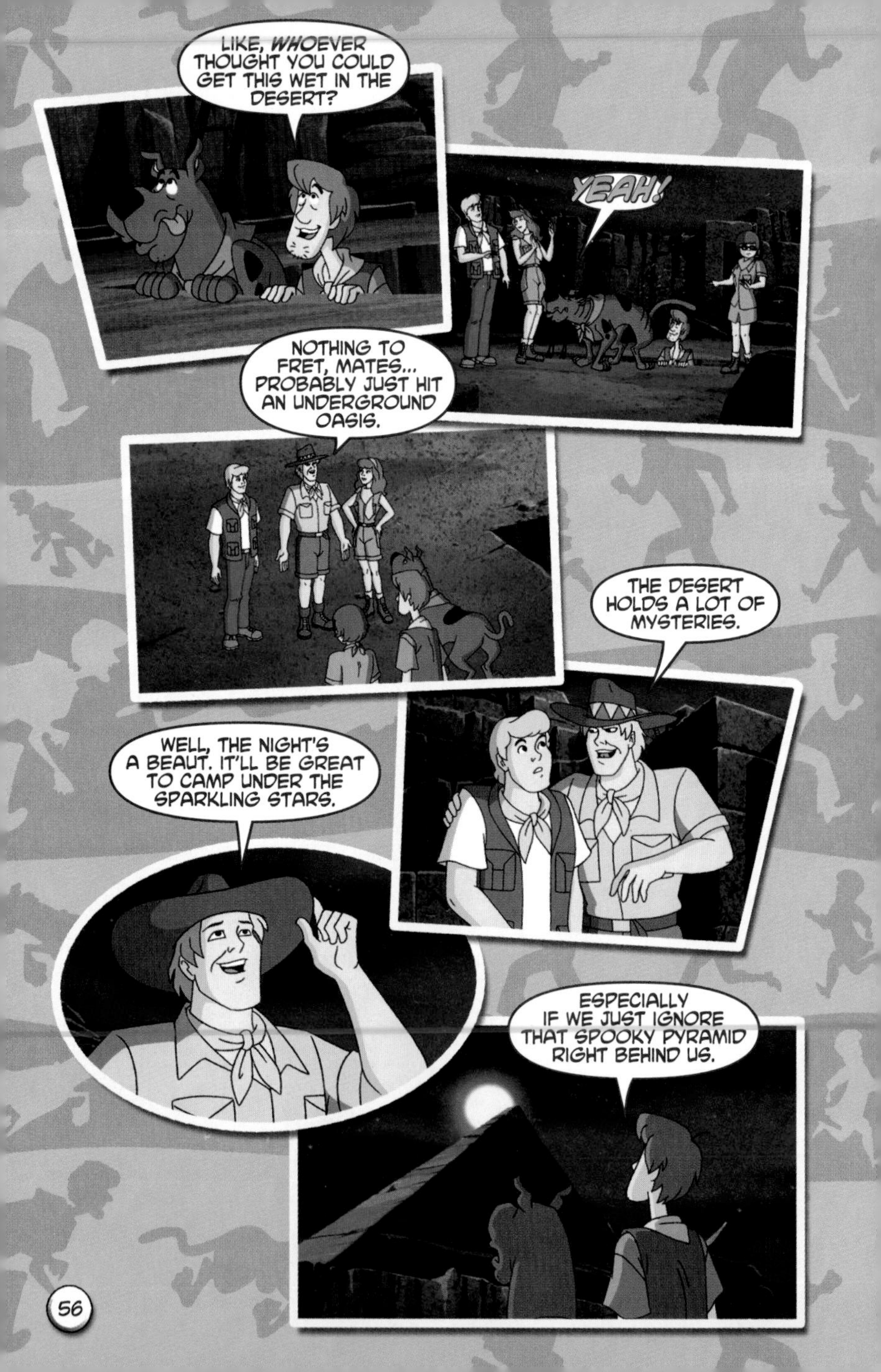
LIKE, WHOEVER THOUGHT YOU COULD GET THIS WET IN THE DESERT?
YEAH!
NOTHING TO FRET, MATES... PROBABLY JUST HIT AN UNDERGROUND OASIS.
THE DESERT HOLDS A LOT OF MYSTERIES.
WELL, THE NIGHT'S A BEAUT. IT'LL BE GREAT TO CAMP UNDER THE SPARKLING STARS.
ESPECIALLY IF WE JUST IGNORE THAT SPOOKY PYRAMID RIGHT BEHIND US.

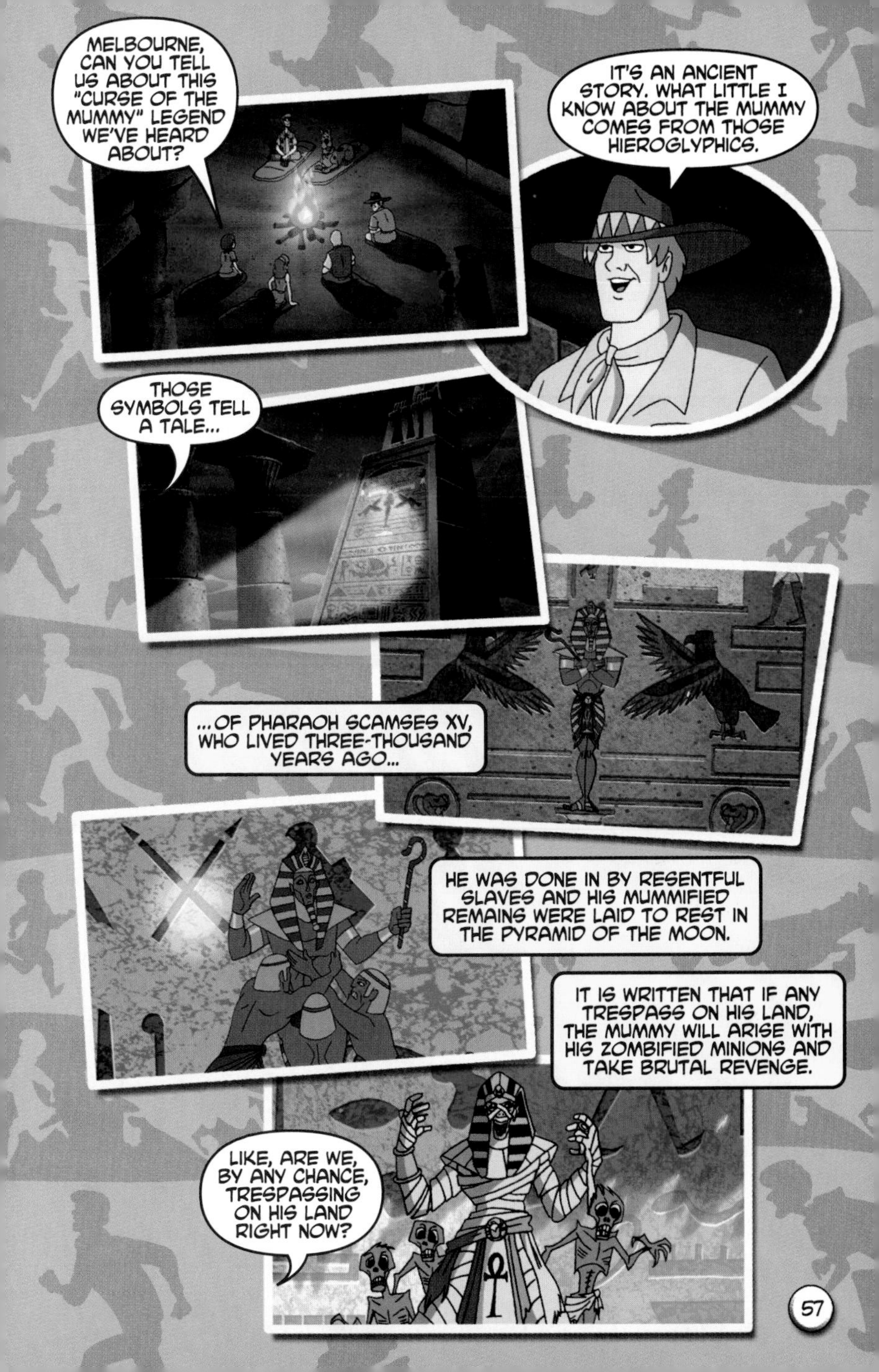

MELBOURNE, CAN YOU TELL US ABOUT THIS "CURSE OF THE MUMMY" LEGEND WE'VE HEARD ABOUT?
IT'S AN ANCIENT STORY. WHAT LITTLE I KNOW ABOUT THE MUMMY COMES FROM THOSE HIEROGLYPHICS.
THOSE SYMBOLS TELL A TALE...
...OF PHARAOH SCAMSES XV, WHO LIVED THREE-THOUSAND YEARS AGO...
HE WAS DONE IN BY RESENTFUL SLAVES AND HIS MUMMIFIED REMAINS WERE LAID TO REST IN THE PYRAMID OF THE MOON.
IT IS WRITTEN THAT IF ANY TRESPASS ON HIS LAND, THE MUMMY WILL ARISE WITH HIS ZOMBIFIED MINIONS AND TAKE BRUTAL REVENGE.
LIKE, ARE WE, BY ANY CHANCE, TRESPASSING ON HIS LAND RIGHT NOW?

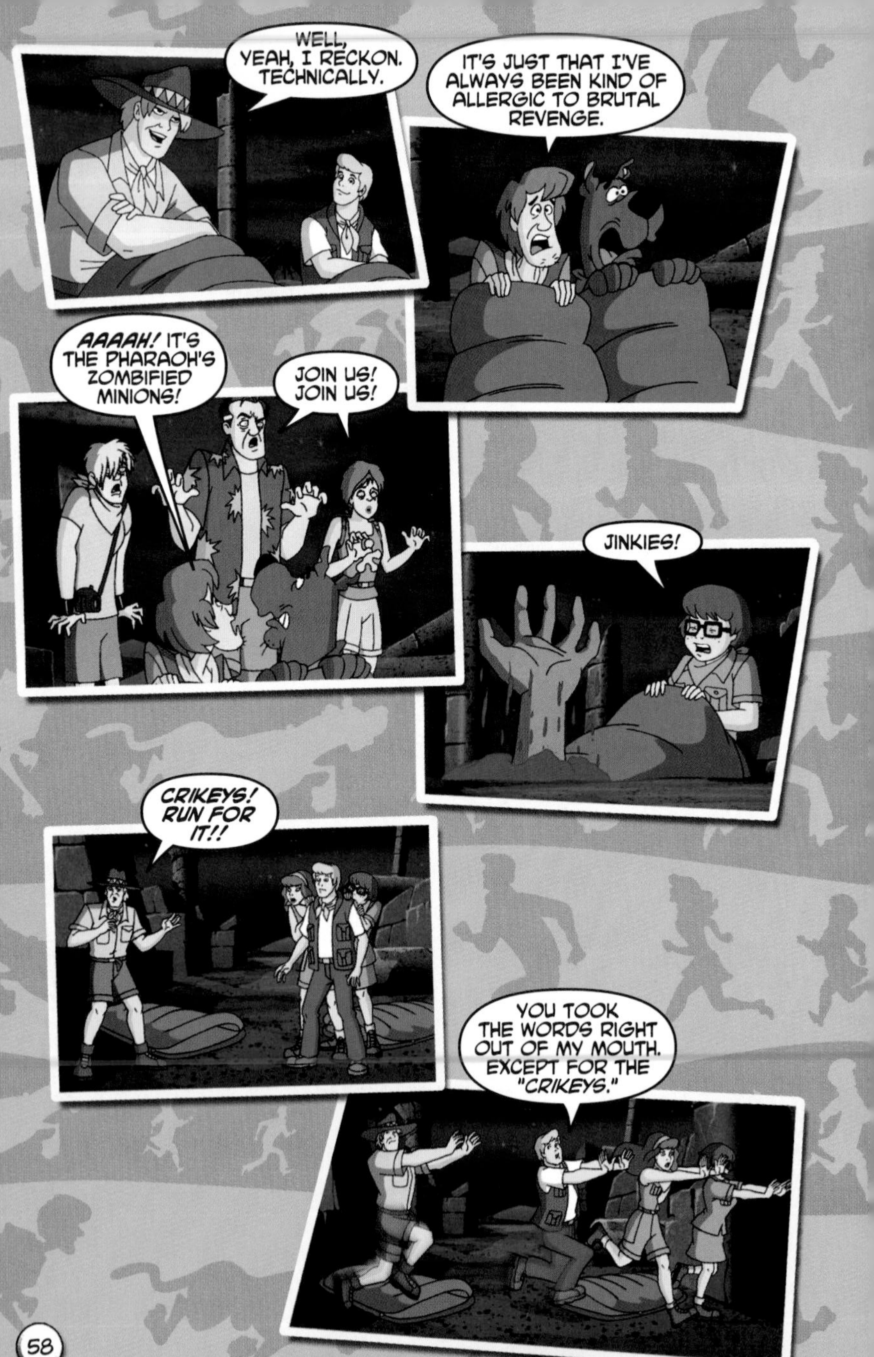
WELL, YEAH, I RECKON. TECHNICALLY.
IT'S JUST THAT I'VE ALWAYS BEEN KIND OF ALLERGIC TO BRUTAL REVENGE.
AAAAH! IT'S THE PHARAOH'S ZOMBIFIED MINIONS!
JOIN US! JOIN US!
JINKIES!
CRIKEYS! RUN FOR IT!!
YOU TOOK THE WORDS RIGHT OUT OF MY MOUTH. EXCEPT FOR THE "CRIKEYS."

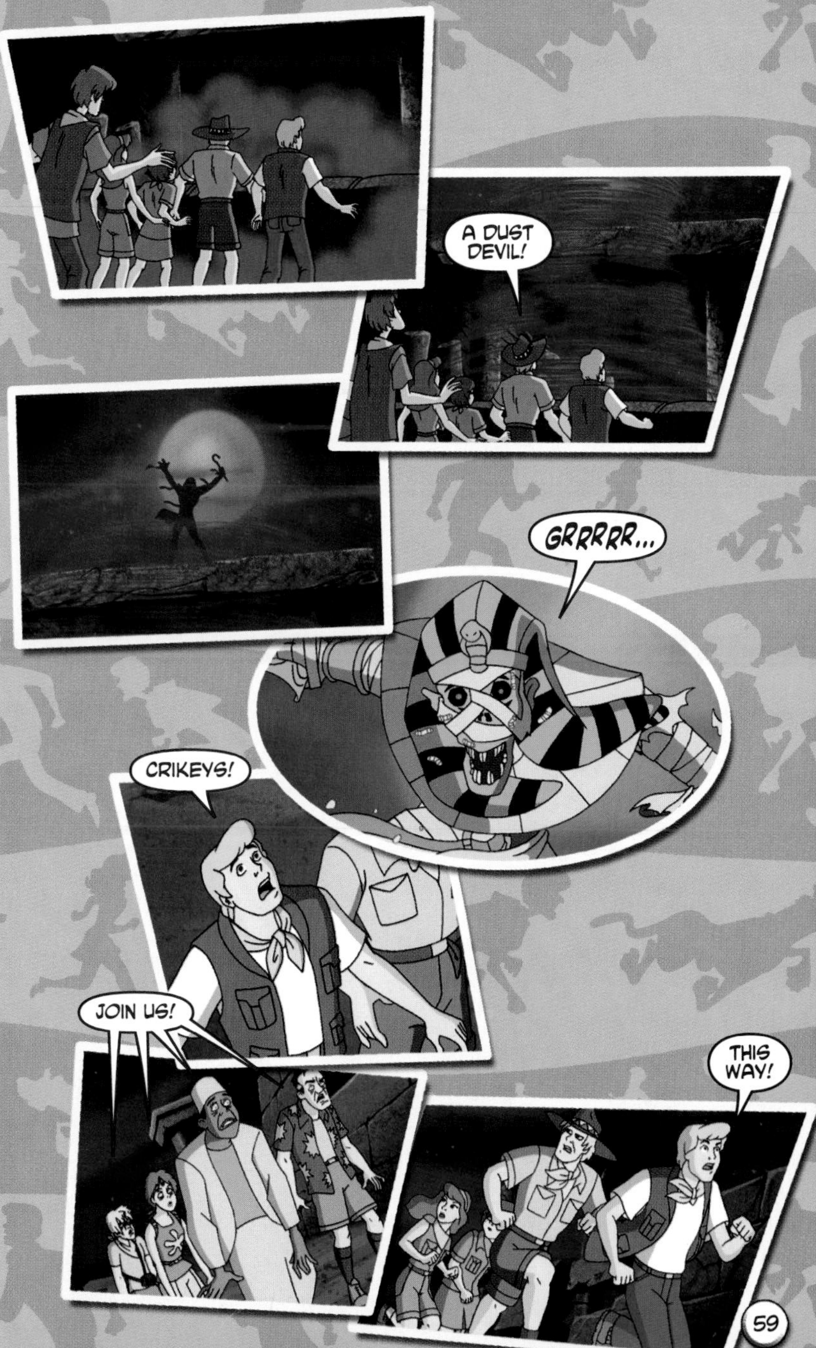
A DUST DEVIL!
GRRRRR...
CRIKEYS!
JOIN US!
THIS WAY!

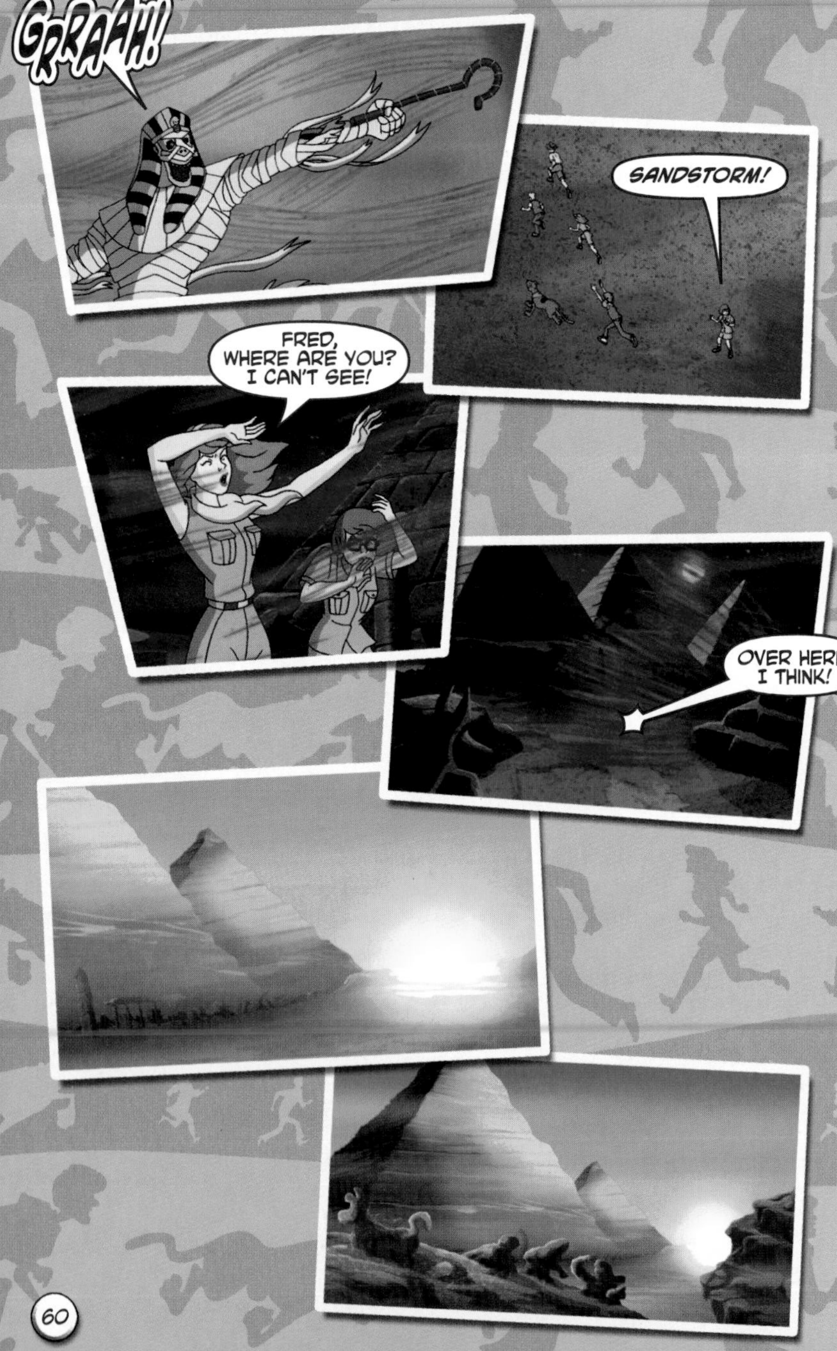
GRRAAAH!
SANDSTORM!
FRED, WHERE ARE YOU? I CAN'T SEE!
OVER HERE, I THINK!

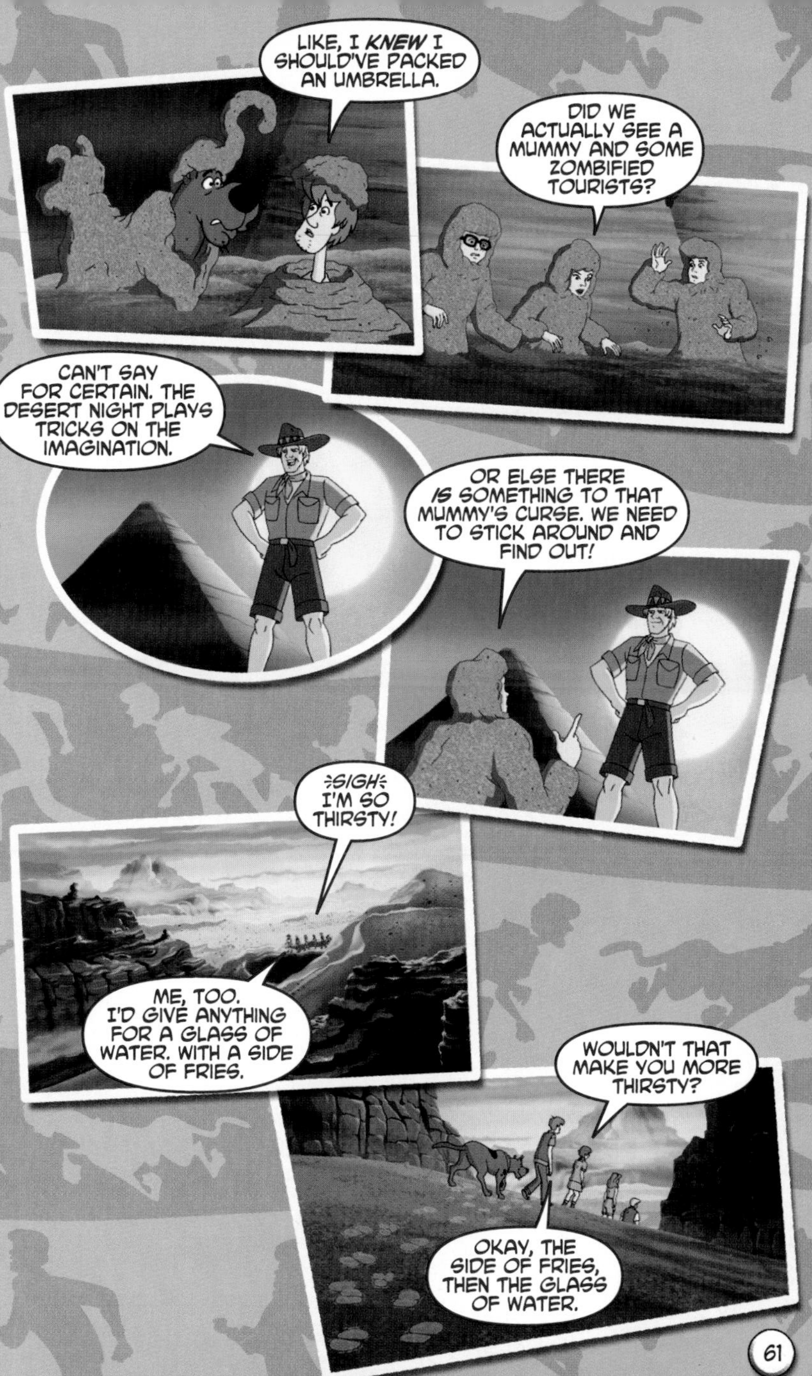
LIKE, I KNEW I SHOULD'VE PACKED AN UMBRELLA.
DID WE ACTUALLY SEE A MUMMY AND SOME ZOMBIFIED TOURISTS?
CAN'T SAY FOR CERTAIN. THE DESERT NIGHT PLAYS TRICKS ON THE IMAGINATION.
OR ELSE THERE IS SOMETHING TO THAT MUMMY'S CURSE. WE NEED TO STICK AROUND AND FIND OUT!
SIGH I'M SO THIRSTY!
ME, TOO. I'D GIVE ANYTHING FOR A GLASS OF WATER. WITH A SIDE OF FRIES.
WOULDN'T THAT MAKE YOU MORE THIRSTY?
OKAY, THE SIDE OF FRIES, THEN THE GLASS OF WATER.

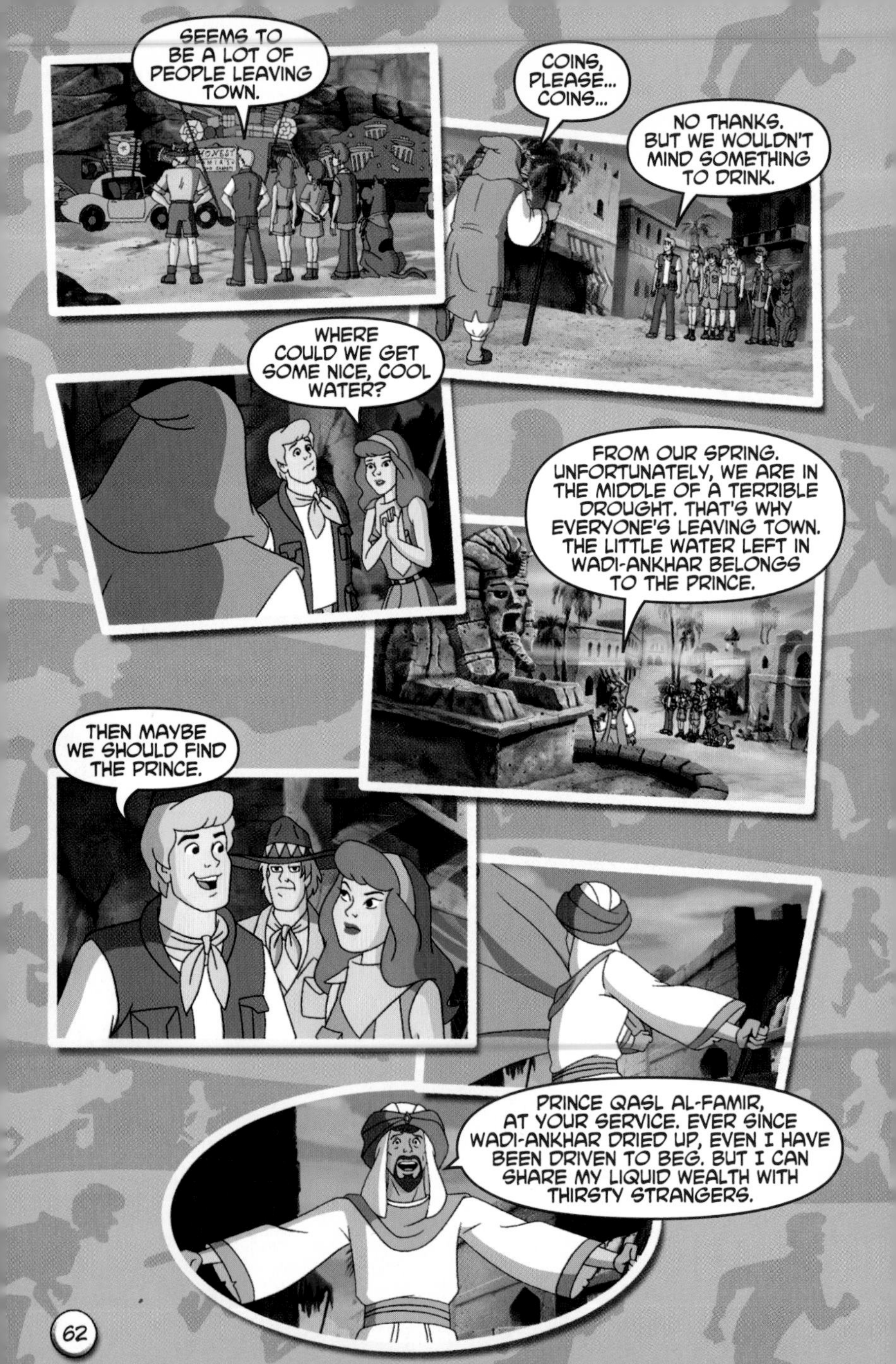
SEEMS TO BE A LOT OF PEOPLE LEAVING TOWN.
COINS, PLEASE... COINS...
NO THANKS. BUT WE WOULDN'T MIND SOMETHING TO DRINK.
WHERE COULD WE GET SOME NICE, COOL WATER?
FROM OUR SPRING. UNFORTUNATELY, WE ARE IN THE MIDDLE OF A TERRIBLE DROUGHT. THAT'S WHY EVERYONE'S LEAVING TOWN. THE LITTLE WATER LEFT IN WADI-ANKHAR BELONGS TO THE PRINCE.
THEN MAYBE WE SHOULD FIND THE PRINCE.
PRINCE QASL AL-FAMIR, AT YOUR SERVICE. EVER SINCE WADI-ANKHAR DRIED UP, EVEN I HAVE BEEN DRIVEN TO BEG. BUT I CAN SHARE MY LIQUID WEALTH WITH THIRSTY STRANGERS.

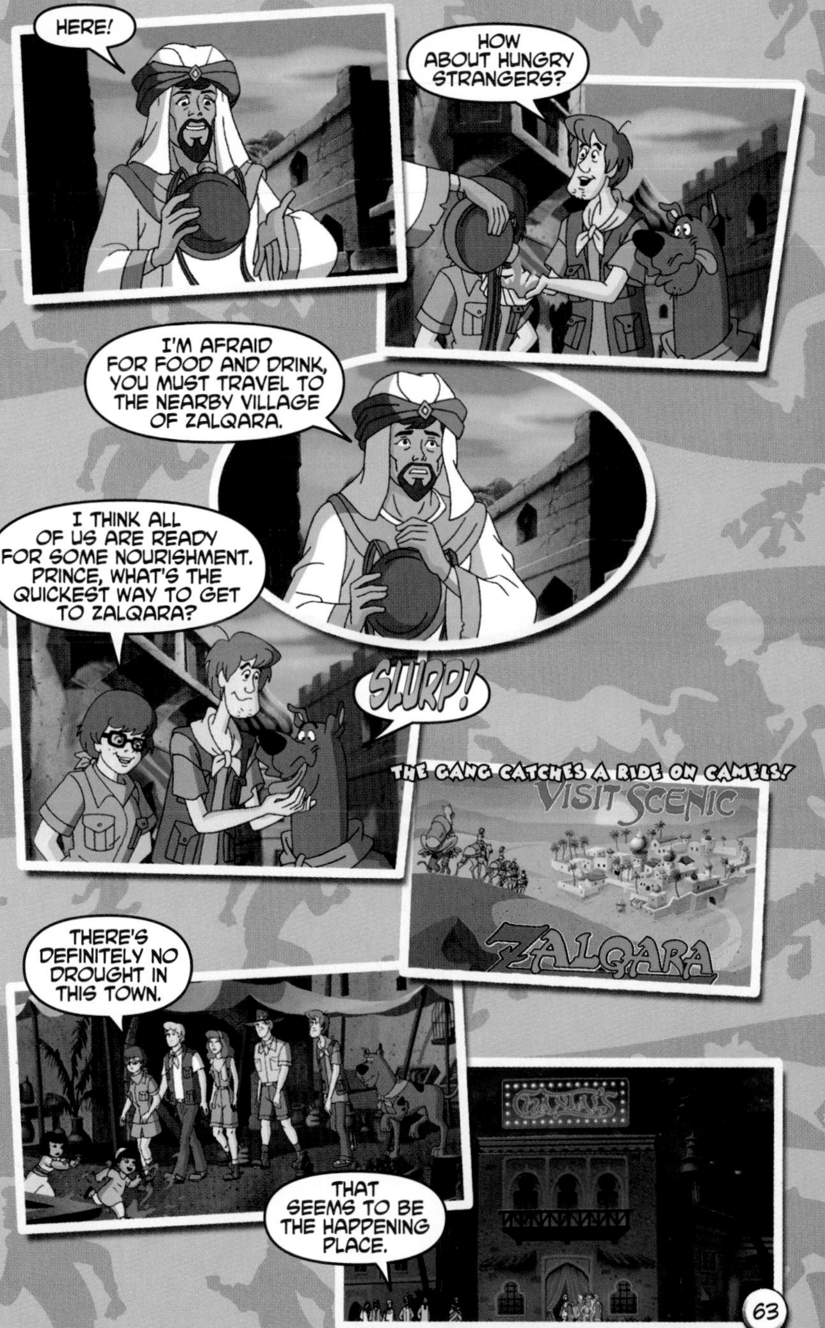
HERE!
HOW ABOUT HUNGRY STRANGERS?
I'M AFRAID FOR FOOD AND DRINK, YOU MUST TRAVEL TO THE NEARBY VILLAGE OF ZALQARA.
I THINK ALL OF US ARE READY FOR SOME NOURISHMENT. PRINCE, WHAT'S THE QUICKEST WAY TO GET TO ZALQARA?
SLURP!
THE GANG CATCHES A RIDE ON CAMELS!
VISIT SCENIC
ZALQARA
THERE'S DEFINITELY NO DROUGHT IN THIS TOWN.
THAT SEEMS TO BE THE HAPPENING PLACE.

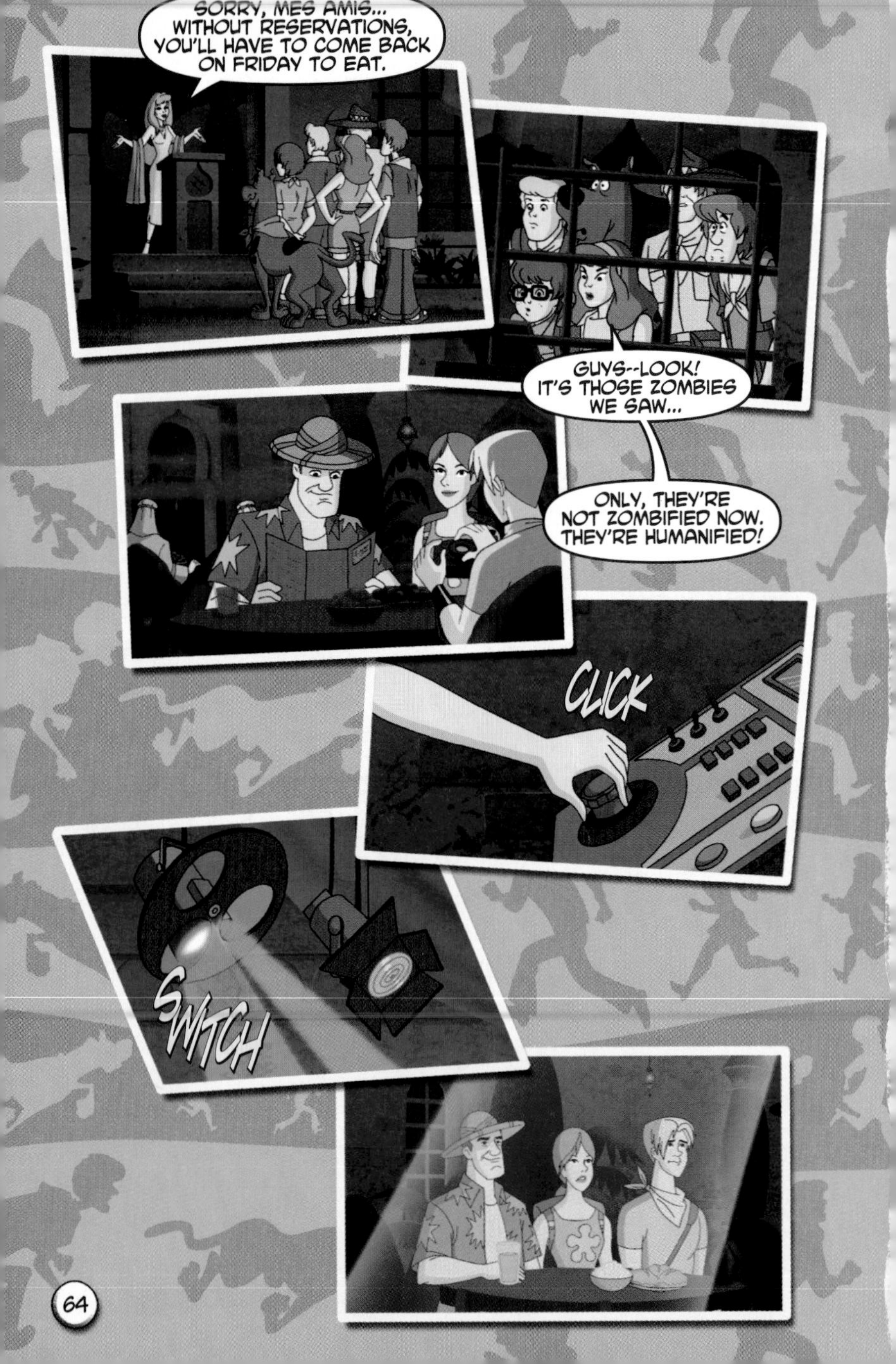
SORRY, MES AMIS... WITHOUT RESERVATIONS, YOU'LL HAVE TO COME BACK ON FRIDAY TO EAT.
GUYS--LOOK! IT'S THOSE ZOMBIES WE SAW...
ONLY, THEY'RE NOT ZOMBIFIED NOW. THEY'RE HUMANIFIED!
CLICK
SWITCH

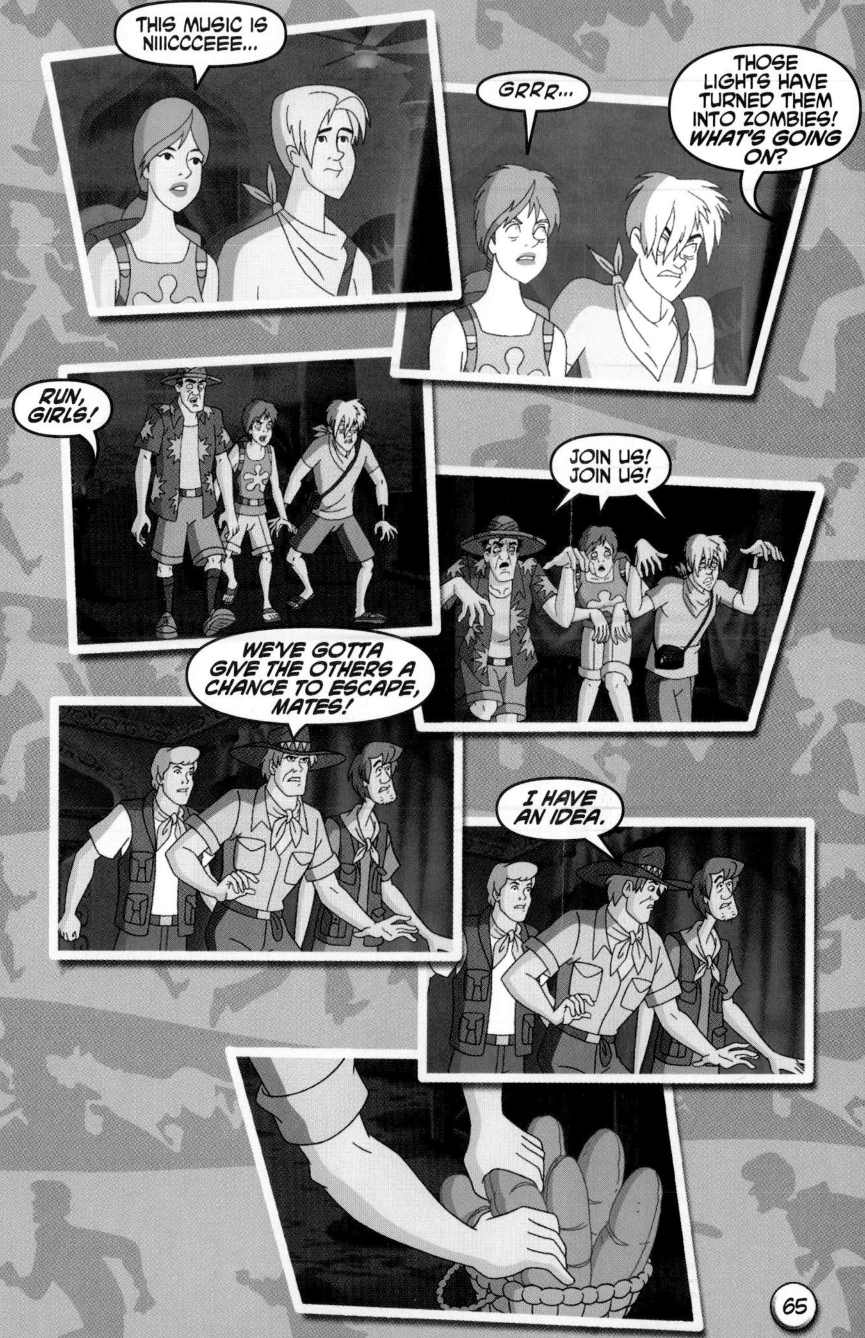
THIS MUSIC IS NIIICCCEEE...
GRRR...
THOSE LIGHTS HAVE TURNED THEM INTO ZOMBIES! WHAT'S GOING ON?
RUN, GIRLS!
JOIN US! JOIN US!
WE'VE GOTTA GIVE THE OTHERS A CHANCE TO ESCAPE, MATES!
I HAVE AN IDEA.

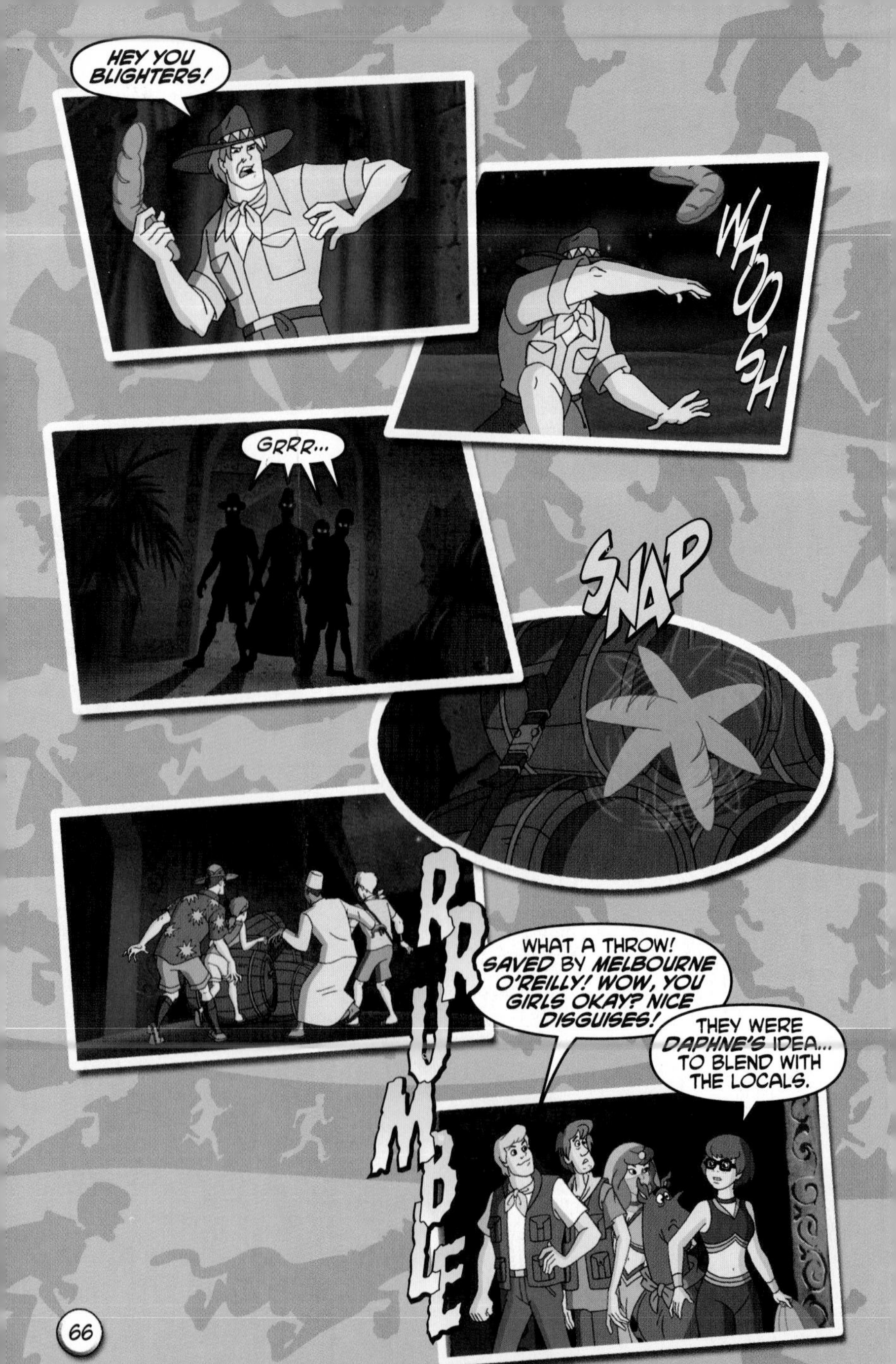
HEY YOU BLIGHTERS!
WHOOSH
GRRR...
SNAP
RRUMBLE
WHAT A THROW! SAVED BY MELBOURNE O'REILLY! WOW, YOU GIRLS OKAY? NICE DISGUISES!
THEY WERE DAPHNE'S IDEA... TO BLEND WITH THE LOCALS.

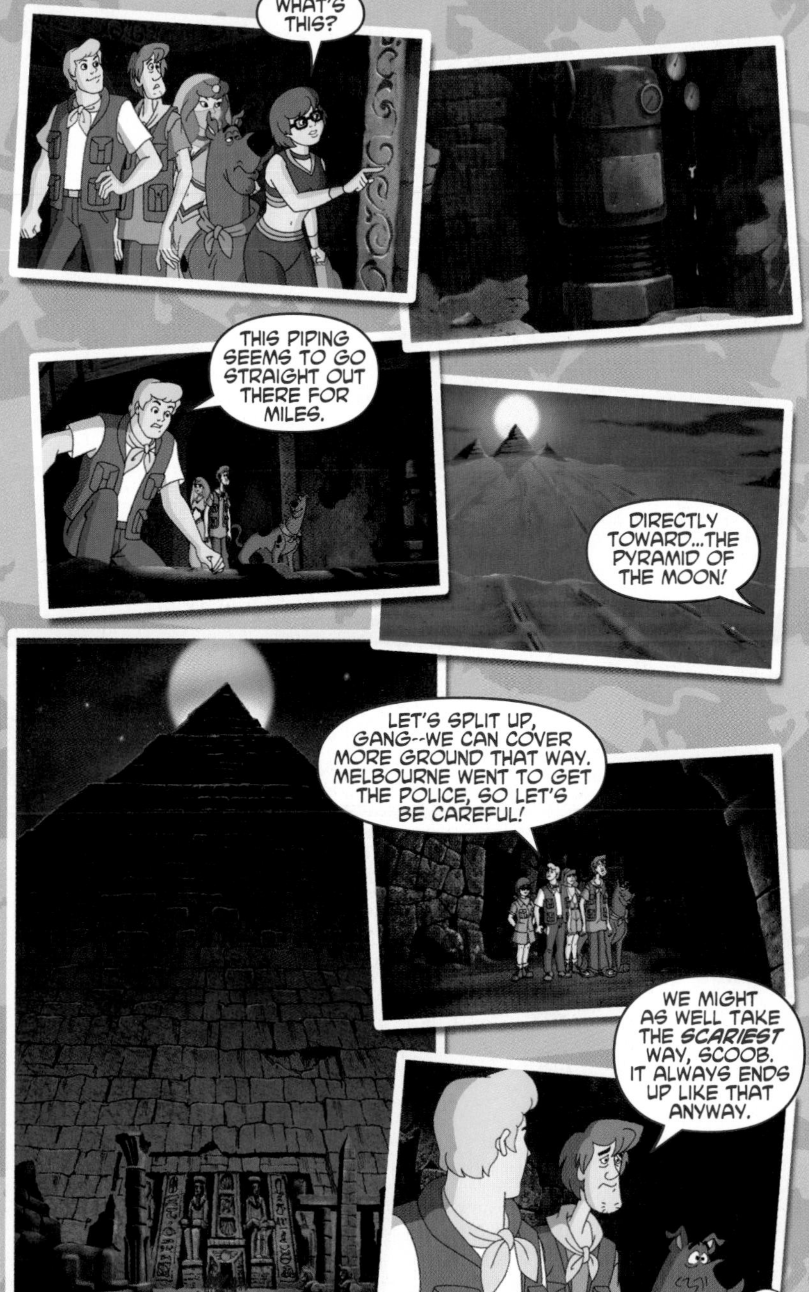
WHAT'S THIS?
THIS PIPING SEEMS TO GO STRAIGHT OUT THERE FOR MILES.
DIRECTLY TOWARD...THE PYRAMID OF THE MOON!
LET'S SPLIT UP, GANG--WE CAN COVER MORE GROUND THAT WAY. MELBOURNE WENT TO GET THE POLICE, SO LET'S BE CAREFUL!
WE MIGHT AS WELL TAKE THE *SCARIEST* WAY, SCOOB. IT ALWAYS ENDS UP LIKE THAT ANYWAY.

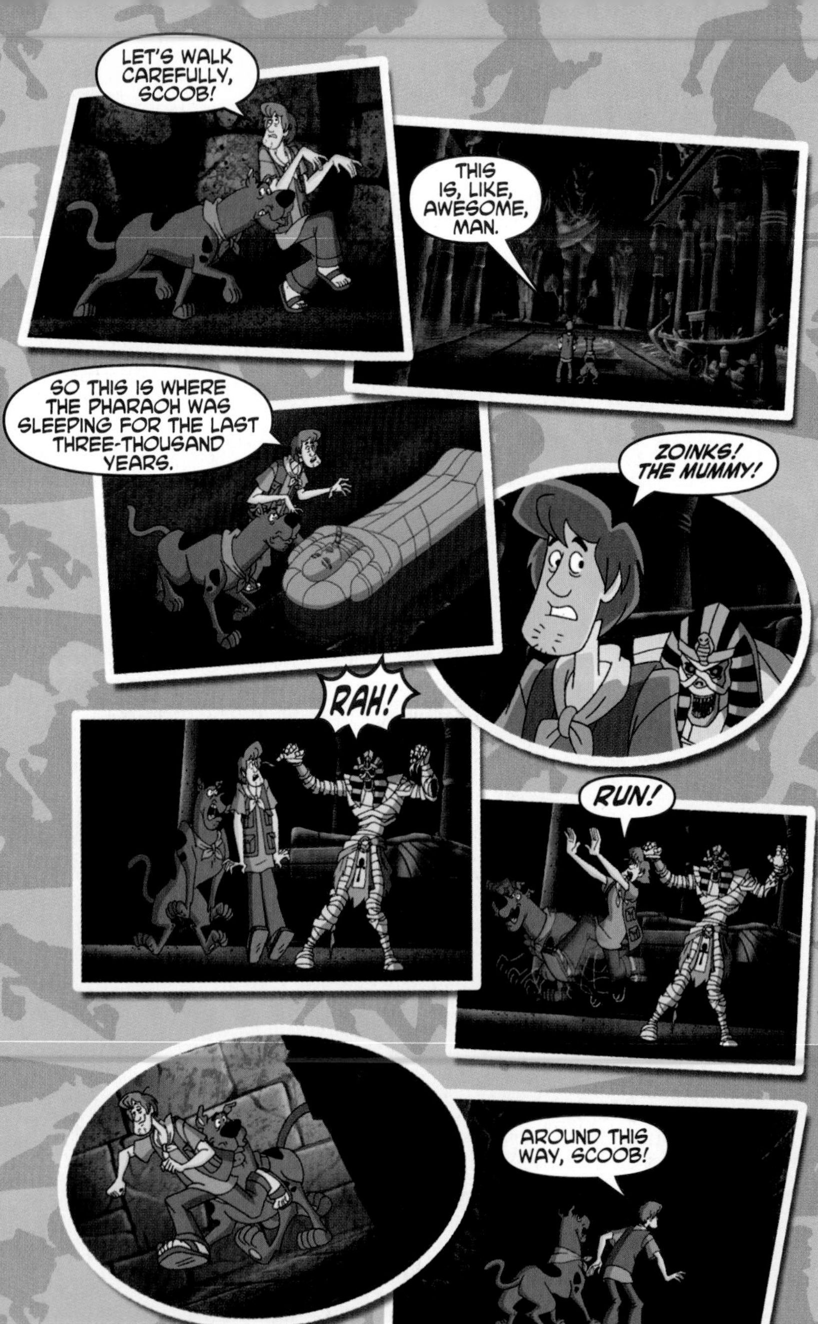
LET'S WALK CAREFULLY, SCOOB!
THIS IS, LIKE, AWESOME, MAN.
SO THIS IS WHERE THE PHARAOH WAS SLEEPING FOR THE LAST THREE-THOUSAND YEARS.
ZOINKS! THE MUMMY!
RAH!
RUN!
AROUND THIS WAY, SCOOB!

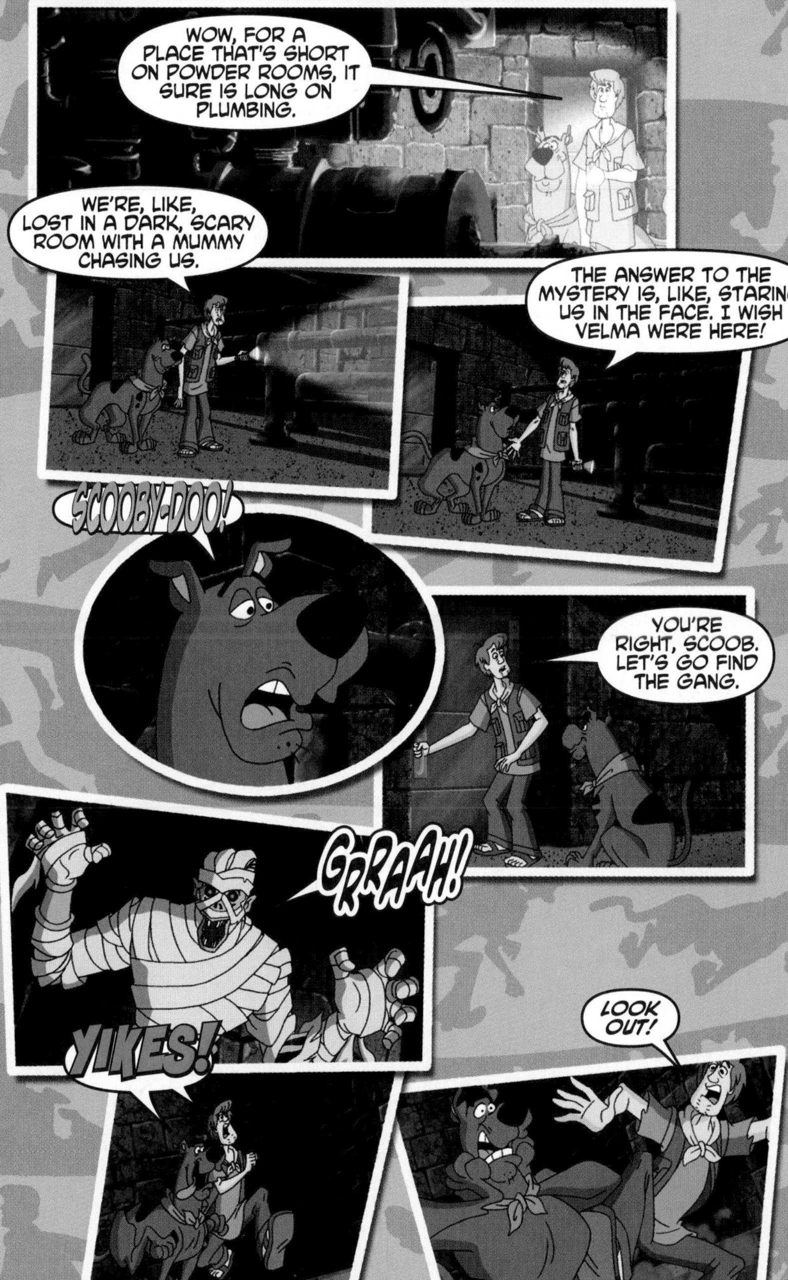
WOW, FOR A PLACE THAT'S SHORT ON POWDER ROOMS, IT SURE IS LONG ON PLUMBING.
WE'RE, LIKE, LOST IN A DARK, SCARY ROOM WITH A MUMMY CHASING US.
THE ANSWER TO THE MYSTERY IS, LIKE, STARING US IN THE FACE. I WISH VELMA WERE HERE!
SCOOBY-DOO!
YOU'RE RIGHT, SCOOB. LET'S GO FIND THE GANG.
GRRAAAH!
YIKES!
LOOK OUT!

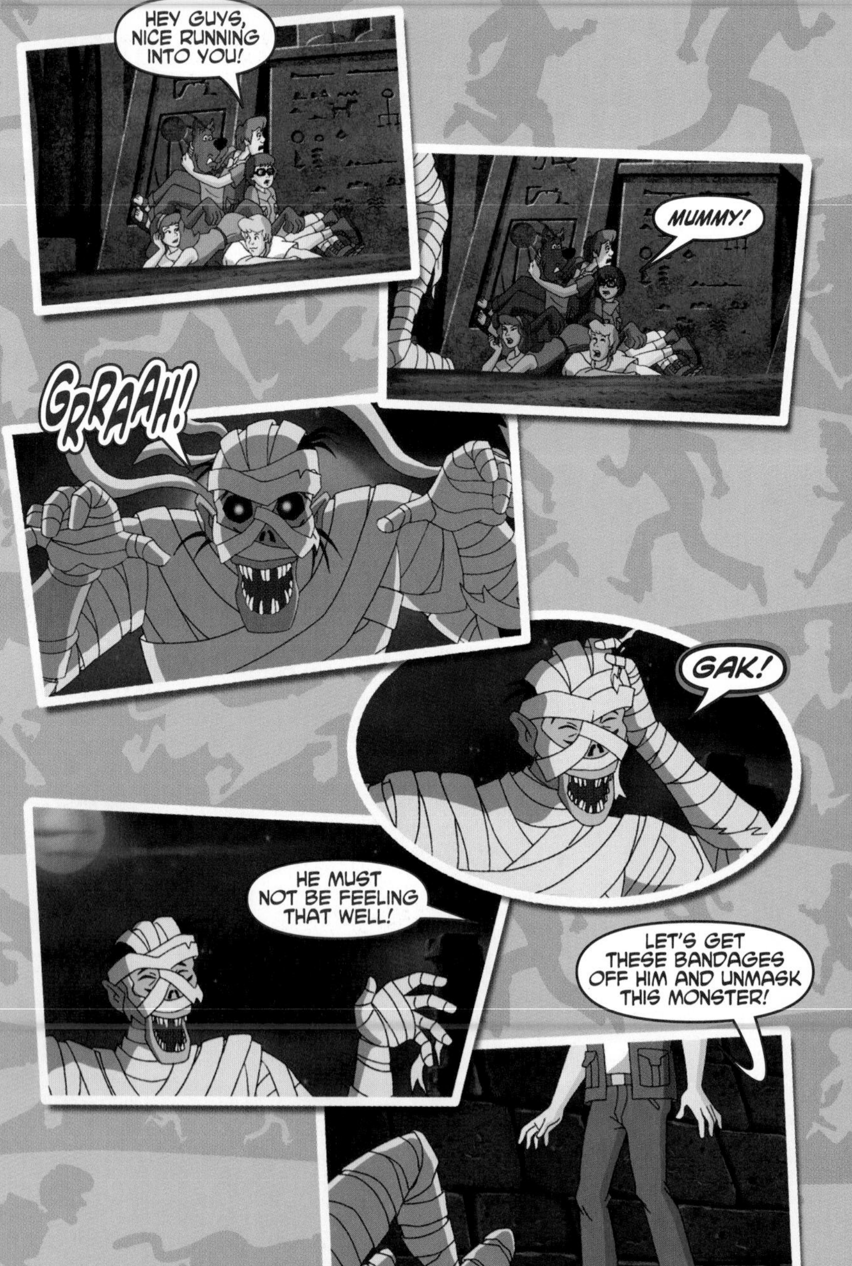
HEY GUYS, NICE RUNNING INTO YOU!
MUMMY!
GRRAAH!
GAK!
HE MUST NOT BE FEELING THAT WELL!
LET'S GET THESE BANDAGES OFF HIM AND UNMASK THIS MONSTER!

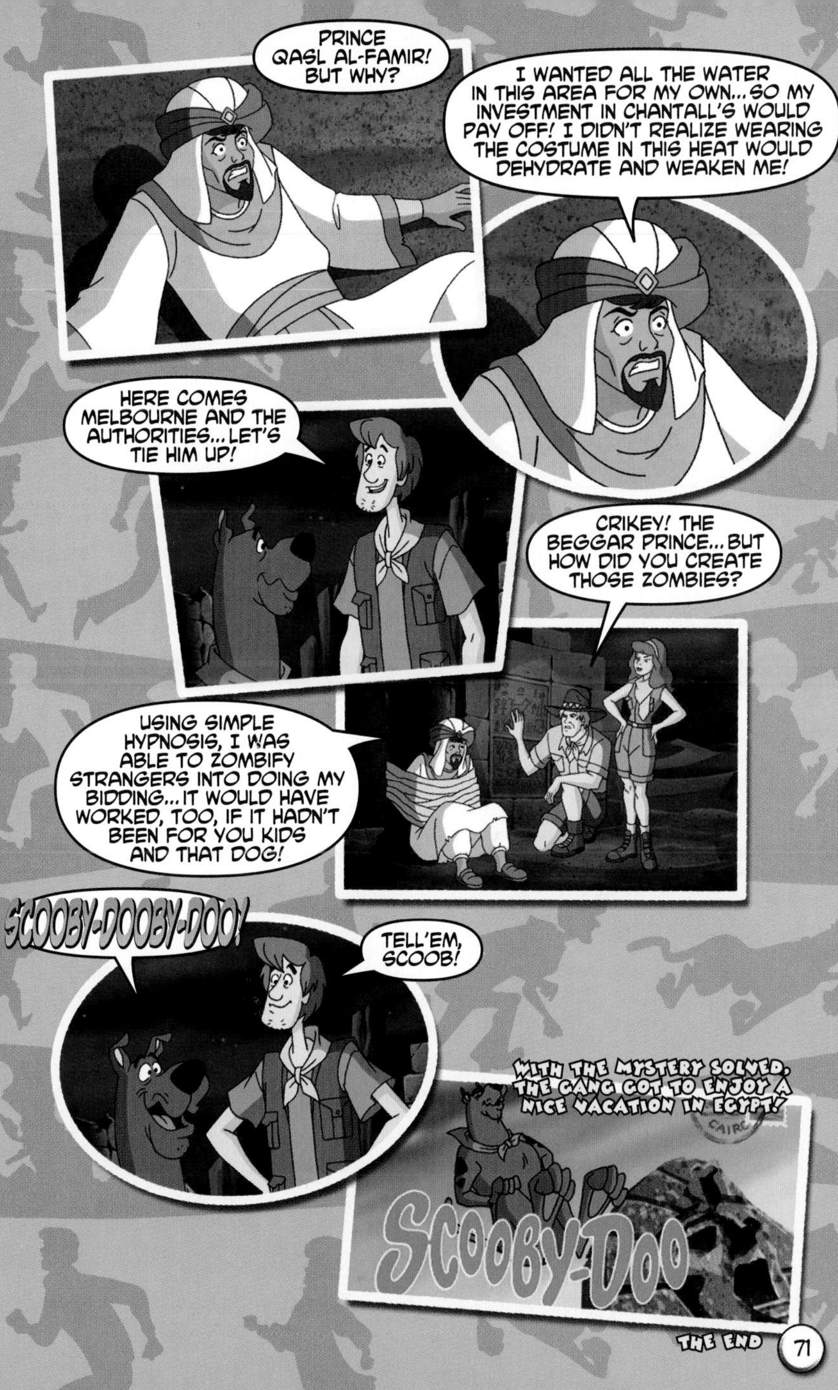
PRINCE QASL AL-FAMIR! BUT WHY?
I WANTED ALL THE WATER IN THIS AREA FOR MY OWN... SO MY INVESTMENT IN CHANTALL'S WOULD PAY OFF! I DIDN'T REALIZE WEARING THE COSTUME IN THIS HEAT WOULD DEHYDRATE AND WEAKEN ME!
HERE COMES MELBOURNE AND THE AUTHORITIES... LET'S TIE HIM UP!
CRIKEY! THE BEGGAR PRINCE... BUT HOW DID YOU CREATE THOSE ZOMBIES?
USING SIMPLE HYPNOSIS, I WAS ABLE TO ZOMBIFY STRANGERS INTO DOING MY BIDDING... IT WOULD HAVE WORKED, TOO, IF IT HADN'T BEEN FOR YOU KIDS AND THAT DOG!
SCOOBY-DOOBY-DOO!
TELL'EM, SCOOB!
WITH THE MYSTERY SOLVED, THE GANG GOT TO ENJOY A NICE VACATION IN EGYPT!
CAIRO
SCOOBY-DOO
THE END

XIAOLIN SHOWDOWN

"Like a Rock"

**Original Television Script Written by
Bill Motz and Bob Roth**

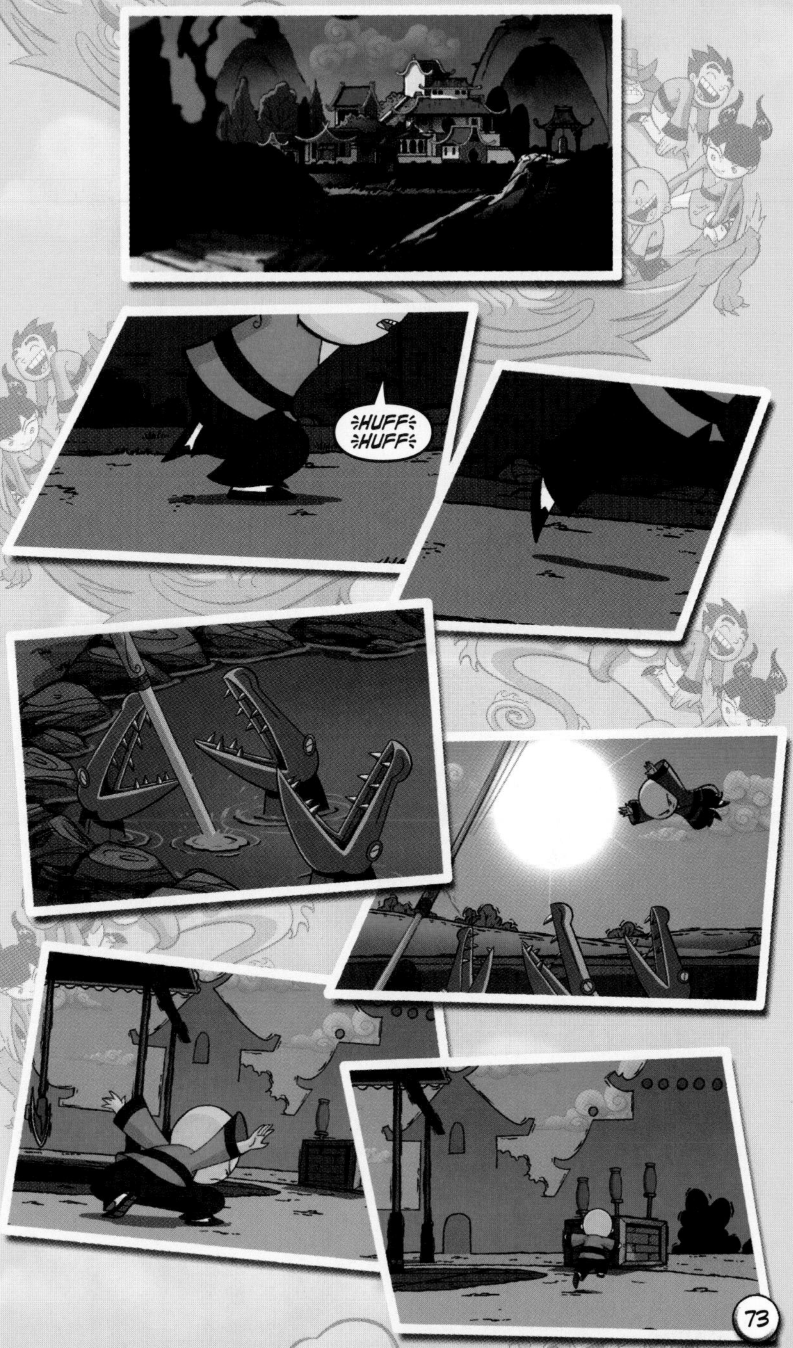
HUFF HUFF

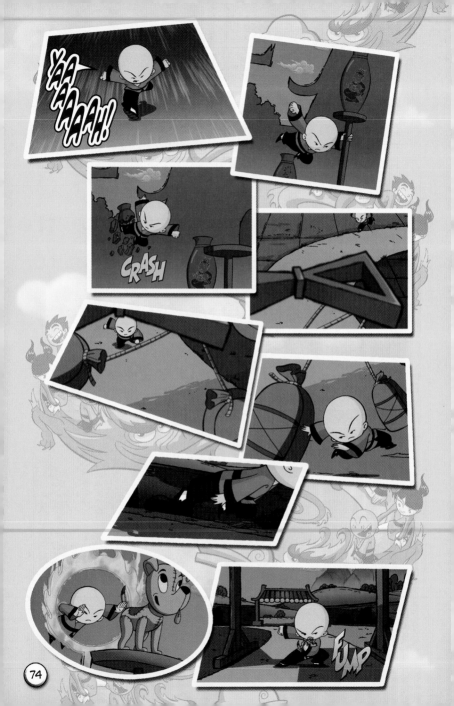

YAAAAAAAH!

CRASH

FUMP

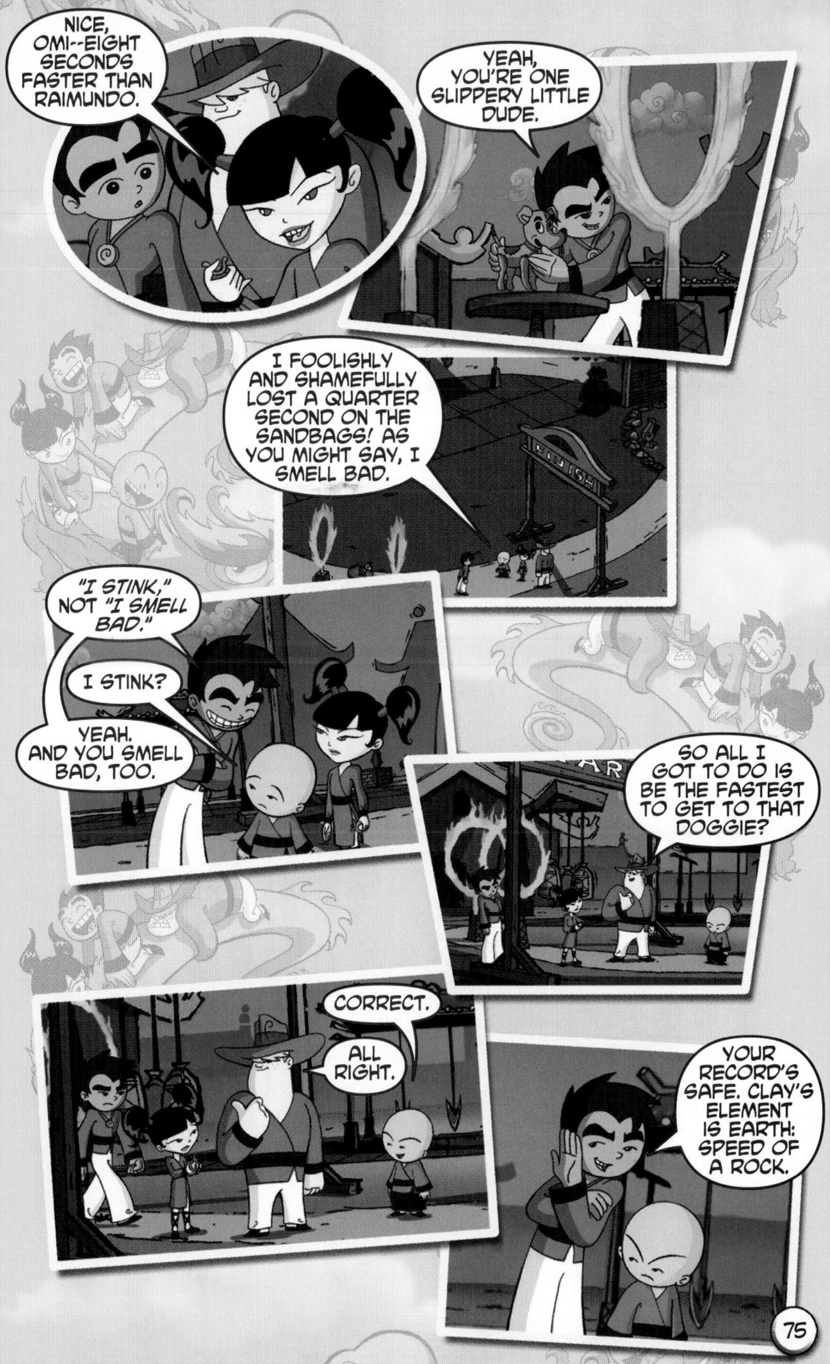
NICE, OMI--EIGHT SECONDS FASTER THAN RAIMUNDO.
YEAH, YOU'RE ONE SLIPPERY LITTLE DUDE.
I FOOLISHLY AND SHAMEFULLY LOST A QUARTER SECOND ON THE SANDBAGS! AS YOU MIGHT SAY, I SMELL BAD.
"I STINK," NOT "I SMELL BAD."
I STINK?
YEAH. AND YOU SMELL BAD, TOO.
SO ALL I GOT TO DO IS BE THE FASTEST TO GET TO THAT DOGGIE?
CORRECT.
ALL RIGHT.
YOUR RECORD'S SAFE. CLAY'S ELEMENT IS EARTH: SPEED OF A ROCK.

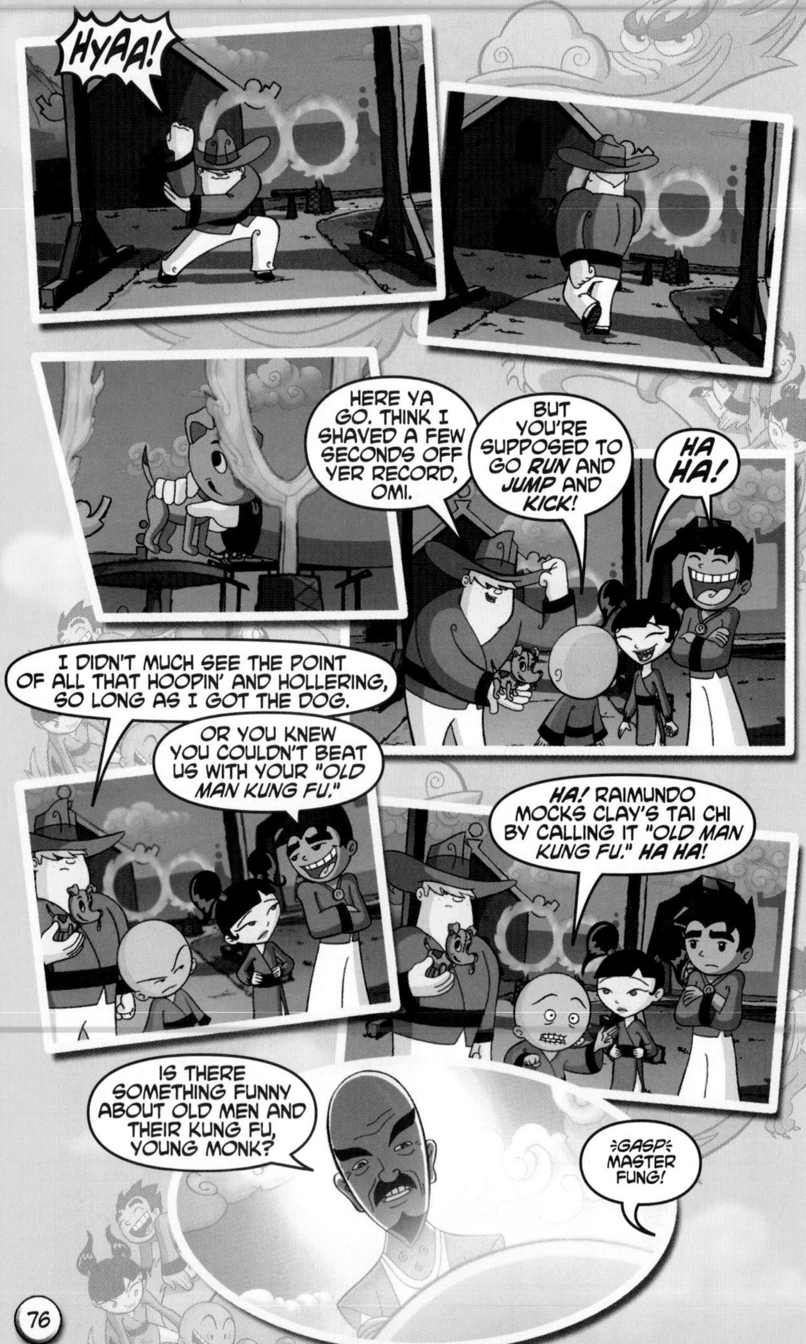
HYAA!
HERE YA GO. THINK I SHAVED A FEW SECONDS OFF YER RECORD, OMI.
BUT YOU'RE SUPPOSED TO GO RUN AND JUMP AND KICK!
HA HA!
I DIDN'T MUCH SEE THE POINT OF ALL THAT HOOPIN' AND HOLLERING, SO LONG AS I GOT THE DOG.
OR YOU KNEW YOU COULDN'T BEAT US WITH YOUR "OLD MAN KUNG FU."
HA! RAIMUNDO MOCKS CLAY'S TAI CHI BY CALLING IT "OLD MAN KUNG FU." HA HA!
IS THERE SOMETHING FUNNY ABOUT OLD MEN AND THEIR KUNG FU, YOUNG MONK?
GASP MASTER FUNG!

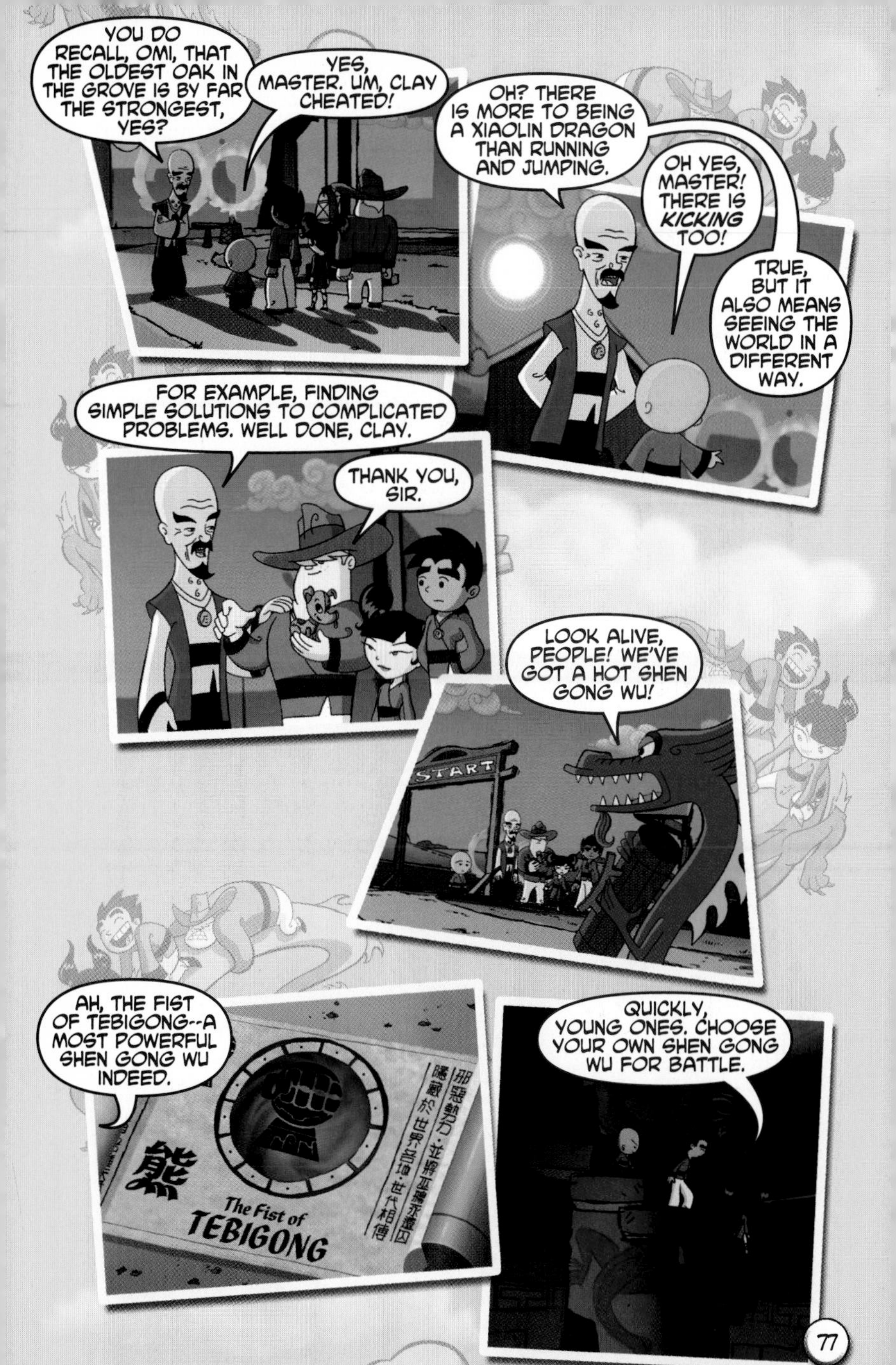

YOU DO RECALL, OMI, THAT THE OLDEST OAK IN THE GROVE IS BY FAR THE STRONGEST, YES?
YES, MASTER. UM, CLAY CHEATED!
OH? THERE IS MORE TO BEING A XIAOLIN DRAGON THAN RUNNING AND JUMPING.
OH YES, MASTER! THERE IS *KICKING* TOO!
TRUE, BUT IT ALSO MEANS SEEING THE WORLD IN A DIFFERENT WAY.
FOR EXAMPLE, FINDING SIMPLE SOLUTIONS TO COMPLICATED PROBLEMS. WELL DONE, CLAY.
THANK YOU, SIR.
LOOK ALIVE, PEOPLE! WE'VE GOT A HOT SHEN GONG WU!
START
AH, THE FIST OF TEBIGONG--A MOST POWERFUL SHEN GONG WU INDEED.
The Fist of TEBIGONG
QUICKLY, YOUNG ONES. CHOOSE YOUR OWN SHEN GONG WU FOR BATTLE.

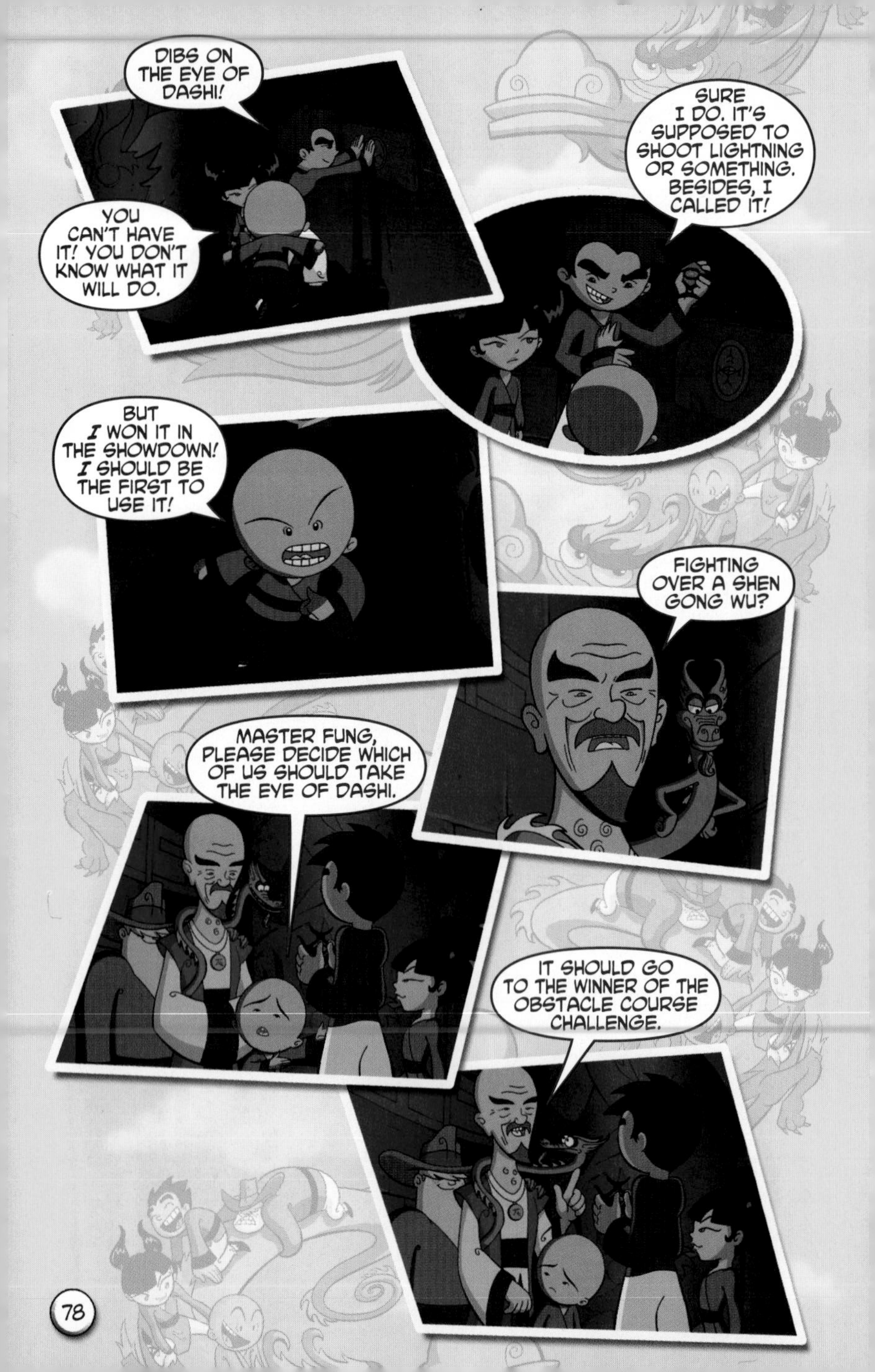

DIBS ON THE EYE OF DASHI!
YOU CAN'T HAVE IT! YOU DON'T KNOW WHAT IT WILL DO.
SURE I DO. IT'S SUPPOSED TO SHOOT LIGHTNING OR SOMETHING. BESIDES, I CALLED IT!
BUT *I* WON IT IN THE SHOWDOWN! *I* SHOULD BE THE FIRST TO USE IT!
FIGHTING OVER A SHEN GONG WU?
MASTER FUNG, PLEASE DECIDE WHICH OF US SHOULD TAKE THE EYE OF DASHI.
IT SHOULD GO TO THE WINNER OF THE OBSTACLE COURSE CHALLENGE.

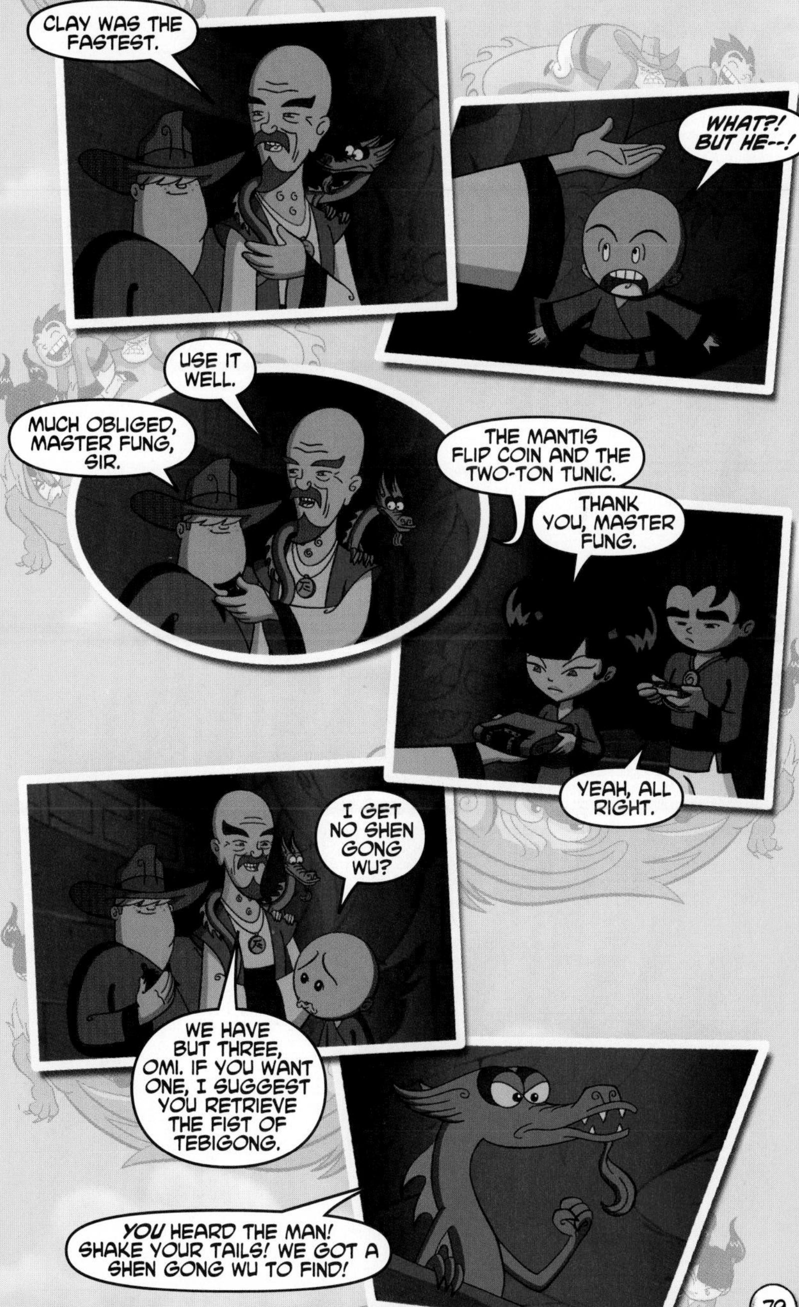
CLAY WAS THE FASTEST.
WHAT?! BUT HE--!
USE IT WELL.
MUCH OBLIGED, MASTER FUNG, SIR.
THE MANTIS FLIP COIN AND THE TWO-TON TUNIC.
THANK YOU, MASTER FUNG.
YEAH, ALL RIGHT.
I GET NO SHEN GONG WU?
WE HAVE BUT THREE, OMI. IF YOU WANT ONE, I SUGGEST YOU RETRIEVE THE FIST OF TEBIGONG.
YOU HEARD THE MAN! SHAKE YOUR TAILS! WE GOT A SHEN GONG WU TO FIND!

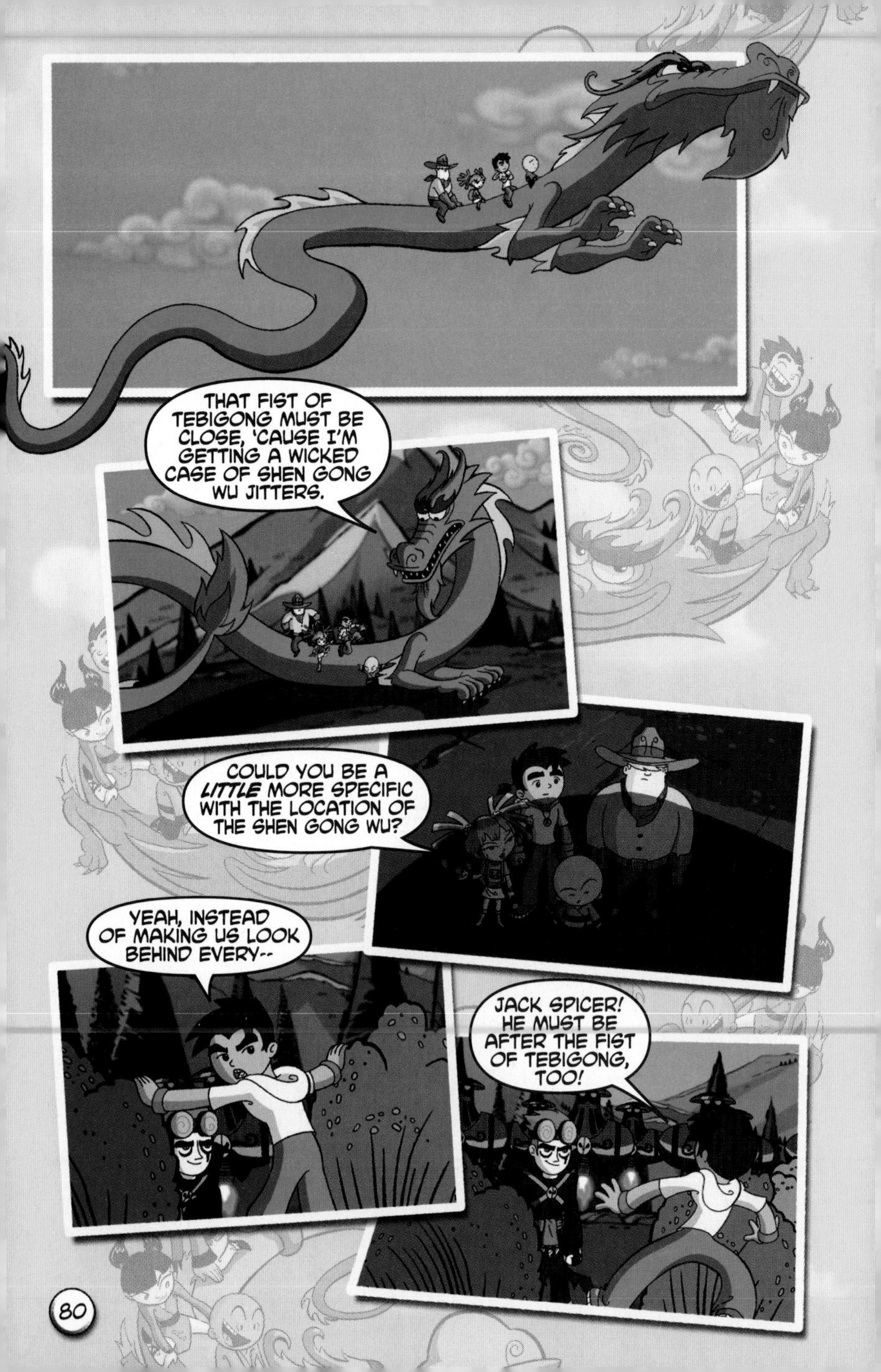
THAT FIST OF TEBIGONG MUST BE CLOSE, 'CAUSE I'M GETTING A WICKED CASE OF SHEN GONG WU JITTERS.
COULD YOU BE A *LITTLE* MORE SPECIFIC WITH THE LOCATION OF THE SHEN GONG WU?
YEAH, INSTEAD OF MAKING US LOOK BEHIND EVERY--
JACK SPICER! HE MUST BE AFTER THE FIST OF TEBIGONG, TOO!

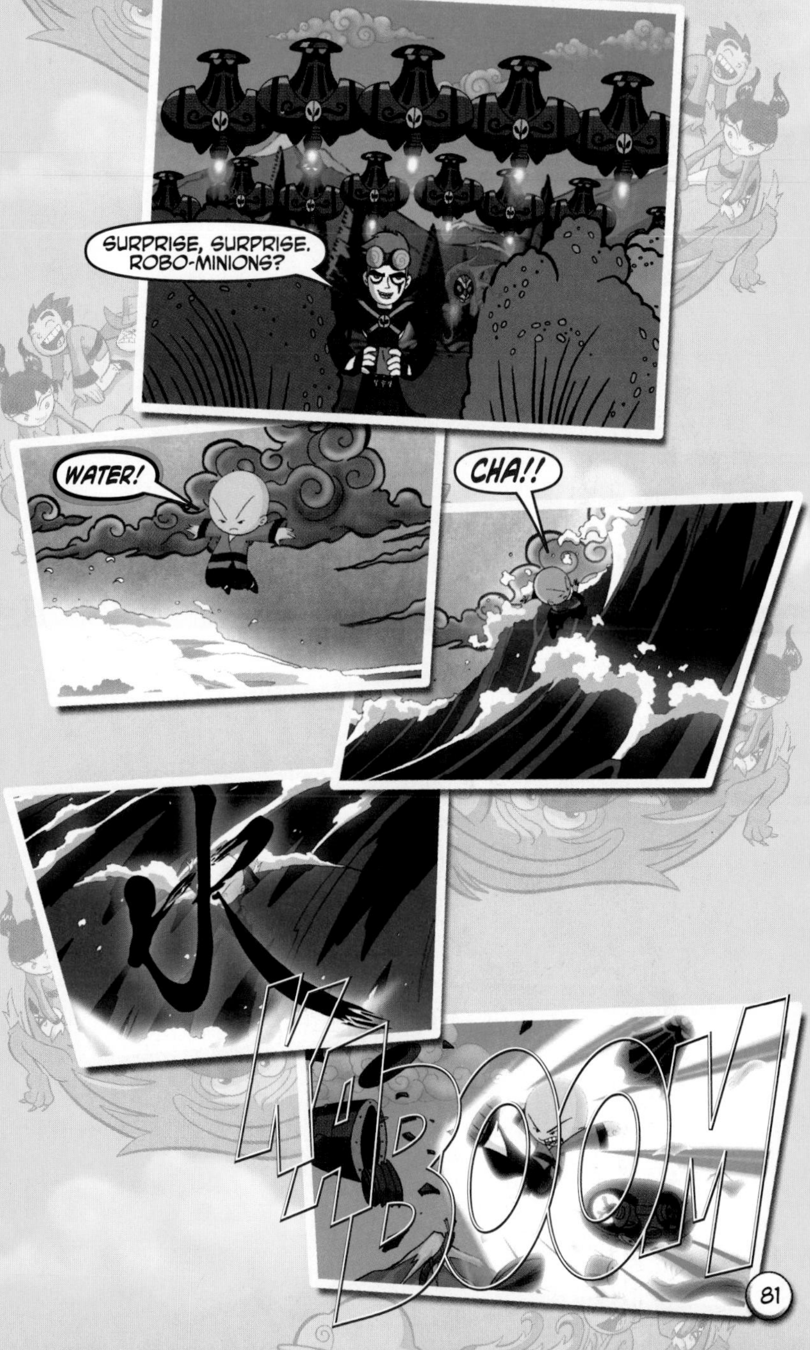
SURPRISE, SURPRISE.
ROBO-MINIONS?
WATER!
CHA!!
KA-BOOM

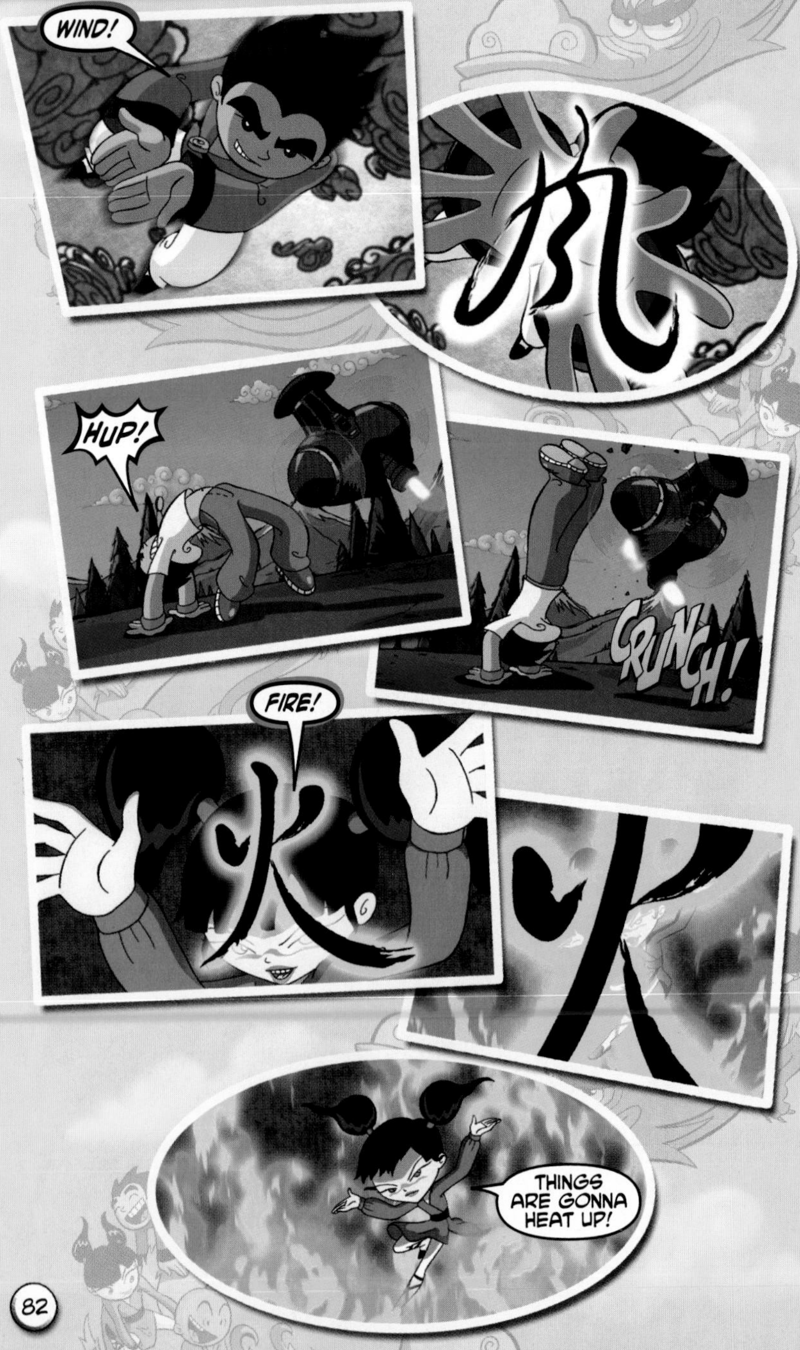
WIND!
HUP!
CRUNCH!
FIRE!
THINGS ARE GONNA HEAT UP!

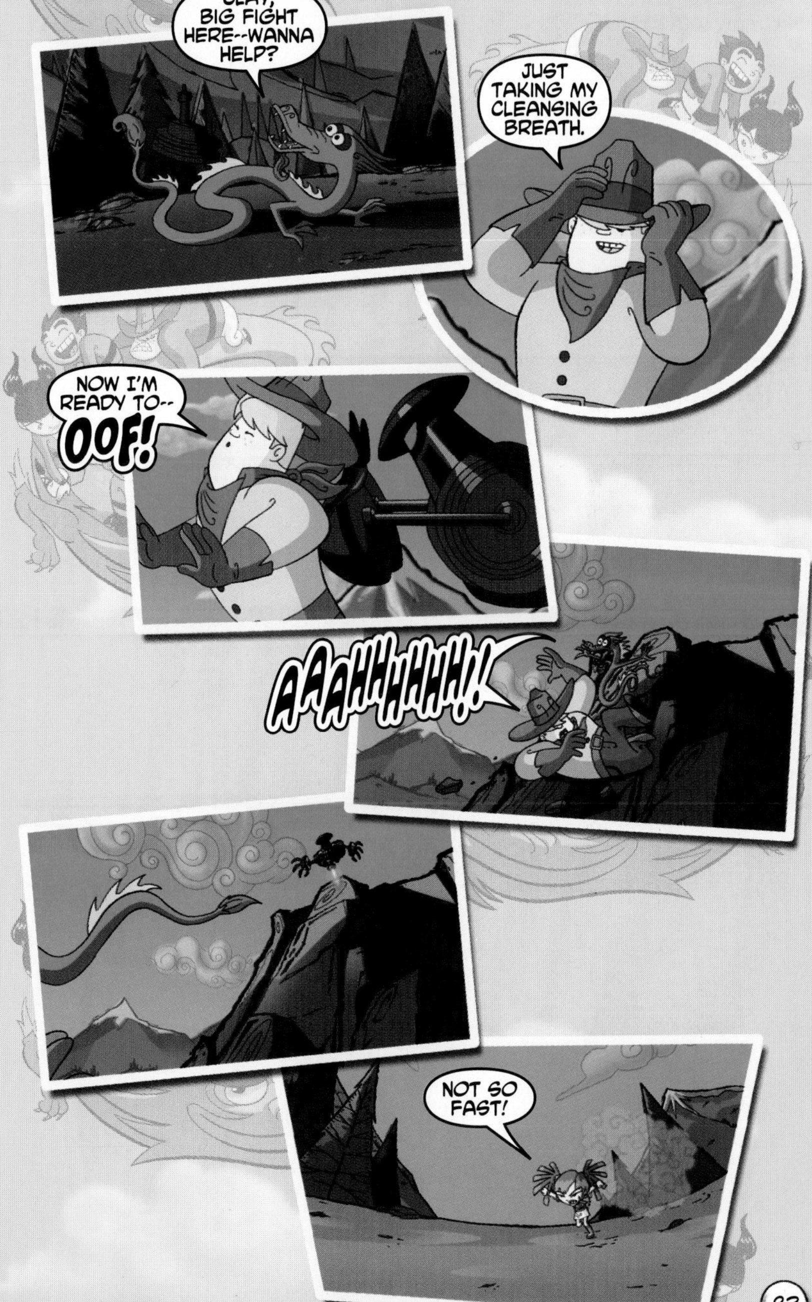
CLAY, BIG FIGHT HERE--WANNA HELP?
JUST TAKING MY CLEANSING BREATH.
NOW I'M READY TO--
OOF!
AAAHHHHHH!!
NOT SO FAST!

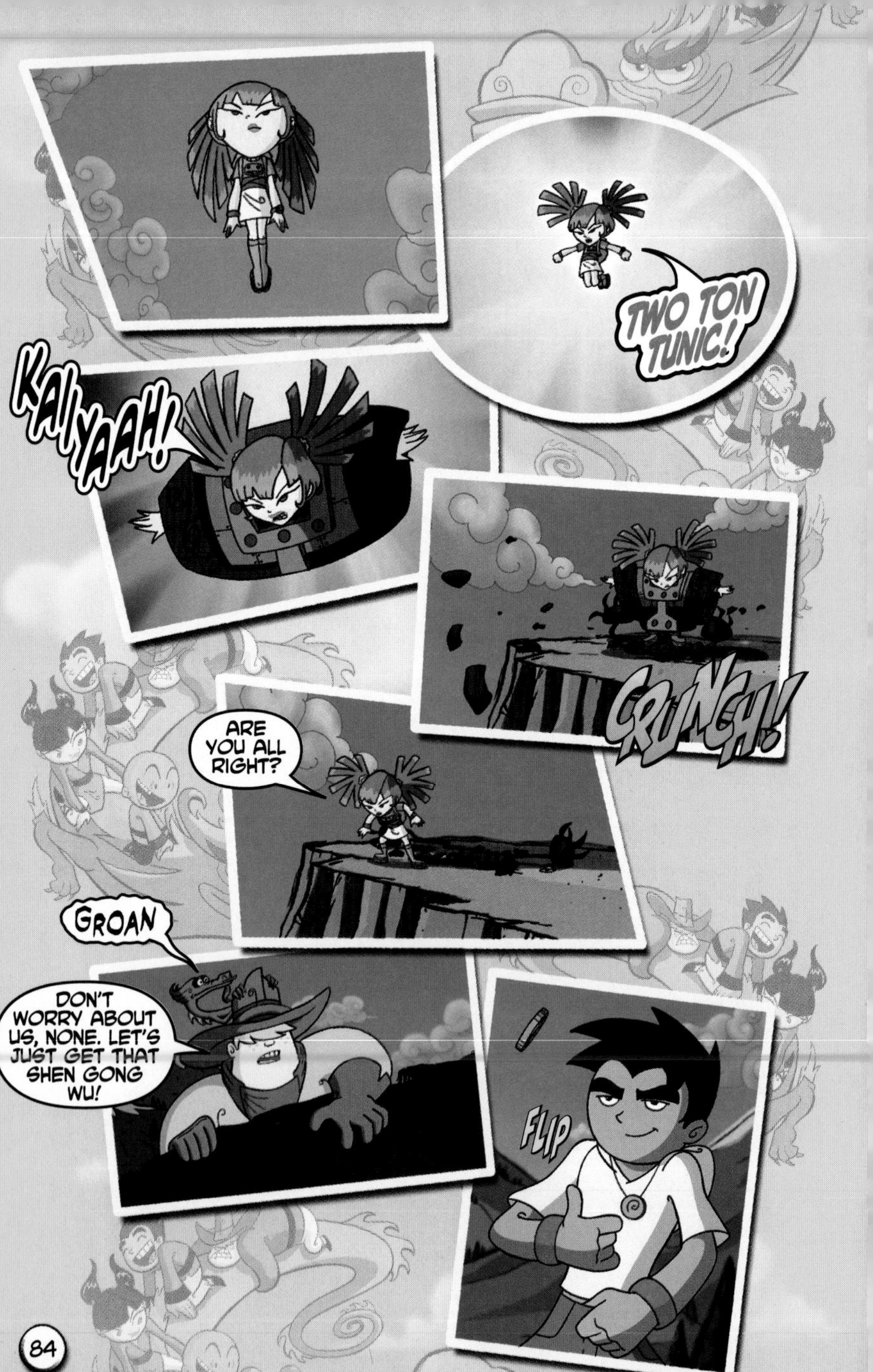
TWO TON TUNIC!
KAIIYAAH!
CRUNCH!
ARE YOU ALL RIGHT?
GROAN
DON'T WORRY ABOUT US, NONE. LET'S JUST GET THAT SHEN GONG WU!
FLIP

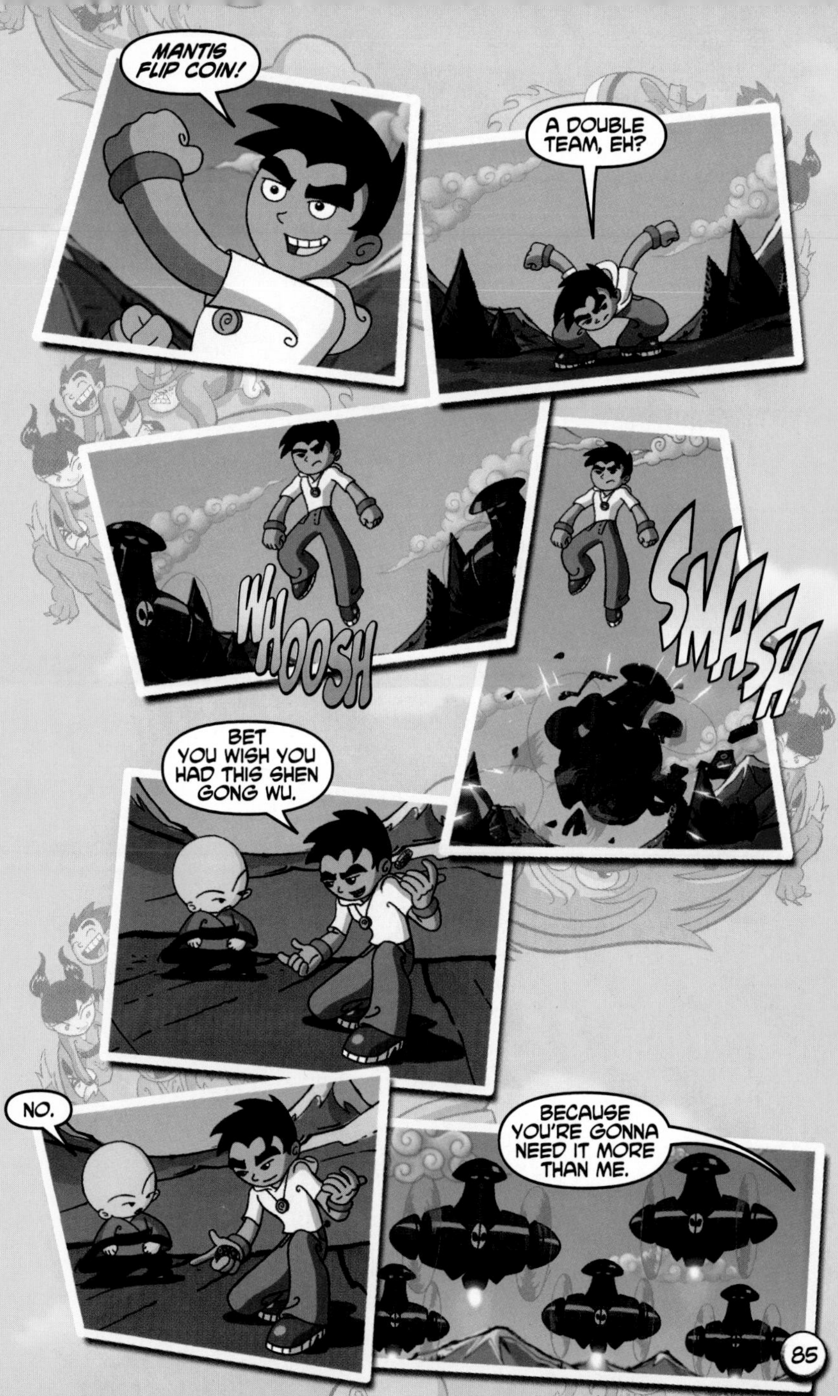
MANTIS FLIP COIN!
A DOUBLE TEAM, EH?
WHOOSH
SMASH
BET YOU WISH YOU HAD THIS SHEN GONG WU.
NO.
BECAUSE YOU'RE GONNA NEED IT MORE THAN ME.

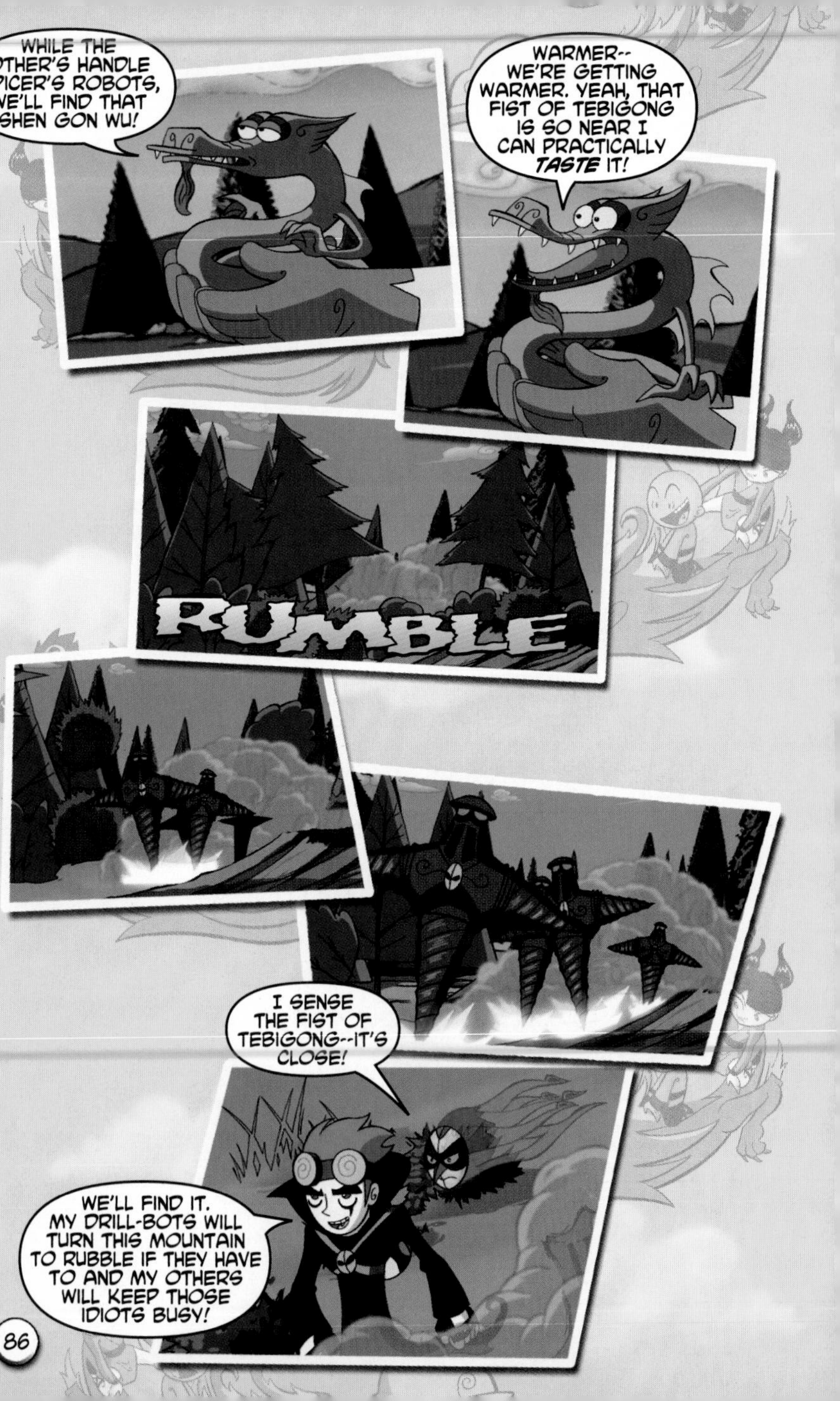
WHILE THE OTHER'S HANDLE SPICER'S ROBOTS, WE'LL FIND THAT SHEN GON WU!
WARMER-- WE'RE GETTING WARMER. YEAH, THAT FIST OF TEBIGONG IS SO NEAR I CAN PRACTICALLY *TASTE* IT!
RUMBLE
I SENSE THE FIST OF TEBIGONG--IT'S CLOSE!
WE'LL FIND IT. MY DRILL-BOTS WILL TURN THIS MOUNTAIN TO RUBBLE IF THEY HAVE TO AND MY OTHERS WILL KEEP THOSE IDIOTS BUSY!

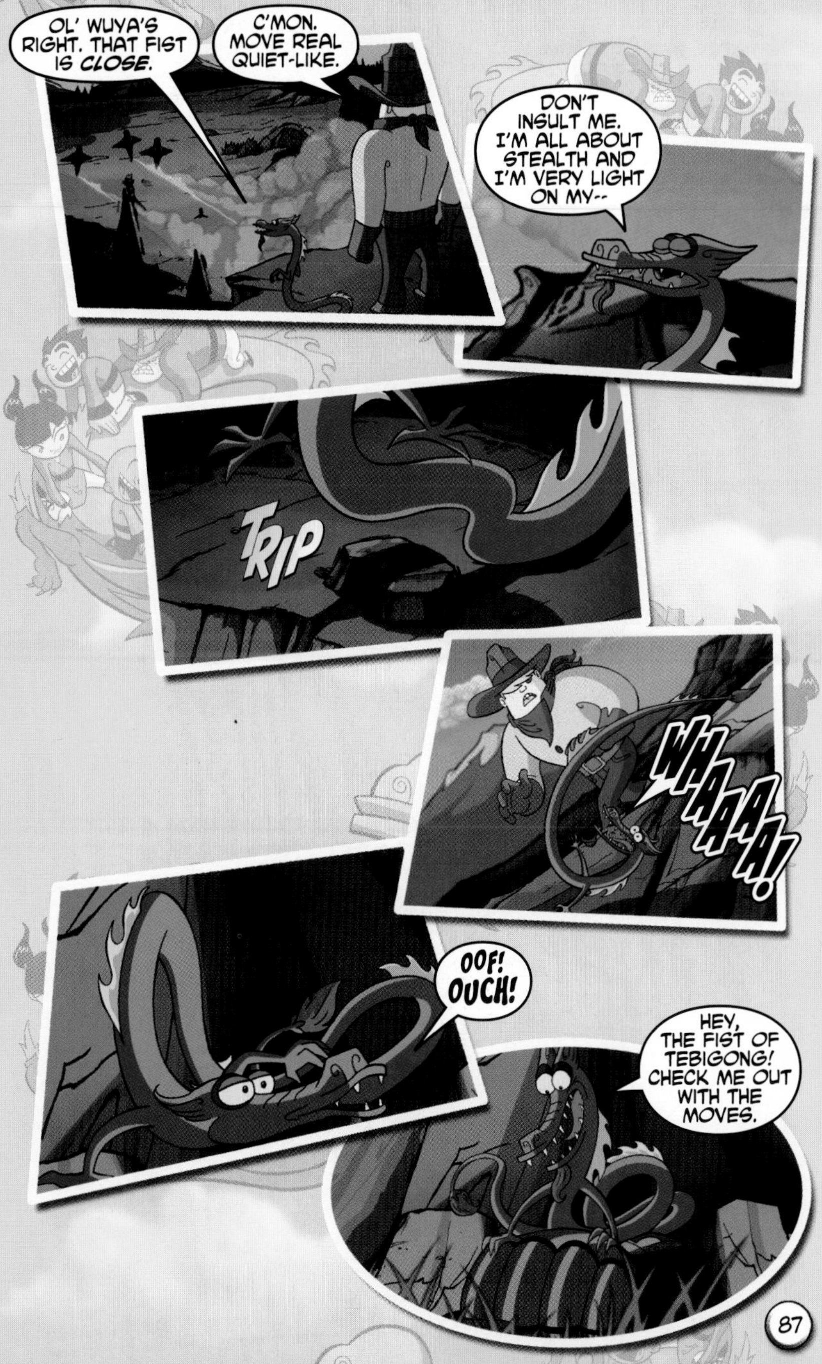
OL' WUYA'S RIGHT. THAT FIST IS *CLOSE*.
C'MON. MOVE REAL QUIET-LIKE.
DON'T INSULT ME. I'M ALL ABOUT STEALTH AND I'M VERY LIGHT ON MY--
TRIP
WHAAAA!
OOF! OUCH!
HEY, THE FIST OF TEBIGONG! CHECK ME OUT WITH THE MOVES.

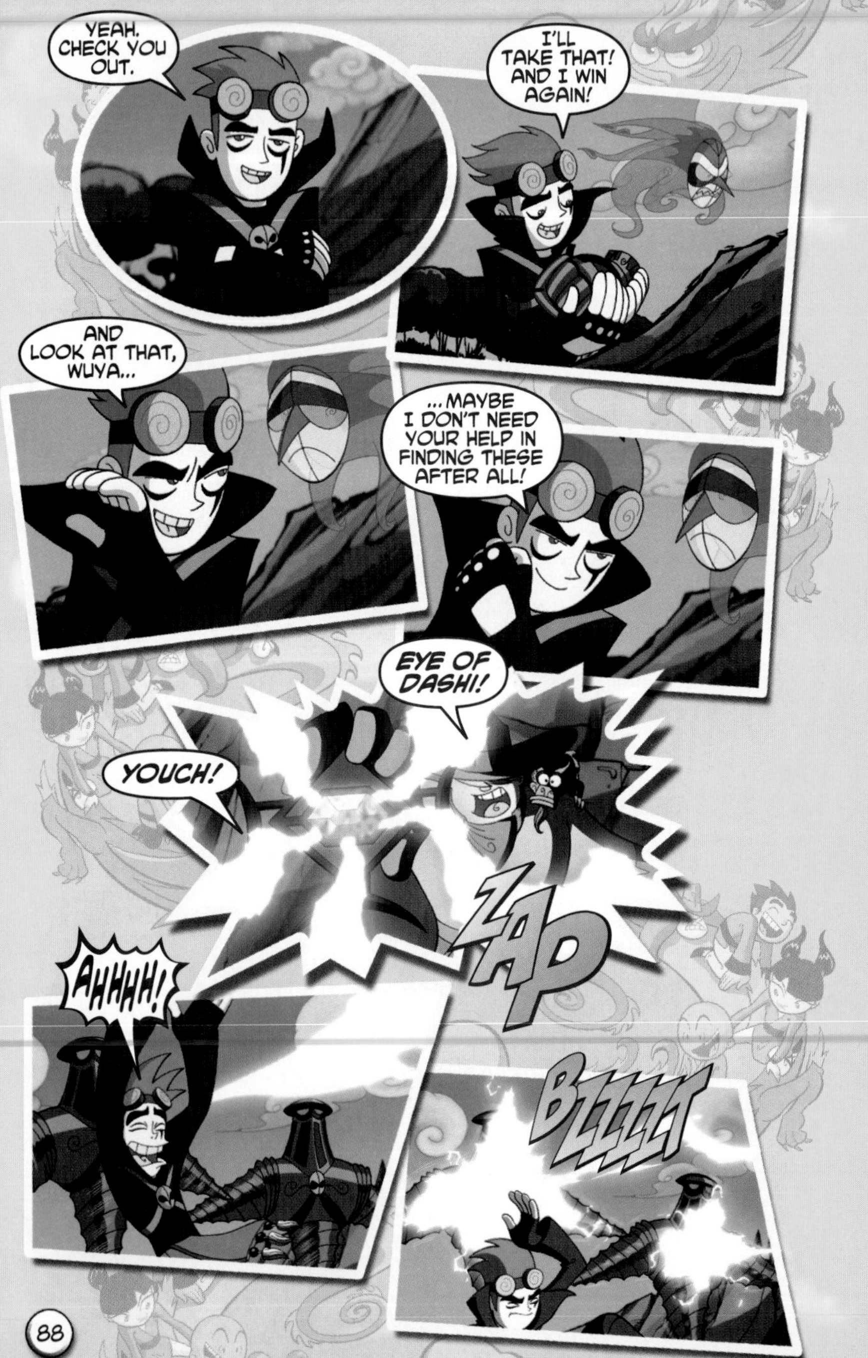
YEAH. CHECK YOU OUT.
I'LL TAKE THAT! AND I WIN AGAIN!
AND LOOK AT THAT, WUYA...
...MAYBE I DON'T NEED YOUR HELP IN FINDING THESE AFTER ALL!
EYE OF DASHI!
YOUCH!
ZAP
AHHHH!
BZZZZT

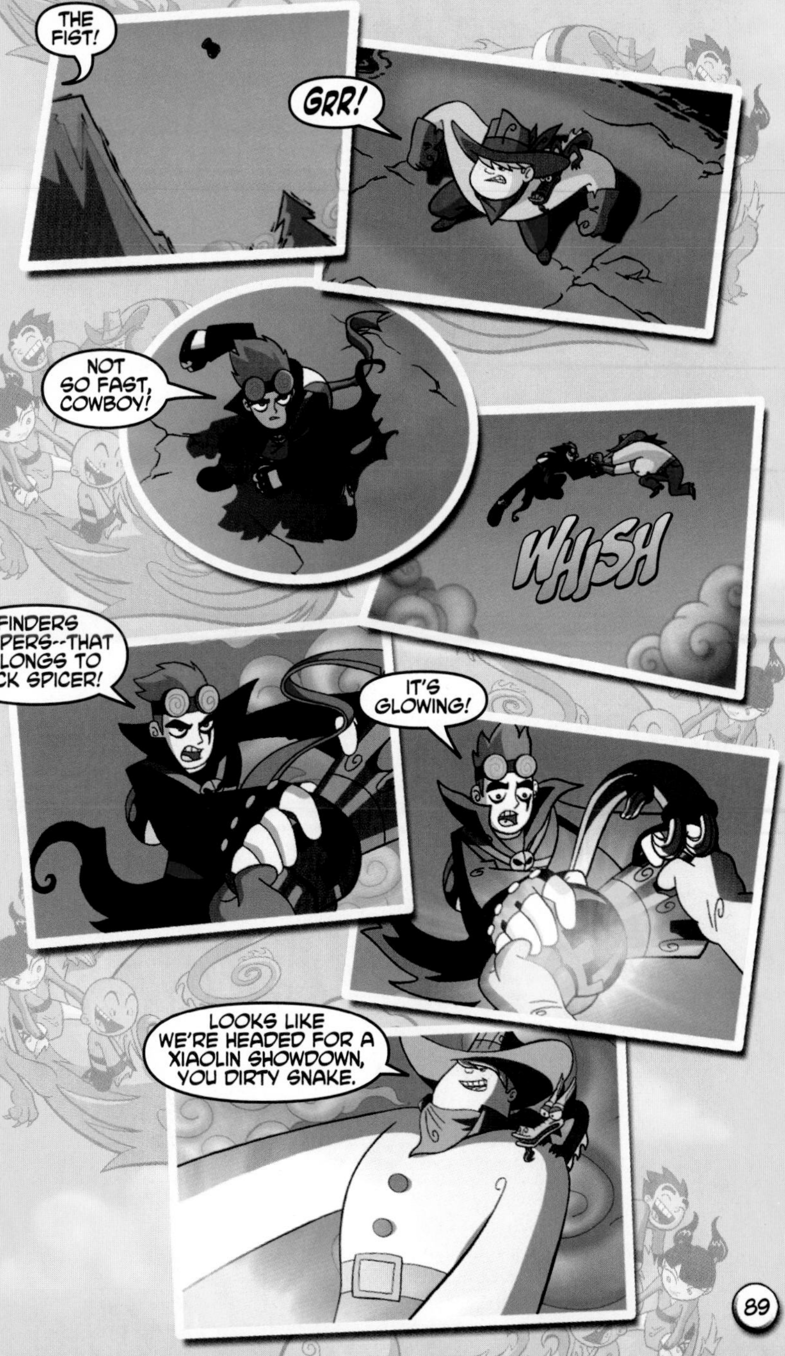
THE FIST!
GRR!
NOT SO FAST, COWBOY!
WHISH
FINDERS KEEPERS--THAT BELONGS TO JACK SPICER!
IT'S GLOWING!
LOOKS LIKE WE'RE HEADED FOR A XIAOLIN SHOWDOWN, YOU DIRTY SNAKE.

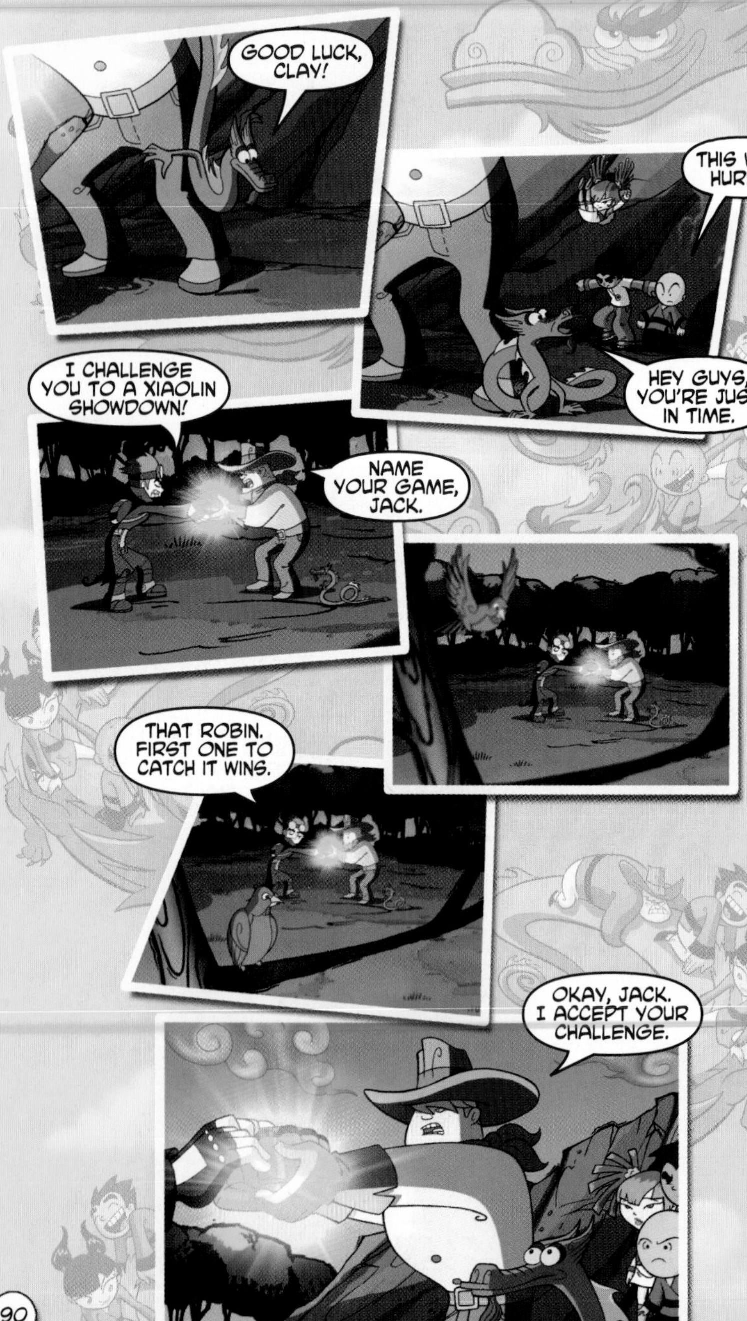
GOOD LUCK, CLAY!
THIS WAY! HURRY!
HEY GUYS, YOU'RE JUST IN TIME.
I CHALLENGE YOU TO A XIAOLIN SHOWDOWN!
NAME YOUR GAME, JACK.
THAT ROBIN. FIRST ONE TO CATCH IT WINS.
OKAY, JACK. I ACCEPT YOUR CHALLENGE.

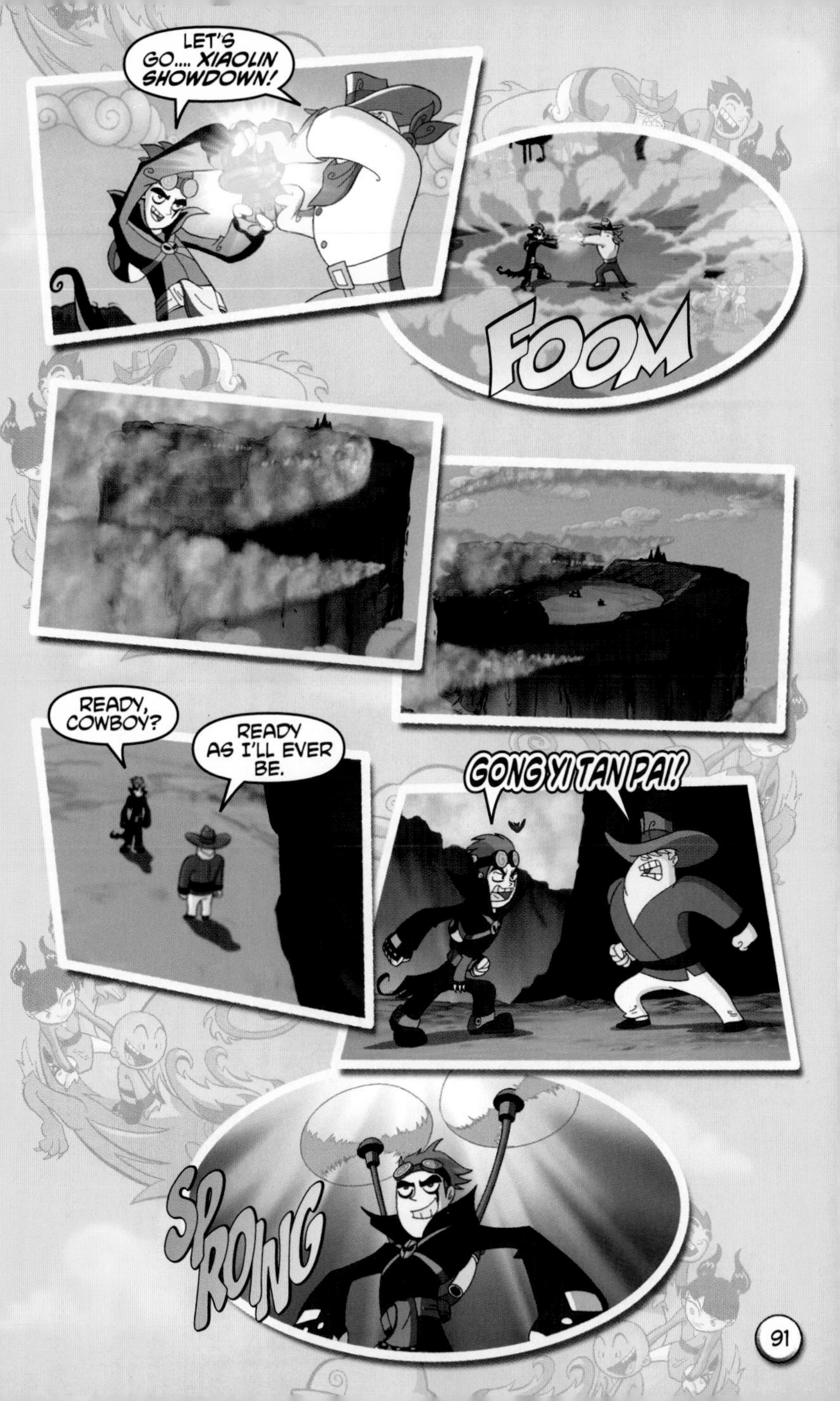
LET'S GO.... XIAOLIN SHOWDOWN!
FOOM
READY, COWBOY?
READY AS I'LL EVER BE.
GONG YI TAN PAI!
SPROING

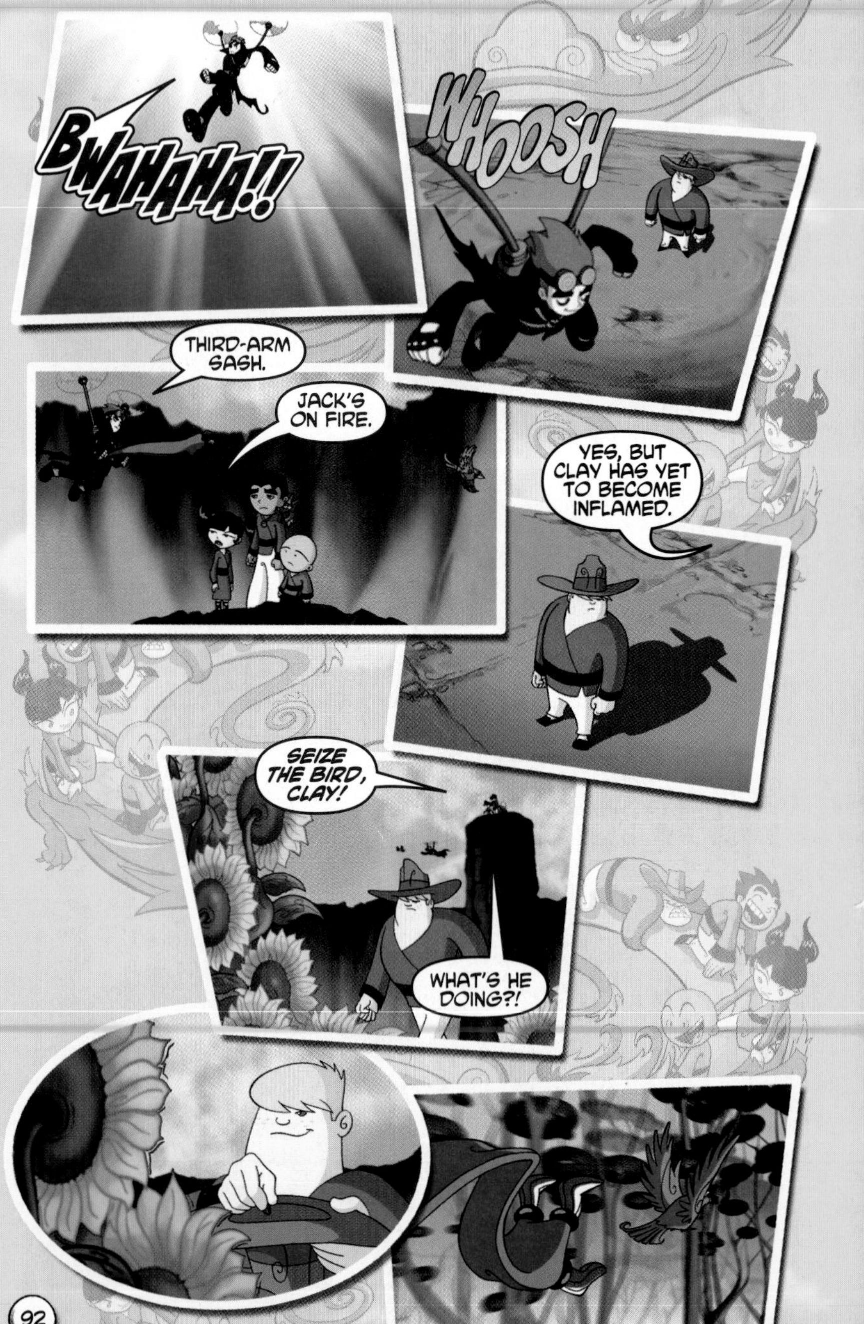
BWAHAHA!!
WHOOSH
THIRD-ARM SASH.
JACK'S ON FIRE.
YES, BUT CLAY HAS YET TO BECOME INFLAMED.
SEIZE THE BIRD, CLAY!
WHAT'S HE DOING?!

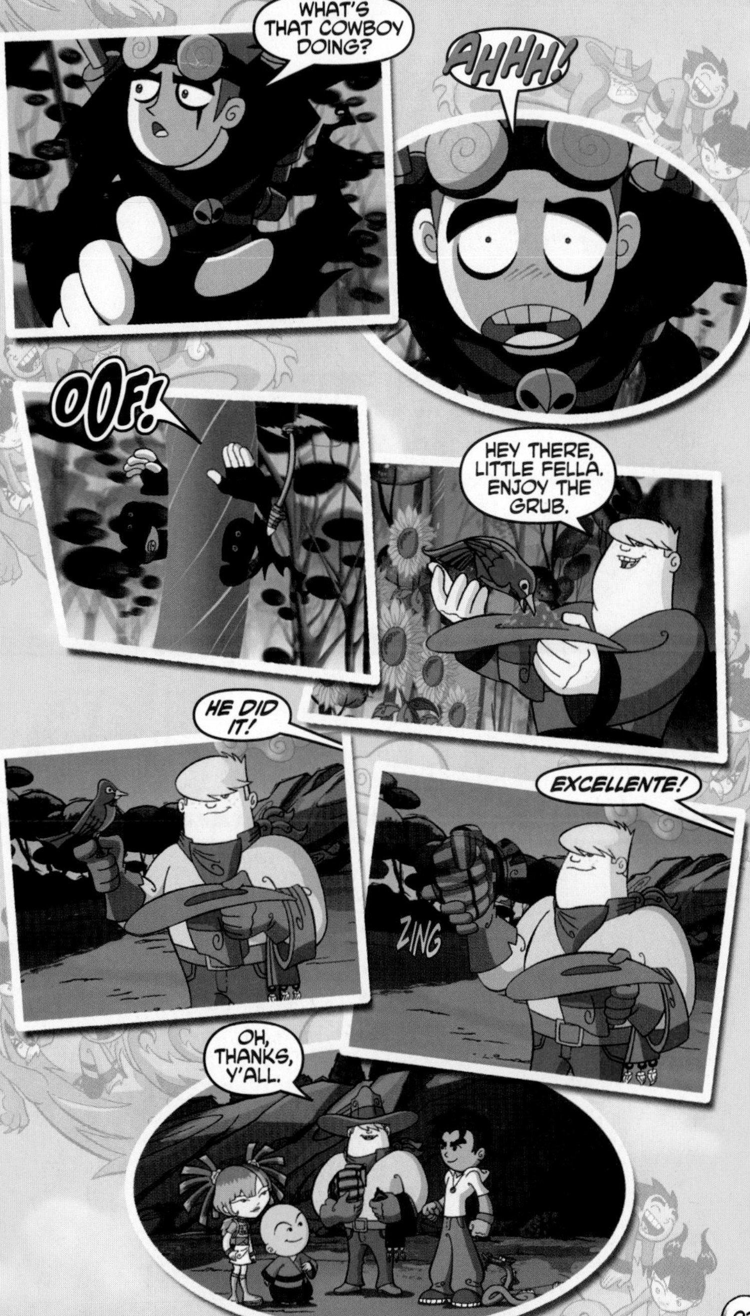
WHAT'S THAT COWBOY DOING?
AHHH!
OOF!
HEY THERE, LITTLE FELLA. ENJOY THE GRUB.
HE DID IT!
EXCELLENTE!
ZING
OH, THANKS, Y'ALL.

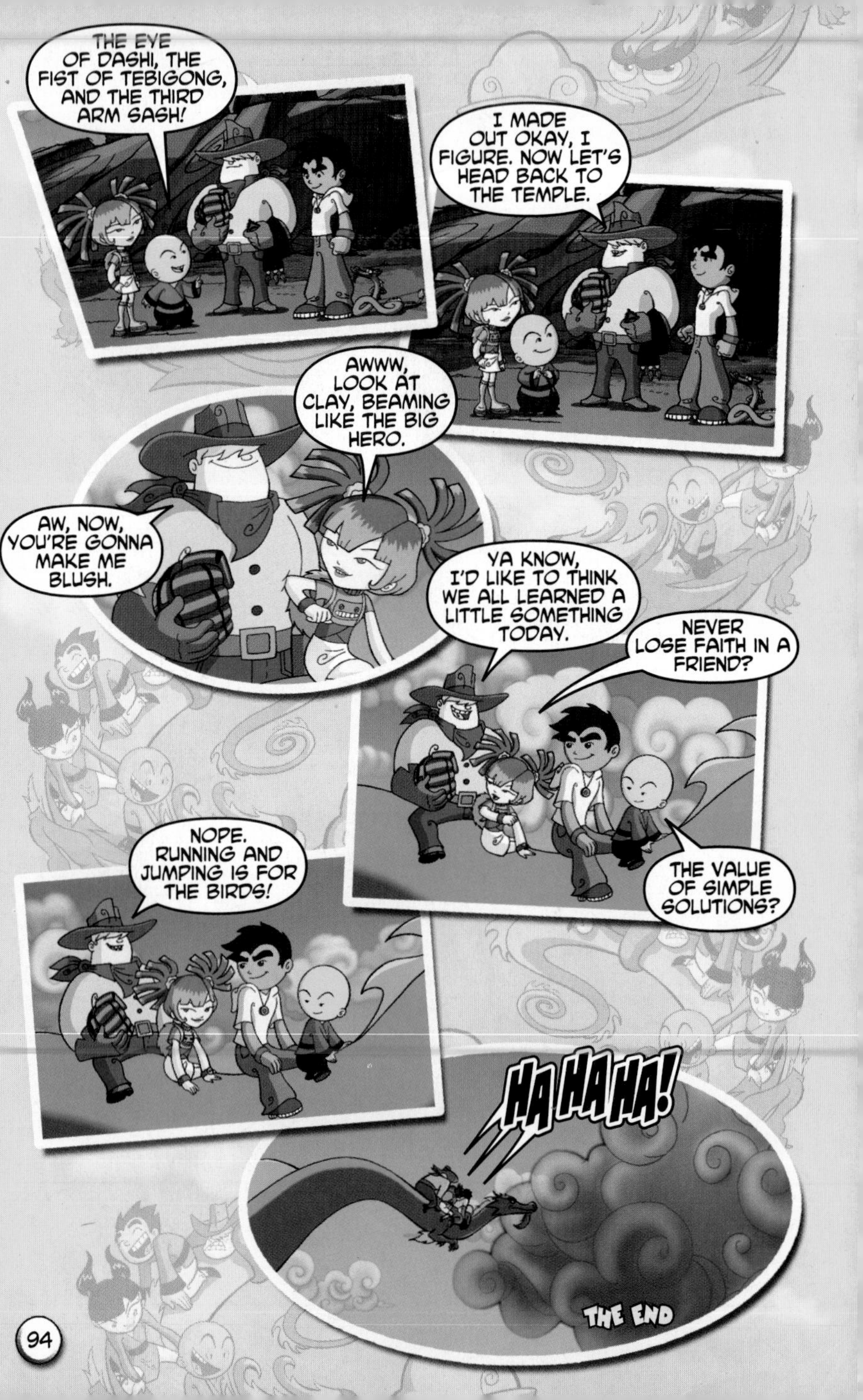
THE EYE OF DASHI, THE FIST OF TEBIGONG, AND THE THIRD ARM SASH!
I MADE OUT OKAY, I FIGURE. NOW LET'S HEAD BACK TO THE TEMPLE.
AWWW, LOOK AT CLAY, BEAMING LIKE THE BIG HERO.
AW, NOW, YOU'RE GONNA MAKE ME BLUSH.
YA KNOW, I'D LIKE TO THINK WE ALL LEARNED A LITTLE SOMETHING TODAY.
NEVER LOSE FAITH IN A FRIEND?
THE VALUE OF SIMPLE SOLUTIONS?
NOPE. RUNNING AND JUMPING IS FOR THE BIRDS!
HA HA HA!
THE END

Hey kids! Hungry for some CARTOON NETWORK™ Jam Packed Action?

This book features the red-hot new series from Cartoon Network...and includes the first episode of Megas XLR on DVD!

Also featuring episodes of:
The Grim Adventures of Billy and Mandy,
Codename: Kids Next Door,
and Samurai Jack!

OTHER BOOKS OF INTEREST

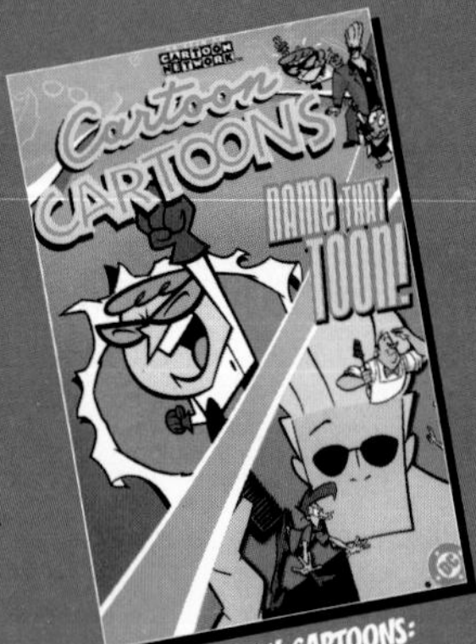
CARTOON NETWORK
Cartoon CARTOONS
NAME THAT TOON!

CARTOON CARTOONS:
NAME THAT TOON!

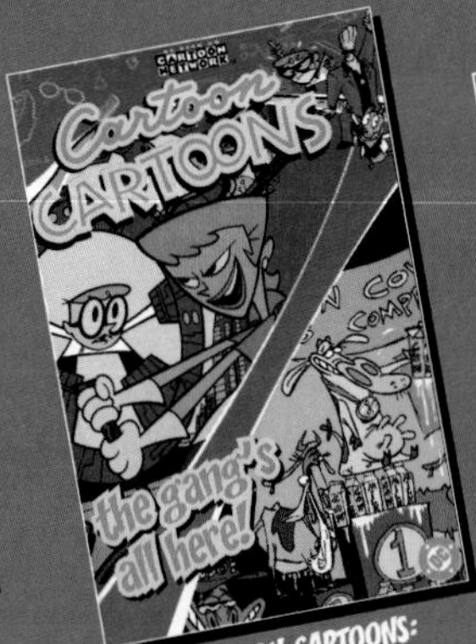
CARTOON NETWORK
Cartoon CARTOONS
the gang's all here!

CARTOON CARTOONS:
THE GANG'S ALL HERE!

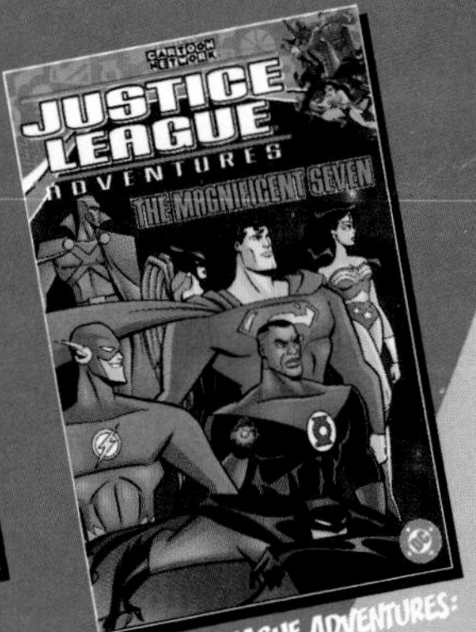
CARTOON NETWORK
JUSTICE LEAGUE
ADVENTURES
THE MAGNIFICENT SEVEN

JUSTICE LEAGUE ADVENTURES:
THE MAGNIFICENT SEVEN

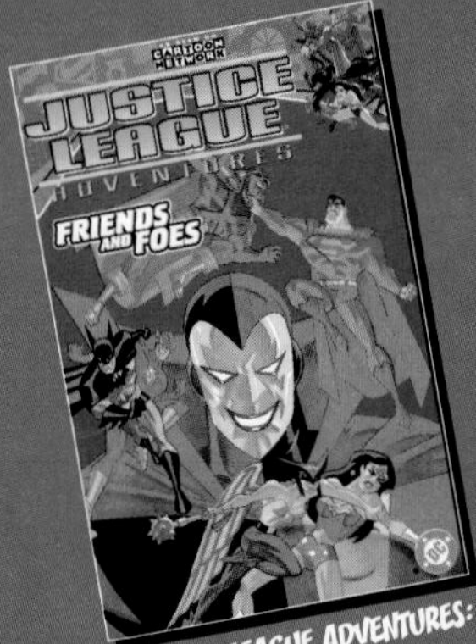
CARTOON NETWORK
JUSTICE LEAGUE
ADVENTURES
FRIENDS AND FOES

JUSTICE LEAGUE ADVENTURES:
FRIENDS AND FOES

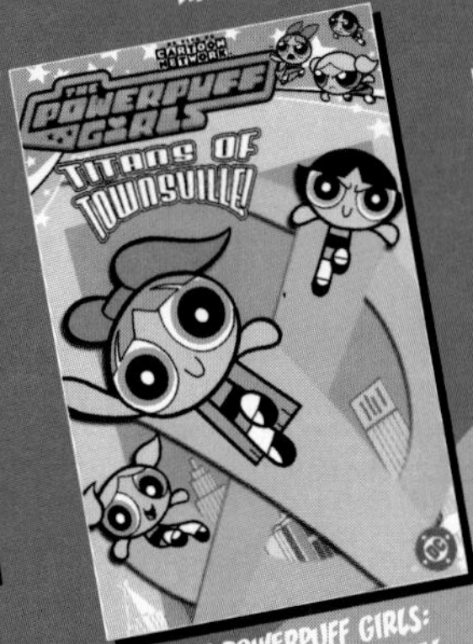
CARTOON NETWORK
THE POWERPUFF GIRLS
TITANS OF TOWNSVILLE!

THE POWERPUFF GIRLS:
TITANS OF TOWNSVILLE!

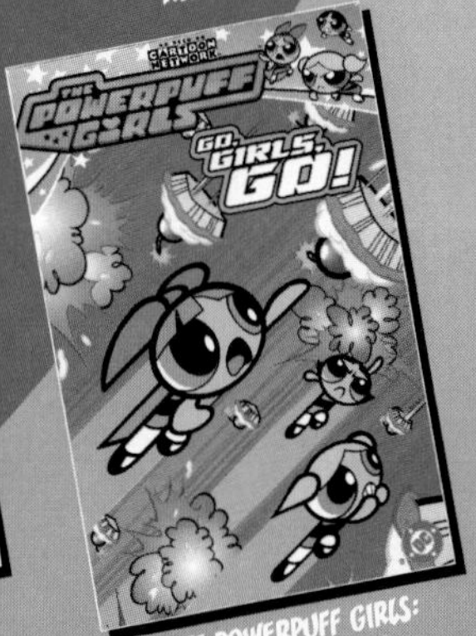
CARTOON NETWORK
THE POWERPUFF GIRLS
GO, GIRLS, GO!

THE POWERPUFF GIRLS:
GO, GIRLS, GO!

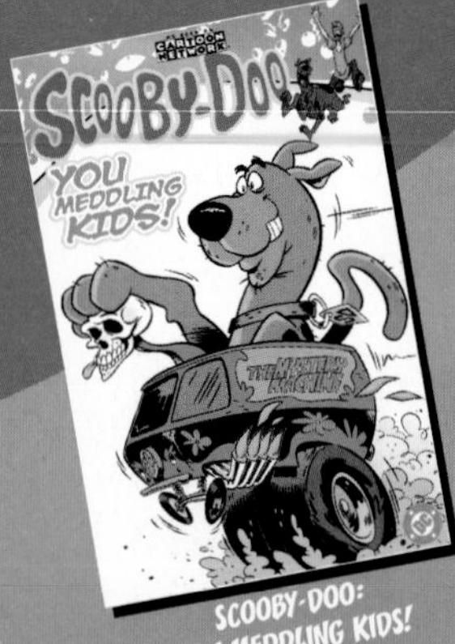
CARTOON NETWORK
SCOOBY-DOO
YOU MEDDLING KIDS!
THE MYSTERY MACHINE

SCOOBY-DOO:
YOU MEDDLING KIDS!

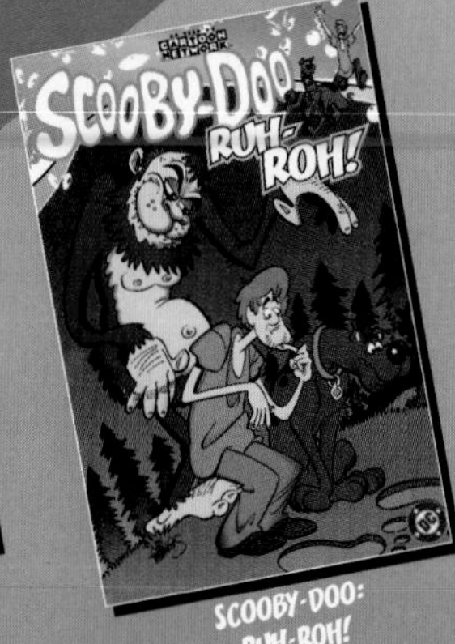
CARTOON NETWORK
SCOOBY-DOO
RUH-ROH!

SCOOBY-DOO:
RUH-ROH!

Comic Shop Locator Service:
1-888-COMIC BOOK